GLASNC

Larry Jeram-Croft

Also by Larry Jeram-Croft:

Fiction:

The 'Jon Hunt' series about the modern Royal Navy:

Sea Skimmer
The Caspian Monster
Cocaine
Arapaho
Bog Hammer
Glasnost
Retribution
Formidable
Conspiracy
Swan Song

The 'John Hunt' books about the Royal Navy's Fleet Air Arm in the Second World War:

Better Lucky and Good

The Winchester Chronicles:

Book one: The St Cross Mirror

The Caribbean: historical fiction and the 'Jacaranda' Trilogy.

Diamant

Jacaranda
The Guadeloupe Guillotine
Nautilus

Science Fiction:

Siren

Non Fiction:

The Royal Navy Lynx an Operational History
The Royal Navy Wasp an Operational and Retirement History

Prologue

The Autumn equinox is when the days and nights are the same length. It is also the time when the boundary between polar air and the moist air of the Azores High starts to migrate south as the sun starts to move more into the southern hemisphere. This volatile boundary is the birthplace of Atlantic depressions. Gaining energy from the massive temperature differences of the air masses and twisted into circulation by the coriolis forces of the Earth's rotation, they are the primary cause of all the gales that hit England throughout the long winter.

This particular depression had actually started out slightly differently. In recent months it had been called Hurricane Mary and had already crossed the Atlantic once from its birthplace over the African continent. It had only managed to wind up into a Category One hurricane and had missed all the land masses and islands that it might have devastated as it curved slowly north along the Eastern seaboard of the United States. By the time it arrived off Newfoundland, it was merely a small circulation. However, it found new energy once it collided with the polar air mass coming down to meet it. As it started its eastwards track, driven by the jet stream, it started to grow. The Gulf Stream below it was unusually far north this year and that also fed its appetite for raw energy. By the time it was in mid-Atlantic, the central pressure was starting to reach record lows. Meteorologists in Europe started to pay it more than their usual attention.

The Commander in Chief Fleet's headquarters at Northwood just outside London are mainly underground in a massive concrete bunker known as 'The Hole.' Designed to survive even a direct hit from a large nuclear warhead, it contains everything the Royal Navy needs to survive and continue to manage the naval war. Including, some would say, some of the prettiest female staff in the navy. However, to suggest to any of them that they were chosen to be breeding stock for a post nuclear world would not be tactful.

One of the key elements to running a navy is to understand the weather and the oceans. Hence the Fleet Weather and Oceanography Centre is one of the units stationed well below ground on the fourth floor of The Hole. It has its fair share of attractive female staff as Lieutenant Mark Simpson reflected as he took his seat for his watch and

1

a shapely pair of legs glided by. In this case, the legs were owned by Leading Seaman Elaine Pagett and he was in the fortunate position of having to share this office with her for the next six hours. Apart from his forecasting duties, one of the tasks he had set himself was to make sure that the lovely Elaine agreed to go out to dinner with him tomorrow night when they were both off watch. Fraternisation between officers and the lower ranks was frowned on in the navy but Mark had already decided that once out of uniform and away from work the rules didn't need to apply. He just hoped that she would agree.

Elaine knew the Lieutenant fancied her. She had been avoiding his advances for some weeks now, ever since she joined the section. It wasn't that she didn't quite like him. It was just that she felt she really ought to stick to the rules. She knew her resolve was slowly weakening and maybe if he asked her out, while they were on watch together tonight, she might just finally give in.

She busied herself in the little kitchenette off to one side of the main forecasting office and made them both a coffee. He liked his black, she liked hers 'Julie Andrews' as the joke went, 'white, nun'. She still smiled when she thought of it. When the kettle had boiled, she filled the two cups and went back into the main office.

Handing one mug to Lieutenant Simpson, she looked over his shoulder at the surface pressure chart he was studying. Although not a qualified forecaster herself, she had done several courses on the subject and was fairly knowledgeable. She definitely knew that the whirlpool that was spinning in the mid-Atlantic looked fairly nasty.

'Is that one going to cause any trouble Sir?' she asked.

Mark looked up at her pretty face so close to his and smiled. 'It would if it was heading for us but luckily the Jetstream hasn't come far south enough yet. It'll clobber the Shetlands and Norway but we don't have any ships that far north.'

'But that's quite a long Cold Front trailing behind it. Won't that be a problem?'

'Good question.' Mark knew that Elaine was pretty clued up. As her Divisional Officer he would probably be recommending her for promotion soon. 'The only ship we have in the South Western approaches is HMS Prometheus, on her way back from the States and she should arrive home well before the worst hits her.'

Their watch continued through the night. Elaine collated all the weather report signals from the various warships currently at sea around the world. Mark looked at the data as well as liaising with the

Meteorological office in Bracknell. He started to produce a new set of forecast charts to be sent via High Frequency facsimile to all naval ships.

It was Elaine who spotted it first. 'Sir, that trailing Cold Front. The latest prognostication from Bracknell is showing a definite kink in the isobars about half way down.'

'Show me,' he replied and Elaine pointed out the feature.

Mark looked at several other reports he had on his desk. 'Ever since that bloody hurricane the other year, the Met Office seem to be paranoid about missing another one. But I'll tell you what, this could be exactly that. The upper air chart is also showing a disturbance about there. With the main low pressure winding up so fast, that front is pretty active and if a secondary low forms there could be some very serious winds around it.'

They spent the rest of their watch focusing on the developing weather system out in the grey Atlantic. Their suspicions seemed to be bearing fruit and by the end of the watch a weather warning had been sent out both from Fleet and the Met Office to all shipping in the area. As Mark finally went off watch he made his way to his cabin in the wardroom. He realised, much to his chagrin, that he had been so caught up in the unfolding drama he had completely forgotten to make his move on the lovely Elaine.

Chapter 1

HMS Prometheus was corkscrewing down a large Atlantic swell. As each roller lifted her stern she would try to slide off course like a wilful child causing the Leading Seamen who was steering her to curse as he applied large amounts of wheel to compensate. The ship would then roll. With six tons of radar on the top of her main mast, she always rolled, even in a mill pond. However, her ship's company had got used to her ways and no one even noticed. Another reason for the crew to be unconcerned was that they would be home in two days and everyone was focusing on their reunions when they arrived in Devonport. Three months in the States on exercise with the US Navy had been testing and fun in equal measure. The social life had been pretty extraordinary as well to the point that many on board were actually glad to be leaving it all behind. That said, there were several sailors actively concerned that when they arrived, there could be certain American ladies waiting for them on the jetty, as well as their wives.

Commander Jonathon Hunt DSO and Bar, the ship's Commanding Officer, was sitting in his chair on the ship's bridge looking out over the grey horizon. He was looking forward to getting home just as much as everyone else. Although in this case, his anticipation was tempered by the knowledge that when they arrived, he would be saying goodbye to his wonderful ship. The two years he had commanded her had passed in a blur. The first had been really tough. Their actions in the Gulf had resulted in the Frigate returning to England in a mess. A massive gash in her side and damage to nearly every weapon system had put her in dock for months. It had even been touch and go whether she would ever go to sea again but in the end, the engineers had prevailed. With the War in the Gulf over and Iraq's invasion of Kuwait in full swing, the Royal Navy needed every hull it could get. But now they were returning for the last time and Jon would have to sit down with his appointer and see what the navy had in store for him next.

'Penny for your thoughts Sir?' Jon's reverie was broken by the voice of his operations officer and close friend, Brian Pearce.

'Oh sorry Brian, I was miles away. I was just wondering what the powers that be have in store for me when I leave the ship.'

'Not heard anything from your appointer?'

'Not a Dicky Bird I'm afraid. I don't mind what it is as long as I don't end up back in that bloody mausoleum in Whitehall again.'

4

'Hmmph, yes and maybe a job where you will be able to see your wife every night.'

'Now there's a thought. Can't see it working though, unless I can her off to Portland to fly the Lynx.'

'Why not have a word with her appointer as well. Maybe you can arrange to be at the same place. Bloody hell, the navy owes you after your success in the Gulf last year.'

'Since when did her Majesty's Navy actually do gratitude?'

'Good point. Oh, changing the subject we've just had a signal in from Fleet warning us of some rather nasty weather coming up our chuff. We should be snug in Devonport by the time it comes through but they wanted us to know.'

'Oh, how bad?'

'Nasty little secondary low, with possible record low pressure and winds of at least Force Ten on the bad side. A proper little miniature hurricane by the looks of it. We should be past the Lizard before we even feel any serious wind, so we could always run into Falmouth if it gets that bad.'

'OK just keep an eye out behind us. It's always best to be forewarned. There was a nasty red sky at dawn this morning. Red sky at night, Shepherds delight.....'

'Red sky in the morning, Shepherds house on fire,' Brian joined in the old joke and they both chuckled.

Fifty miles astern of HMS Prometheus Petter Olafson, the Master of the Motor Vessel Ocean Wanderer was not in such a sanguine mood as the Captain of the warship to the east of him. His Chief Engineer had just told him that they had discovered contamination in their fuel tanks. The Chief was reasonably certain that they had enough clean fuel to reach the Channel and then if necessary they could put into Falmouth or even Portland should they not be able to reach Southampton. However, he had also just seen the latest ocean weather forecast from the Met Office and there was some very rough weather brewing up behind them. He was now seriously considering running for shelter in Southern Ireland or even Brest.

At the rear of the bridge was a barometer and it was plunging, literally. He hadn't seen such a pressure drop in all his years at sea. Every alarm bell, that thirty years of experience had given him, was starting to ring. He got up from his seat and looked at the barometer once more and then the sky astern of them. The sea was really starting to get up and the sky was now a dark grey. It was already blowing a full Force Eight and he was sure it would soon be more than that.

He made his decision. It would be Crosshaven in Southern Ireland. It was the closest shelter he could get to, even if it meant heading further north and more into the path of the storm. He could travel almost as fast as the depression was moving and stay ahead of the worst of the weather. His alternative, of Brest, was further to go and a lee shore should he be delayed in any way. He ordered the helmsman to come another twenty degrees to port.

Just then, his First Officer came onto the bridge. Jorgen Olafson was also his brother in law and they had both grown up together in the town of Stavanger on Norway's wild, west coast.

Petter looked at his friend. 'The barometer is plunging Jorgen. I've decided we need to head for shelter and Crosshaven is the closest. It means crossing the path of this little depression but then we will be safe.'

His brother in law was a man of few words and simply nodded as he stared out of the bridge windows over the vast deck stretched out ahead of them. He finally spoke, 'the cargo Petter.'

'Yes I understand. I remonstrated with the owners before we sailed as you well know. I presume you are talking about the main hold?'

'Yes it should be full and it's not.'

'So, what is your assessment?'

Jorgen thought carefully as he chose his words. 'I've done some calculations. If it shifts, it has enough leverage to capsize the ship. Five thousand tons of iron ore can do that.'

'But the baffles should hold it surely? You're starting to get me worried.'

'Yes the baffles should hold but we are already rolling hard. If it starts to shift over them then we could be in trouble.'

'Alright but the sea shouldn't get any worse than this. We are moving at the same speed as the storm and well ahead of it.'

Jorgen nodded. He was just about to speak again when they all felt the motion of the ship change. The vibration of the ships massive diesel engine, that had been ever present since they sailed five days ago, had suddenly disappeared. Almost immediately, the helmsman reported that he could no longer hold course and the speaker above Petter's head woke into life.

'Captain, this is the Chief Engineer, I'm sorry but it looks like the fuel was worse than we thought. We've lost propulsion for the moment and I can't guarantee the generators for long either.'

As he spoke all the bridge lights went out and the Chief Engineers voice was cut off.

Petter looked at Jorgen as a sharp stab of fear shot through him. 'Do what you can to secure the cargo. I'm going to put out a distress call. We may not have much time.'

Jon was about to leave the bridge and grab a few hours sleep. He knew that as soon as they closed land he would be kept busy. Then the bridge VHF suddenly broke into life.

'Mayday, Mayday, Mayday,' a strongly accented voice called. 'This is the Motor Vessel Ocean Wanderer. My position is Fifty degrees, Twenty One minutes north, Ten degrees, Fifty Five point Two minutes west. We have suffered a total power failure and we are not under command. We are carrying a partial load of iron ore which is in danger of shifting. I have thirty six souls on board. Is there any vessel that can assist? Over.'

Before Jon could request it, the Officer of the Watch reported, 'fifty two miles astern of us Sir, should I alter course?'

Jon thought for a second. No other ship had answered the call. 'Yes please Officer of the Watch. Yeoman, answer the call please and tell them we are turning to assist. We should be with them in about three hours.'

Jon knew that once they were heading to the west they would be slamming into this large sea. If they could do even twenty knots he would be very surprised. He grabbed the ships main broadcast. 'D'you hear there, Captain speaking, the ship is about to turn across the sea and may roll heavily. The reason is that we have received a Mayday from a merchantman astern of us and we are going to their assistance. I would like the First Lieutenant, MEO, Ops Officer and Flight Commander to come to the bridge now please.' He then had to grab hold of his seat as the ship gave a massive lurch and roll to starboard as they turned into the trough of the swell. Several crashes could be heard from below the bridge ladders. Jon just hoped they weren't from his cabin.

The ship quickly steadied up on the new course and now instead of rolling hard she was pitching into the large rollers coming from almost dead ahead. A sound like a shot gun blast was heard as the first waves broke over the bow and slammed into the bridge windows. For a

7

moment all outside view was obliterated as the curtain of sea water streamed down the glass. Jon and the Officer of the Watch both reached forward at the same time and turned on the large windscreen wipers in front of them not that it was going to make that much difference from now on.

'Try twenty knots Terry,' Jon called to the Officer of the Watch. 'And we'll see how she takes it.'

Just then Des Slater, the First Lieutenant and Brian appeared. They were closely followed by Andy Cummings, the ship's Mechanical Engineer Officer, and finally Jerry Thompson the ship's Flight Commander and pilot of the Lynx helicopter. Jon was glad that Jerry was finally back on board. He had been quite badly injured during their foray into the Gulf the previous year but had now made a full recovery.

Jon outlined the situation as far as it was known. He then turned to Jerry. 'Well Flight Commander, this could be interesting, what are your thoughts on being able to operate in this weather?' As he spoke, another wave smashed into the bridge windows and they all had to grab on to something as the ship shuddered.

Jerry looked grim. 'If you can give me a decent course and speed Sir, I reckon I could get off the deck, not too sure about getting back on again though.'

'Agreed, the ship in distress is about a hundred and twenty five miles from the closest point of land which is Southern Ireland, so if we have to take people off, you should be able to make that, especially with the wind behind you.'

'Yes Sir but I can only carry about nine people at the most and I doubt I would be able to get back to you any time soon. Honestly, I don't think I could land back on board for more fuel in this sea state.'

Brian looked at Jon. 'I think we'd better put a call into Culdrose Sir. A Sea King has the endurance and much more carrying capacity. We would HIFR them if they needed fuel.'

'Good point Brian, make it so. Maybe get one on the way. It can stop at Cork for fuel. We don't know yet whether this ship is in real danger. They've quite rightly put out a Mayday but they're still afloat and who knows they might be able to get underway again.'

The discussion went on for several more minutes as all options were considered but in the end they all knew they would have to wait until they arrived on the scene. The team left to make preparations, leaving Jon on the bridge to ponder the situation. He wondered who would be flying the Sea King that Culdrose would send.

Chapter 2

Lieutenant Helen Hunt was sitting in the crewroom of 771 Squadron at the Naval Air Station at Culdrose looking out over the windswept airfield. All training flying had been cancelled as the wind was now blowing hard, over twenty five knots and the visibility was dreadful. She didn't care, Jon would be home tomorrow. They hadn't seen each other for months and she couldn't wait for his ship to come alongside in Devonport where she would be waiting tomorrow afternoon. She knew what it would be like. This would be the third time he had returned from a foreign deployment but that only made the anticipation higher.

With the weather clamped in and a Friday afternoon in the offing, most of the aircrew had repaired to the bar on the other side of the airfield. She had come off duty that morning and although they hadn't been called out, she was still feeling tired. She never slept well when there was a radio bleeper beside her bed which could go off at any moment. Maybe she should sneak off home and get a good sleep so that she was ready for Jon's return. Her thoughts were interrupted by the Squadron Senior Pilot putting his head around the door.

'Duty crew off your arses please. We've got a shout and it could be a big one.'

The three aircrew, who had been lounging on some of the faded armchairs, jumped up and shot out to the briefing room. Helen thanked her stars she wasn't on call. The thought didn't last long as the Senior Pilot looked around and caught her gaze. 'Helen, we're probably going to need two cabs on this one. Are your team still here?'

With a sinking feeling, she nodded. 'Yes SPLOT, I'll get them into the briefing room. They're all around somewhere.'

Five minutes later, the duty officer was standing in front of the briefing room detailing the situation to the two crews that were now assembled.

'We've got a Norwegian Ore carrier called the Ocean Wanderer in distress about a hundred miles south west of Ireland. She's put out a Mayday as she's lost all power and there is a shitty piece of weather about to clobber her in a few hours time. She is still afloat but they are worried that the cargo could shift, in which case she will need help immediately. You two crews are to man up and fly to Cork where you will refuel and await developments. You may not be needed but if you are then we need to get you as close to the scene as we can.'

Helen, along with the other aircrew was busy writing notes down on her kneepad. However, she wasn't surprised by the duty officer's next point. She had already worked it out in her head.

'One further thing, we have a warship in the area. HMS Prometheus has turned to offer assistance and will be standing by shortly. Helen, that's your old man's steamer isn't it?'

She nodded but didn't say anything.

'Well her Lynx is serviceable and they believe it would feasible to launch her. She would have the endurance to get ashore to Cork but as you all know, the Lynx is far too small to take off the whole crew and anyway it may well be dark by the time it gets serious and they have no night Search and Rescue capability.'

The door suddenly opened and a slightly dishevelled Lieutenant appeared with a large briefcase in his hand.

'Right, I'll hand over to the Met man and then you lot better get airborne.'

Prometheus had at last reached the position of the Ocean Wanderer and had been able to slow down to a more sensible speed. Jon, Des and the Officer of the Watch were looking at the stricken ship which was rolling horribly in the massive swell.

She's rolling more to port than to starboard,' Jon observed, as he studied her through his binoculars.

Des agreed. 'She's a large ship though, at least twenty thousand tons, maybe she can take it.'

Jon nodded. He had the microphone of the VHF radio in his hand. He raised it to his mouth. 'Ocean Wanderer, this is Prometheus, we have you visual, what is your situation now over?'

There was a few seconds silence then a voice answered. 'Prometheus, thank you for coming, as we expected our main cargo has started to shift. I have no option but abandon ship if that's possible in this sea state. Do you have any recommendations?'

'Ocean Wanderer, yes I do, we have two Sea King helicopters standing by in Southern Ireland. They have enough capacity to take all your crew. But confirm you wish to abandon over?'

'Affirmative, once this sort of cargo starts to move there is no chance to stop it. And the weather is going to get much worse before it gets better.'

Jon could hear the undercurrent of fear in the man's voice. 'Understood Ocean Wanderer, we will get the helicopters on their way.

10

They will take about an hour and half to get here. Do you think you can last that long?'

'We can only pray. If we can't, we have a lifeboat and life rafts but launching them and getting into them will be very difficult in this sea state.'

Jon could only agree. The wind was now a good Force Nine. He was even starting to worry about damage to his own ship. He turned to the First Lieutenant, 'Des, work up what contingencies we might have if they have to use the liferafts and the helicopters can't get here. I'm afraid there's no way we can launch the Lynx now, so it's a worst case scenario but we have to be prepared.'

Des nodded and left the bridge as Jon took up the microphone to the Ops room. 'Ops call Culdrose and get them to contact the Sea Kings and get them to launch. Tell them to get here as soon as they can.'

Cork airfield hardstanding was barely visible in driving rain. Helen was sitting in the right hand seat of Rescue Five Zero looking glumly over towards the other machine, Rescue Five Five. Her crew had gone inside to the small terminal building to try and find some coffee but she had elected to stay in her seat and stay dry. Every now and then the aircraft rocked to a gust of wind and a rotor blade dipped down in front of the cockpit.

The flight over had been rough. They had elected to fly in cloud, at altitude and so there had been nothing to see until the approach radar at Cork had guided them down almost to the threshold of the main runway before anything became visible. There had been no word about whether they would be needed yet but a refuelling bowser had topped up their tanks. Now it was simply a matter of waiting.

For some reason that Helen couldn't shake off she had an unusual feeling of apprehension about this mission. There was no logical reason for it. She had flown in such bad conditions before. The Sea King was rugged and reliable, and she knew she was on top of her game. She smiled inwardly at herself when she remembered the first time she had flown in one of these metal monsters at Yeovilton several years ago. She had been awed that such an inanimate lump of machinery could even fly, let alone fly gracefully. The cockpit had seemed like a nightmare of incomprehensible switches and gauges. Now, it seemed like home. She found she even liked the smell of flying machines, a mixture of burned kerosene and grease. Half the time, she found that she was doing the various cockpit checks without conscious thought and flying was second nature. So why was she feeling so concerned? Maybe it was because she had been looking forward to seeing Jon again for so long and now there could be a delay. She also knew that when he was back and they had some time together, they were going to have to have a very serious talk. Unlike her husband, she had slowly been realising that although she loved the navy, there had to be something else in her life. She had something very important to tell him.

Her thoughts were interrupted by the banging of the small personnel door opening behind her and the damp face of Robbie, her second pilot, appeared, smiling and holding out two steaming paper mugs of what she hoped was coffee. She grabbed them from him as he then proceeded to clamber into the left hand seat. He didn't bother to strap in.

'What ho Helen, you made the right decision there. The departure lounge is just about empty and there's nothing inside except for a crappy old coffee machine. I got soaked just getting there and back. Thank goodness we're wearing goon bags today at least they keep the rain out.'

'Any news on what's going on with the ship out there?'

'Derek is in the control tower now and I reckon we should hear something soon.'

No sooner had he spoken and a door at the base of the tower opened and a green clad figure was running towards them waving his hands over his head in a circular motion.

Helen knew exactly what it meant and so did Robbie. Annoyed that she hadn't even taken a sip of her coffee, she threw the contents out of her side window, jammed the paper cup into her nav bag and started to wake the sleeping beast back into life.

Chapter 3

The Sea King was being buffeted hard by the relentless gale. The sea, only a few hundred feet below them, was almost pure white. The tops of the waves were being blown off by the force of the wind and great streams of spume were streaming away from their crests. They had taken off a few minutes behind Five Five to allow for a safe separation as the first part of the trip was in cloud. As soon as the aircraft's radar had confirmed that they were clear of the Irish coast they had carefully descended and broken through the cloud base at just less than two hundred feet.

Derek, the Observer, was watching his radar and Doppler navigation system. 'We've got a wind at about forty five degrees to our track and so our ground speed is only seventy knots, can't we go any faster?'

Helen had been flying at their normal airspeed maximum of one hundred knots. 'Alright Derek, we'll wind her up to maximum but be prepared for a rough ride.'

She pulled the collective lever up until both engine torque meters were at one hundred per cent and kept the aircraft attitude steady. The airspeed increased to just over one hundred and fifteen but the vibration, in the already shaking machine, was now severe.

'These bloody things were originally designed to do a hundred and twenty,' Robbie muttered.

'Not at such a high all up weight,' Helen responded. 'But it won't matter for a little while. What's our ETA now Derek?'

'With that extra fifteen knots you've managed to get we should be there in another fifty minutes. If we could climb and get the wind to veer more it would cut down the ahead component and that would also help.'

'Good idea,' replied Helen. 'Let's try it. I'll creep up to a thousand feet and we'll see the effect.'

Although they were back in cloud, the wind did indeed veer and they gained another ten knots ground speed. 'Derek, tell Five Five what we've done,' Helen called to her Observer.

The call was acknowledged and the other machine also climbed to take advantage of the wind shear.

The lead aircraft then called ahead. 'Prometheus, this is Rescue Five Five, with Five Zero a few minutes behind me. We estimate arriving on scene in thirty five minutes request Sitrep over.'

The ship immediately responded. 'Rescue Five Five, Roger, I hold you both on my zero two five at forty five and fifty miles. The casualty has a list of over thirty degrees now and the crew are all mustered at their emergency stations. Get here as fast as you can, over.'

'This is Five Five understood. Can you describe the deck layout and wind conditions please?'

A new voice came on the radio and Helen's heart leapt. She recognised it immediately. 'Rescue helicopters, this is the Commanding Officer speaking, I'm ex aircrew, so will talk you through some ideas.'

Robbie grinned over at Helen knowing that it was her husband on the radio. She didn't notice.

'The ship is beam on to the wind and can't manoeuvre. She is rolling very heavily. The list is to port, which is the downwind side. The deck layout is simple. There is a large superstructure aft and long well deck ahead up to the bow. There is plenty of room but there are a number of loading derricks along the deck. There is no way you can land on and even winching a crewman down could be problematical. My suggestion would be to winch from just ahead of the main superstructure, over.'

'Five Five copied all that. Any casualties reported?'

'Negative, nothing serious but they have some walking wounded. They also have a portable radio with them and will be listening on sixteen, so I suggest you call them when you get closer.'

'This is Five Five, all copied thank you.'

The next twenty minutes passed all too quickly. Helen and the crew talked over various ideas. Tiny, the Aircrewman, who had stayed in Helen's crew all through her time on the squadron, was keen to try to go down to the ship. He knew how important someone on deck could be. However, Helen also knew how almost suicidally brave he could be. 'Now listen everyone, Five Five will get there first and I doubt very much whether there will be room for two of us to winch at the same time, so let's just see what they come up with first.'

It wasn't long before they had the two ships on radar and soon after that they were able to descend back below the cloud and slow down to a more comfortable speed.

'Fucking hell, the sea's even rougher, if that's possible,' Robbie observed, looking down as they emerged from the cloud.

Helen could only agree but now they could see the victim in the distance as well as the much smaller grey shape a few hundred yards away from her.

The other Sea King flew around the disabled ship carefully assessing the situation. Helen slowed down to seventy knots which was their best speed to conserve fuel and orbited away from the scene to allow the other aircraft to operate safely.

For such a violent scene, all started off well. Five Five made a careful approach and was soon established in a high hover over the deck of the ship. They made no attempt to lower a winchman, which Helen wholeheartedly agreed with but spent several minutes on the radio explaining to the crew of the ship what needed to be done. One by one, an orange clad figure ran from the shelter of the superstructure and grabbed the winch horsecollar once it had settled on deck. The Sea King then snatched the body quickly upwards and despite several wild swings gathered it into the cabin door to safety. The process seemed to take forever. Helen was starting to worry about fuel and the fact that it was starting to get dark.

Derek confirmed with Prometheus that they had Helicopter in Flight Refuelling hoses ready on deck. The Sea King could go down and hover alongside and use its winch to pull up a hose to get fuel. However, Helen wasn't that keen on doing the manoeuvre in such a sea state.

Just as she was considering biting the bullet and asking for a HIFR, Five Five called. 'All stations this is Five Five. I have twenty four casualties on board. I can't take any more and anyway must leave now to get home with at least some gas in the tanks. Five Zero, it's your turn now.'

Derek acknowledged as the other machine transitioned away from the stricken ship and headed away to the north east.

'Alright everyone', Helen called over the intercom. 'We've not been using lots of fuel like the other cab. We've still got over two hours endurance, so we won't ask for a HIFR. Let's just get down there before it gets totally dark and get the other twelve guys off.'

Helen repeated the previous aircraft's approach and was soon in a high hover over the ship's well deck. The superstructure off to her right gave her enough visual references to hold a reasonable hover and the conning instructions coming from Derek in the cabin door was enough to finish the job.

Although it was starting to get fairly dark now, she was starting to settle into the routine and the first two survivors were recovered without incident. Suddenly, everything changed. The bridge of the ship which she had been using as her reference stopped coming up past the vertical. She immediately realised what was happening.

'She's starting to list even more guys, be careful,' she called urgently. Her words were too late. The next time the superstructure rolled away from her it kept going and in what seemed like seconds, the whole massive structure was gone, as the whole ship turned turtle.

'I've got one on the wire,' Derek called. 'Just hold steady a few more seconds. Alright, he's in. Helen can you back up and come down twenty feet?'

Helen was having problems of her own. 'Sorry Derek, I'm going to have to transition forward and fly a circuit, I can't see a bloody thing. We'll do an AFCS transition to get back into the hover.'

As she started to circle around, Prometheus called over the radio. 'Five Zero, Sitrep please?'

Helen answered. 'We managed to get three off but that leaves nine unaccounted for. Have you seen anything from where you are?'

'Affirmative, there are at least some bodies in the water downwind of the hull which is now floating upside down. However, I am unable to launch a sea boat in these conditions.'

'I understand Jon,' she replied. 'I am going round to get into a hover and should be able to find them.' She hadn't realised her automatic use of Jon's name and no one else mentioned it.

Within two minutes, she was back facing into the wind and had engaged the Automatic Flight Control System that would bring the helicopter into the hover using its Doppler radar. It was now pitch black and they turned on their powerful search lights as soon as they were established in the hover. With the help of Prometheus, who had been maintaining a plot of the position of the survivors in the water, they had managed to find a group of four men clinging to each other. This time Helen allowed Tiny to go down on the wire and the first two casualties were retrieved safely. However, the second time Tiny came up, his goon suit had been ripped open and despite his protestations Helen refused to let him go down again. She applied the same veto to Derek who immediately volunteered to take over. It took longer but the other two men were recovered, although the last man came up with the winch wire tangled around his legs.

'Five more men out there. Derek, can you ask the last guys to come up if they know what happened to them?' Helen asked.

'Hold on Helen,' Derek replied. After a few minutes, he called back. 'They're not sure Helen. One of the men said he thought he saw their skipper swimming but no one else saw anything.'

Helen looked at their fuel gauges. 'Derek, how long to get back to Cork?'

'With the tail wind we should get, about forty five minutes and much less than that to get to land of course.'

'We can't just leave without looking for the others. Right, we'll drop back a little and then do a ladder search into wind. We've got fuel enough for another fifteen minutes then we either HIFR or head home.'

Within minutes, they came across two more casualties and successfully recovered them. Derek called from the rear. 'Helen one of these guys is the First Officer. He says his brother in law is the ship's master and he was in the water but they got separated. He has no idea where he is now.'

Helen knew that the survival time in these waters was a matter of minutes. She had enough fuel to fly for an hour and a half. If she broke off the search, even for the fifteen minutes or so it would take to get fuel from Prometheus, they would probably be dead by the time they resumed. If she didn't and they couldn't get fuel and HIFR had been known to go wrong, then they could end up in the water themselves. Jon had told her about his unplanned landing of a Sea King on a Leander Frigate some years earlier but then the sea had been relatively flat. Today, such an evolution would be suicide.

She made her decision. 'Right guys, we keep looking, any objections?'

There were none. Twenty minutes later, just as Helen was about to give up, Robbie spotted something in the water off to the left. It was a faint light. Robbie took control and manoeuvred towards it until it could be picked up in the searchlight. It was a body and it didn't seem to be moving.

'Derek, you are going to have to go down on the wire I'm afraid,' Helen called. 'But don't risk anything if it's clear he's dead alright?'

Derek acknowledged the call and Tiny took over the con. Two minutes later, a very shaken Derek was winched back up with a body in the other harness.

'He's conscious Helen and the other guy back here confirms it's his brother in law. He says he sure there are no other survivors. The other guys were with him and they've gone.'

'Right, let's get some gas and go home,' Helen was sorry for the other men but this rescue wasn't over yet. They still had to reach dry land.

The HIFR was a nightmare. Jon had told her how much Prometheus rolled but saying it and actually having to hover alongside the ship were two different things. It took ten minutes of the combined efforts of Tiny and Derek just to get the hose connected to the refuelling point. All the time, Helen was having to fight the Sea King to remain even remotely in position. Robbie was in no position to help from the other seat as he could barely see the Frigate. Eventually, the fuel gauges started to creep up. When they had reached two thousand pounds Helen called a halt. She really ought to have taken more but she was getting exhausted. With the hoses returned to the deck, they gratefully transitioned away and she handed control over to her second pilot.

'Five Zero, this is Prometheus, very well done, that was a brilliant piece of flying. Your vector to Cork is zero two seven at ninety six miles.'

Helen replied. 'I bet you say that to all the girls. Thank you Prometheus, see you when you get in.'

She turned and smiled at Robbie, while speaking over the intercom to them all. 'Bloody well done all of you, that wasn't easy, any of it. Derek, how are the casualties?'

'We've got at least one broken arm and several incipient hypothermias but nothing life threatening as long as we can get back soon.'

Helen sighed and relaxed back in her seat. It was a mistake. There was a loud bang from above her head and the whole aircraft shook.

'What the hell?' She queried as she scanned the instruments. She suddenly saw the problem. 'Robbie, lower the lever, come back to seventy knots and fly with as little power as possible.'

'Oh shit, the Power Turbine Inlet Temperatures, I've got it.' As Robbie lowered the collective to reduce power, the number two engine recovered.

'What the fuck's going on Helen?' Derek called from the back.

'The number two engine just surged Derek. We must have salt build up in the engine intakes. Put out a Pan call. Although I don't think Prometheus can help.' There was serious concern in her voice but after all they had been through she was damned if she was going to let this latest problem stop them reaching land.

Both pilots knew the problem. Continued flying in a salt laden atmosphere could allow a crust of salt to form in the engine intakes and leading edges of the rotor blades. Eventually, this could lead to the engines being choked, which is what had just happened.

'Derek get on the radar, can you see any rain around?' she called urgently.

'Hang on, turn left twenty degrees. Something's showing up a few miles ahead.'

Robbie turned the aircraft and also climbed as much as he could. With both engines now restricted on power, he didn't dare pull too much but if they could get into cloud, the water vapour might help clean the salt off. Suddenly rain started to hit the windscreen. Both pilots watched the engine PTIT gauges and with relief saw them start to creep down slightly. Unfortunately, the rain quickly stopped.

'Turn us around Robbie,' Helen instructed. 'See if we can get back into the rain.'

Carefully monitoring the engine gauges, Robbie banked the helicopter and reversed their course. They were soon back in the rain and once again the engine temperatures cooled further. At the same time the ride became smoother as the airframe vibration decreased.

'Must have been a lot of salt on the rotor blades as well. We just didn't notice it as it slowly built up.' Robbie observed. 'I reckon we should be able to get back on heading now Helen.'

Helen agreed and they turned for Ireland.

On the bridge of Prometheus they had heard the helicopter's distress call. Jon, as an ex Sea King pilot, had immediately understood what the problem was. He also realised there was absolutely nothing he could do about it. So it was with a rush of relief that he heard them call that they had managed to clear some of it in a rain cloud. He knew it would not have removed all the salt but they seemed confident of reaching land and it could be washed off properly once on the ground.

Brian was standing next to him the whole time. 'Well Sir, that was a bloody good bit of aviating all round. Helen deserves a bloody medal.'

Jon looked at his friend. 'They all do and I'm going to recommend them for one even, if one of them is my wife.'

Chapter 4

Jon watched, as at first light, the remains of the Ocean Wanderer finally slipped below the waves. Despite the Observer in Helen's Sea King saying that one of the survivors had reported that the last few men had died, he didn't want to give up until he was sure. The ship had stayed afloat for hours and provided an excellent datum for them to search from but he had to admit now that there was no point in staying. The sea temperature was fourteen degrees and no one could have survived the night in those temperatures, even if they were wearing full immersion gear.

Even so, it was with a degree of reluctance that he gave the order to turn for home. The weather had moderated enormously. The sky was clear with a few scudding showers and the wind was a balmy Force Seven. The sea state was still high but with the ship now heading down the swells, they were no longer slamming although Prometheus was back to her old tricks and rolling like a pig.

With a start, Jon realised that he hadn't slept all night and suddenly he felt exhausted. With a quick word to the Officer of the Watch, he went down the starboard bridge ladder and entered his day cabin. Jenkins his steward was there and offered him coffee and breakfast but Jon realised he was just too tired. With a brief instruction to be woken at noon, he went into his sleeping cabin and was asleep as soon as his head hit the pillow.

He woke to the smiling face of his steward, who had a large mug of coffee ready for him. Thanking him profusely, Jon then shooed him away and headed for his shower. As the water hit him and he started to feel properly awake, he started to contemplate getting home and seeing Helen again. At the thought of his wife, he looked down. His body's reaction reminded him just how much he had missed her. Hearing her voice on the radio last night hadn't helped. Determinedly, he turned the water to cold. There would be plenty of time for that later.

Refreshed, even if he was still a little tired, he made his way to the bridge. Brian had just taken over the afternoon watch.

'Afternoon Sir,' Brian called cheerily. 'ETA Plymouth is twenty hundred tonight. It will still be light, so flag Officer Plymouth is happy for us to come straight in.'

'Any word that the press are going to be there Brian? They're normally quick at picking up on things after a rescue.'

'And you and Helen hardly stay out of the limelight but I've not heard anything, so fingers crossed.'

The bedside telephone woke Helen up from a deep sleep. For a second she couldn't remember where on earth she was but looking around she saw the familiar curtains of her bedroom. The events of the previous night and day quickly flooded back. They had dropped their casualties off at Cork and then with another quick refuel, had made the final run back to Culdrose. Robbie had done most of the flying for which she had been grateful. When they finally arrived back at base, they had given Station Ops a quick debrief and she had managed to get away to her married quarter. She realised she had absolutely no recollection of going to bed.

She looked at the bedside table and saw, with surprise, that it was almost noon. She must have slept a good eight hours. Grabbing the telephone, she sat up and tried to settle her thoughts. 'Helen Hunt, can I help?'

The voice at the end of the telephone caught her by surprise. 'Lieutenant Hunt, this is Captain Morgan. I'm sorry if I woke you and I know it's a Saturday but I would like you to come into the Air Station this afternoon. I want to personally congratulate you and all the other crew on your work last night and the press would also like a word.'

Helen was flattered that the Air Station Commanding Officer had made the effort to call her personally. However, she groaned inwardly when he had mentioned the press. They had been a pain over recent years. It seemed that the navy's golden couple were always good for a story and she would bet a fortune that they had already made the connection with the rescue and the presence of her husband's ship. More stupid interviews, more hopelessly inaccurate reports.

'Helen, are you still there?'

'Oh sorry Sir, I was just contemplating talking to all those reporters again.'

The Captain chuckled. 'Well, that will teach you to do such a bloody good job. Anyway, my office, at two please.' He hung up.

She jumped into the shower and quickly dressed before grabbing a sandwich in the kitchen. With half an hour to spare, she drove back into the Air Station but this time headed over to the administration building by the wardroom where the Captain had his office. As she mounted the steps she saw the rest of her crew, plus those from the other aircraft.

'Oops, am I the last to arrive?' she asked in general.

Robbie answered. 'You're the only one who wasn't on base when the call came to see the great man. Don't worry, we've ten minutes yet.'

Sophie Stevens, the station Public Relations Officer, walked in. She looked around and
was clearly counting heads. 'Good afternoon everyone, the Captain will talk to you all first and then we have a local reporter who would like to interview you.'

Helen noted something in Sophie's voice as she made her last comment.

'Who exactly is the reporter Sophie?'

'Now Helen, he is the only local chap and he is syndicated to all the national newspapers.'

'It's that little shit Simon isn't it? I told you I'd never talk to him again. When Jon got back from the Gulf he interviewed me and Jon and then just made the whole bloody thing up. It was a disgrace.'

'Now look Helen, Simon Gross is a well-respected journalist and we need all the good publicity we can get, you know that.'

Helen had been mortified and disgusted when she read the tissue of half-truths and bare faced lies the man had produced last time. She wasn't going to stand for it again. 'Sorry Sophie, not even the Captain can order me to talk to him and you certainly can't.'

Just then, the door to the inner office opened and the Captain himself came in.

'Well done everyone that was a hell of a rescue you guys pulled off. You will be glad to know that all of the men you rescued are now reported as recovering well. I know some of them didn't make it but frankly, I consider it a miracle that you managed as well as you did. Now look Helen, I overheard your comment about the journo and to a degree, I agree with you. The man is a little weasel but he wants to put this on the front pages of one of the major tabloids. I really don't want to miss the opportunity.'

Helen pursed her lips. 'Sir, I understand what you're saying but I can't face Jon and I being treated like that again.'

'Alright, how about I insist that you see his copy before it's published and he has to accept your approval?'

Helen knew she would have to bow to the inevitable and at least that way she might be able to curb some of the more outrageous excesses that made it into print.

She nodded her acceptance and the Captain talked to them all, querying them about the detail of the rescue, before offering a final thank you to them all. He then left and Sophie the PRO, and a young man with thinning hair and round glasses came in. He smiled at them all.

'Hello everyone, to those who don't know me, I'm Simon Gross and I want to interview you for the National Press. It seems you guys did a fantastic job last night.'

Helen had to admire the man's bare faced cheek and did her best to keep her answers to monosyllables but she had to contain herself several times when he talked to her directly. After half an hour, she looked at her watch. She then excused herself with the statement that she needed to get to Plymouth to meet her husband. She didn't give the journalist time to follow up her remark and slipped out of the office.

Breathing a sigh of relief, she made her way home. It was a weekend and she was not on call, so she was free for the next two days and Jon would be home that night. Putting all other thoughts out of her mind, she changed into civilian clothes and went down to the garage. Jon's present was there. They both normally drove around in an old Ford Capri that Jon had had for years but a few weeks ago, when visiting the Air Station at Yeovilton, she had seen one of these sports cars. She knew Jon had always wanted one. There was a classic car restoration firm nearby and with some time to spare, she scrounged a lift and went to have a look. The result was the bright red Triumph TR5 sports car now gleaming in their garage. As she looked at the immaculate machine, she imagined the look of delight on his face when he saw it. It hadn't been cheap, the TR5 was the most sought after of the whole series and this one had been professionally restored but she had the money and he was worth it. Besides, she loved to drive it as well, so it was a double plus. She had originally intended to let him see it when he got home but it had stopped raining and the sun was shining. She would take the top down and drive to Plymouth, where she had arranged to meet her brother to see Jon's ship come in from the Hoe and then she could give it to him as soon as he arrived.

Chapter 5

The accident on the A30, near the end of the dual carriageway, was a horrible one. The road leading in and out of west Cornwall was the only main artery for tourists and locals alike. In this case, a caravan heading towards Truro and travelling too fast down the hill before the final roundabout, had started to sway. Instead of trying to control it, the driver had done exactly the wrong thing and slammed on the brakes. The oversize caravan had immediately whipped around and jack-knifed the tow car into the opposite lanes. The tow car, with two adults and two children in the back, was already upside down when it was hit by the sports car coming the other way. The lorry driver following, also had no chance to react and ploughed into both vehicles. After that, everyone else managed to stop or take avoiding action. The road was blocked in both directions and despite the help of those on the scene, by the time the ambulances arrived, there were two dead adults and two severely injured children to deal with.

Helen had no idea what had happened ahead of her. All she knew was that, once again, the bloody A30 was blocked. The road was a nightmare for locals and tourists. The standing joke was that the dual carriageway around Bodmin was amazingly efficient at delivering you straight to the permanent traffic jam at the end where it went into single carriageway. Successive governments had promised to do something about it but never actually managed to deliver on their promises. It was definitely one of the major drawbacks to serving at Culdrose. Getting to Plymouth in under three hours was always the aim and all too often not the result.

Knowing that sitting in a traffic jam for an interminable time was definitely not going to get her to Plymouth, she decided to use one of her rat runs. If she could get another half a mile further on, she knew there was the A3058 that would take her down to St Austell and allow her to head towards Plymouth. The traffic was moving in stops and starts and she soon found out why. At least half the cars ahead of her were having the same idea. However, once on the new road, the traffic was at least moving although she knew that once they got into the outskirts of St Austell another jam awaited her. She wasn't worried though because Jon had shown her another route down some rather pretty side roads that bypassed the whole area. With the top down and the sun in the sky it would be a beautiful drive. She loved the car with its straight six engine. It had loads of power and the note from the exhaust was exhilarating.

She spotted the turn off and because it appeared to head in the wrong direction, no one else was bothering with it. Soon, she was flying along a beautiful country lane with the wind in her hair and no other cars in sight. Ahead of her, she could see the white mounds of the China Clay pits that the road skirted around. Looking at her watch, she realised there was still plenty of time to get to Roger, her brother's house and then to go down to Plymouth Hoe to watch Prometheus come in. She knew it was going to be Jon's last evolution in the ship and he would be dreadfully disappointed to leave the Frigate. However, she felt rather differently. They had been separated far too much over the last two years and she had already spoken to her appointer. There were several options that would allow them to be together. She just prayed that Jon would like one of them. A wave of longing washed over her as she thought of being together again.

Up ahead, was a small village pub. She and Jon had stopped there once but it was very much for the locals and although they weren't made unwelcome, she distinctly felt that they were seen as outsiders. Well, there wouldn't be time to stop there anyway. As she sped past the entrance, she didn't see the tattered old green Landrover pull out. At the wheel was a local farmer who had just finished his fourth pint and was now going home for a nap, as he did every day. Pulling out from the car park, he didn't bother to look. No one used the road, so he was startled to see a small red car in his way. Pulling the wheel hard to the right, he thought he had missed it but then there was a small bang and he felt the wheel jerk in his hand.

Although she hadn't seen the Landrover, Helen felt the impact. Suddenly, the car slewed hard to the left and the nose crunched into the hedge. Cornish hedges are notorious for hiding stone walls and this was no exception. As the nose dug in, the car, which was now sideways across the road, started to roll over. Helen had taken the advice of the restoration company who had sold it to her and a roll over bar had been fitted. She just had time to realise it was going to save her life, when the car slammed into the road upside down and then sideways into the hedge. Stunned but still conscious, she was suddenly aware that the engine was still roaring. She reached forward to try and turn it off but the disorientation of being upside down meant she couldn't find the key. Suddenly the engine stopped. Cars designed in the sixties didn't have as many safety features in them as modern cars and in this case the impact had ruptured the fuel lines. Being a fuel injected engine, petrol started to spray into the driver's compartment. The inertial cut off switch hadn't operated and several pints of fuel had been released. Realising the danger, Helen frantically struggled with her seat belt, crying and screaming to Jon for help as she did so. She was too late. With a loud crump the whole car caught fire.

The patrons in the pub had also heard the crash and rushed out. One of them had even got to within feet of the wreck before it burst into flames and forced him back. Unlike the movies, cars don't normally explode and within minutes the fire was subsiding. The onlookers were able to get closer. The first man who looked inside saw Helens charred remains and was promptly and violently sick.

Jon was full of torn emotions. Conning Prometheus back into Devonport was a sad occasion but knowing that Helen would be on the jetty was making up for it. She had said she would be on the Hoe with her brother to wave as they went past. He had been rather busy as he made sure the ship stayed in the narrow channel and he hadn't been able to see her specifically although there were several people waving. But now they were tied up and the families were starting to stream on board.

'Finished with main engines,' he said to the Quartermaster. It was his last direct order to the ship but instead of feeling the loss, suddenly all he wanted was to go home. The ship would be alongside now for some time for maintenance and his relief would be joining in a fortnight. He knew the wardroom were planning some sort of social for him and there was quite a lot of work to do sorting out things for the handover. However, the weekend would be his as soon as Helen arrived. She had been hinting at something special in her letters. He wondered what it was. He made his way down the starboard bridge ladder and into his day cabin. The ship would be left in the tender care of the Duty Watch and Officer of the Day, so that as many of the ship's company could get home as soon as possible.

Just before he entered his cabin, he heard the bright chattering of children and he saw Brian and Kathy his wife, with their two little ones. He waved to them.

'Seen Helen yet Jon?' Kathy asked.

'Not yet, she's probably fighting to get through the scrum on the flight deck.'

'That's odd,' Brian said. 'I left strict instructions with the Quartermaster to ensure the Captain's wife was given priority.'

Jon wasn't worried. 'Maybe she's caught up in traffic. Getting from deepest darkest Cornwall can be a nightmare.'

'That's a good point Jon,' Kathy replied. 'I heard on the radio that there had been yet another accident on the A30. The tail back was for miles. Luckily, I had already gone past it.'

'Ah, that's highly likely then. Anyway, I'm for packing and hopefully she will be here by the time I've finished. We'll see you in the pub tomorrow?'

'Absolutely, as long as the damned road is clear to get back that is.' Brian replied with a smile.

Jon went into his cabin to get changed. His steward had already packed a small bag. He would remove the majority of his stuff over the next week. Once changed, he sat down trying to stifle his impatience. It was unlike Helen to be late but if she had been caught up in traffic he well knew how long it could take to get free.

Eventually, unable to curb his impatience he went down the starboard ship's waist to the flight deck. It was just about deserted now, only the OOD and Quartermaster, who stiffened to attention at the sight of him.

'Stand easy chaps. I don't suppose you've seen my wife driving a tatty old Ford Capri have you?'

Before they could reply, he noticed a strange car come to a stop at the bottom of the gangway. He realised it was a police car, one of the ones you saw on the main roads. Two policemen got out. One was clearly from the MOD Police the other a regular copper.

'Looks like you've got some trade already,' Jon commented to the OOD. 'I wonder who has managed to get themselves in trouble in such a short time. That has got to be something of a record. I'll let you get on with it.' He turned to go back to his cabin when he overheard one of the policemen.

'We're looking for a Commander Jonathon Hunt,' one of them was saying to the OOD.

Jon turned. 'That's me,' he said. 'Can I help?' For no reason that he could pin down, except that the expression on both policemen's faces were grim, a wave of apprehension washed over him.

'Could we talk in private Sir? We have some bad news.'

Chapter 6

The end of the breakwater at the pretty little fishing village of Porthleven was a dangerous place to be when the wind blew hard from the west. In the past, people had been swept to their deaths in an instant. Today was getting to be that sort of day. It was grey, both the sky and the sea. A keen wind blew in from America and the marching ranks of grey rollers broke continuously against the rocks at the base of the man made structure. The air was full of rain and salt spray. It was a dark day made for mourning, contemplation and overwhelming grief.

Jon stood right at the end oblivious to the weather and the surroundings. He didn't even know why he had come here except that it seemed to be a place that would echo his mood. Who knows, he might even be lucky and be swept to a watery grave by a rogue wave. It would certainly solve his problems. Ever since the policemen had told him what had happened to Helen he had felt completely numb. There was a hole in his soul that he knew would never heal. In a stroke his best friend, his lover and companion had been taken from him, for no reason that he could understand. One moment he was full of the anticipation of their reunion, the next it had all just gone, no notice, no reason.

He heard something behind him and immediately recognised Brian's voice. 'Come on shipmate, you can't stay here. They've put the warning signs up and closed the breakwater.'

For a second, Jon was tempted to tell Brian to go to hell but he couldn't treat his old, no his only real friend now in that way.

'I went to the morgue this morning Brian. They didn't want me to see the body. They said they had enough evidence to make an identification. But I had to look, to see her one more time. I've seen burned corpses before you know.'

Brian kept quiet. He knew it was best for Jon to say as much as he could.

'She was a mess but I had been expecting that. It didn't worry me and at least I was able to say goodbye, as much as I could. There was something else though.' His voice tailed off on a choke.

'Go on.'

'Jesus. She was over three months pregnant. That fucking drunk bastard farmer and his pisshead friends in that pub, not only killed my wife but also my unborn child.'

Brian was dumbstruck. That was the last thing he was expecting but Jon kept on. 'It must have been the last night we spent together before we sailed for the States. She told me in her letters that she had a surprise for me. At first, I assumed it was that bloody sports car but now I realise it was something more.' His shoulders slumped and Brian realised he was sobbing.

Brian put his arm around his friend's shoulders. 'Come on mate, let's go home. You stay the night with Kathy and me. We'll all get rat arsed together.'

To his surprise Jon simply let himself be led away.

The next morning, Brian woke with a massive hangover. For a second he couldn't remember why and then it all came back. At least, by getting Jon pissed, he had fallen asleep as he always did. He looked at his watch and was surprised to see how late it was. Just then, Kathy came in with two cups of coffee.

'Think you might need this darling. I've got an even bigger one here for Jon.'

Brian took it gratefully as Kathy went down the corridor to their spare room where Jon was staying. She was soon back.

'Brian, Jon's not in bed and I've looked down the road to his married quarter. His car isn't parked outside. It was there last night.'

'Oh shit, he was talking about going to that damned pub and sorting out the landlord. I hope to Christ he hasn't. Can you remember the name?'

'The Crown, I think.'

'We'd better get the phone book and see if we can warn them. In fact, you do that and I'll get in the car and see if I can head him off.'

'But what if he's gone somewhere else? He could be just going back to the ship.'

'If that's the case then he won't be getting himself in the shit. If he's not there, I'll ring you from the pub and then go on to Plymouth. Also, have a word with the Air Station in case he's gone there.'

'Fine but you drive carefully, we don't want another accident.'

Brian nodded as he struggled into some clothes and then after giving Kathy a quick peck on the cheek, ran out to his car. With no idea how much of a head start Jon had, he put his foot down and prayed he was wrong at the same time. The traffic was reasonably light today and he made good time. Within half an hour, he was driving down the lane that led to the pub and where Helen had died. With his heart in his mouth, he saw a blue flashing light in the pub car park. As he pulled in, he saw a small Panda car and Jon's old Capri but no one was there. He jumped out and made his way into the pub.

Jon was there sitting down at one of the tables with an elderly looking constable at his side. They both looked up as Brian came in.

'Ah, you must be one of this gentlemen's friends,' the policeman said. 'We had a phone call to say you were coming, from your wife I believe.'

Brian nodded and looked at Jon. 'Jees mate, I hope you haven't done anything stupid.'

Jon looked up. 'I only wanted the landlord to know how I felt about what they had done.'

Behind the bar, a rotund greying man looked over at them. His face was ashen. 'We didn't do anything Sir, we tried to help.'

Jon was about to say something but Brian looked at him. 'Jon just shut the fuck up OK? You're only going to make things worse.' And then turning to the constable. 'Has any offence been committed constable?'

'No, your friend here just explained to everyone how he felt. I don't think there would have actually been anything more and I do sympathise with him. The best thing you can do now is to get him home.'

Brian nodded and took Jon by the arm. 'Are you up to driving?'

'I got here didn't I? Sorry Brian, as always you're there to keep me out of the shit. Yes, I'll drive.'

As they were about to leave, the landlord called over. 'I am really very sorry for your loss. I'm going to have to live with it as well. I know that's no real help to you but it is true.'

For a second Jon hesitated. Brian couldn't tell what was going through his mind. Then he shrugged and they left.

Two days later, they held a memorial service at Culdrose. There had been talk of having it at the Fleet Air Arm chapel at Yeovilton but Jon had absolutely refused to contemplate the idea. That was where they had been married and he couldn't face the thought of holding her funeral there as well. In the end, they held the service in 771's hangar as it was the only place large enough to hold all the attendees. There had been a private family ceremony earlier at the local crematorium. Helen had always said she wanted to be cremated.

Jon had been dreading meeting her father as he had always opposed her entrance into the navy.

Just before they went in, he took Jon aside. 'Jon, you know I didn't like Helen's life choices, except for marrying you that is. But this could have happened anywhere at any time. Just in case you think I blame you or the navy for this, I don't, I really don't.' He gave Jon's arm a squeeze and Jon smiled back as they made their way into the small chapel.

Later, in the squadron hangar, he stood at the front of the crowd. He didn't know whether he would actually be able to speak as he looked at the sea of faces, many of which he recognised.

'I'm going to keep this very short. Helen Hunt, my wife, was extraordinary. Only a few days ago she was involved in one of the most dangerous and brave rescue missions I have ever seen. I should know. I was there. She was the first female officer to gain her naval wings and fly operationally. I just hope that she is an inspiration to all aircrew, male or female. I have some glad news, just before this service, I received a telephone call confirming that she has been awarded a posthumous Air Force Cross for her part in that rescue. Other awards for the other aircrew will be announced later. But far more than that, she was my wife and my love. I will miss her forever. I would like to thank you all for coming today. There is just one more thing to be done, if you will excuse me.'

He left the Dias in total silence, which was immediately broken by the sound of approaching aircraft. Seven Sea King helicopters in formation appeared over the perimeter fence. They flew low over the building as the attendees streamed out to watch. One broke off and turned hard to come into land in front of the building, leaving the rest in the famous 'missing man' formation. Suddenly, Jon appeared out of the front door dressed in flying clothing and ran under the rotors of the aircraft clutching something in his hand. He clambered in the large cargo door which slid shut as the aircraft immediately took off.

Sitting in the cabin, wearing a despatcher's harness for safety, Jon held on to the urn containing Helen's ashes. Helen hadn't said in her will how she wanted her ashes scattered but Jon knew she would approve. The aircraft flew out into Mounts Bay. The pilot, who was the 771 Commanding Officer, called over the intercom. 'Whenever you're ready Jon.'

Tiny, the Aircrewman, slid open the large cargo door and a blast of air hit Jon in the face. Outside, he could see the grey sea below him and Saint Michaels Mount in the distance sitting off the long Cornish coast. It was a sight he had seen so many times, both from helicopters and the decks of warships. Suddenly, he didn't want to do it. He clutched the urn to his chest realising it was his last tangible link to that wonderful girl. Then he knew he had to. It was what she would have wanted.

Bracing himself against the slipstream, he threw the urn out and clear of the helicopter. They were at a thousand feet and his eyes tracked it as it fell away towards the sea. Just as he was losing sight of it, there was a puff of what he first thought was smoke and then realised the top must have come off. Just for a second, the cloud seemed to take the shape of a bird flying up towards the clouds and then it dispersed. Jon sat back with tears streaming down his face. Nothing was said as the aircraft turned for home.

Chapter 7

Simon Gross was excited and elated. Ever since the amazing Culdrose rescue and its tragic aftermath, he had been looking for another angle and now he had found it. This time the story would be so good, he would have to be accepted as a major player and a job in London was sure to follow. He had been a journalist in Cornwall now for far too long but reporting on traffic jams and lost kids on the beach was never going to give him the leg up he needed. When the wife of the famous naval Commander had come to Culdrose, he thought he might at last have got the story he needed. But by the time he had got to them, the nationals had all done their pieces and although his work had been taken it wasn't exactly earth shattering despite the extra spins he had included.

However, that was all about to change. The press had picked up on the death of the girl very quickly but her husband had been extremely robust in fending them off. Even he hadn't been able to get near. However, now that the story of the rescue out in the south west approaches was getting headlines, coupled with the tragic death of one of the key players, the whole country was taking an interest. The Air Station had finally called a press conference to announce the awards that had been made. Commander Hunt would also be there as the Commanding Officer of the warship that had stood by. Several major television stations and all the tabloids would be there. Simon was going to make his name.

Jon was extremely angry and frustrated. The last thing he wanted now was more publicity. Everyone, from the Station PRO, to just about every newspaper in the country had tried to interview him. He had told them all to sod off in no uncertain terms. However, the previous day, the Captain of the Air Station had telephoned him. Jon had been back on the ship starting the handover to his relief when the call came.

'Jon this is Captain Morgan, look I know you don't think much of the press and I respect your privacy over your recent loss but we are going to have a press conference tomorrow about the rescue and I want you to attend.'

'Sorry Sir, you can give me a direct order and I will not obey it. Not the least because I am far too busy at the moment and I am not responsible to you. I am responsible to the Captain of the Eighth Frigate Squadron to ensure that the command of this ship is handed over correctly.'

'Actually, I've already spoken to F8 and FOF2 for that matter and they are happy to release you. Look, I know how you feel but this conference is to announce the awards that the aircrew are going to receive and that includes the posthumous one for Helen. More importantly, I want to honour all the brave crews who were involved. Your presence as a famous naval aviator and the eye witness on the scene will be invaluable. Think of the good it will do the navy. Please.'

Jon knew he was in a difficult position. 'Alright Sir, I will attend but I absolutely insist that I will not answer any questions at all about Helen's accident. I'm happy to describe my recollections of the rescue but no more.'

'Fair enough Jon and thank you. We'll see you tomorrow at ten o'clock.'

So now here he was, along with several others, seated on the stage of the Air Station theatre. To Jon's surprise, there was also Petter Olafson the Master of the Ocean Wanderer who had fully recovered. Earlier on, he had come up and thanked him profusely. The auditorium wasn't full of people but there were plenty in attendance, along with a great deal of equipment ranging from microphones to television cameras.

Captain Morgan spoke first and outlined the story of the rescue in general terms. Petter Olafson then described the issues with his ship and how they had got into difficulties. The Commanding Officer of 771 introduced his men and gave the detail of how the rescue had been conducted. Finally, Jon stood and explained his ship's involvement.

Captain Morgan then rose again and announced the honours and awards that had been approved, including Helen's. 'So gentlemen, I will now hand over the floor for questions.'

They came thick and fast. On several occasions, people tried to bring up the subject of Helen's accident and every time it was made clear that it was not going to be discussed.

Sitting near the back, Simon Gross was considering his best approach. He had already asked several innocuous questions but he needed to use his last one to best effect. He had quickly realised that there would be no way he could ask what he wanted during the main session. He would have to conduct a small ambush as things wound up. The BBC Television crew were close by and he had a quiet word with them. With any luck, the whole thing would be caught on tape and that would only make him more well known.

The question session drew to an end and the Captain called time. The panel of naval officers would have to walk down the aisle, next to

Simon, to leave the theatre. He had decided how he would play it. He would start with a standard question and then lead in with the left hook about why Commander Hunt had been to the pub where his wife had died and the police had had to be called to sort out the situation. He was sure it would cause a sensation.

Just as the Commander was about to walk past, he got to his feet and stood in his way. He could see that the BBC crew were already filming. He saw the look of anger and distaste start to appear on the Commander's face. That would soon change once the truth was out.

'Commander Hunt, sorry just one quick question.' he asked in a loud voice to ensure that everyone could hear. 'How do you feel about the accident that your poor wife had on the day after the rescue?'

Jon was taken by surprise by the banality of the question. It was one he had heard journalists often ask and he had always been nonplussed when the recipient had attempted to give an honest answer. But coming from this man and despite all the warnings that had been given about not talking about the subject, he had chosen to ignore them. It made him see red.

He hesitated for a second as his anger mounted. The man seemed to be about to ask something else when everything snapped.

'You want to know how I feel about my wife being killed in a stupid accident, caused by a pissed driver, after risking her life to save the crew of that ship. I'll bloody well show you how I feel.'

Every minute of the anguish and anger of the previous days was behind the punch that Jon threw at the bloody man's face. His fist hit him hard in the mouth, so hard that his lip split as his head snapped back and he crumpled to the floor. The TV crew were grinning delightedly as they caught every part of the exchange on camera.

For a second, Jon didn't know what to do. The red mist was still clouding his eyes although he dimly realised just how much his knuckles now hurt. He felt a pair of hands on his shoulders and a voice in his ear. It was Brian.

'Bloody good right hook old son but probably not the best of times to have used it. Let's get you out of here.'

Simon was starting to get groggily to his feet, helped by one of the camera crew, when someone started to clap. The crews of the two Sea Kings had been sitting in the auditorium and they had witnessed the whole thing. Before Simon could even think about remonstrating with the man who had assaulted him, he realised that the clapping had spread. Within a heartbeat, everyone in the theatre was standing and applauding.

35

Jon was completely taken aback. For a moment he couldn't understand what on earth was going on. Then he smiled for the first time in days as he turned to the journalist. 'Does that answer your question?'

Simon belatedly realised that he had blown it. What was really bad was the TV crew who had also joined in the applause, were still filming. With no choice, he decided to beat a retreat. 'You will be hearing from my lawyers,' was his parting shot, which was met with jeers.

Rear Admiral Peter Beresford, the Flag Officer Second Flotilla and still Jon's effective senior officer until he received a new appointment, stood with his back to Jon looking out of the window of his office. The view before him was of the bustling dockyard at Devonport. Several frigates, all under his overall command, were lined up along the dockyard wall. One was HMS Prometheus.

He turned and looked at Jon who was standing before his desk. 'Sit down Jon, would you like a coffee?'

Convinced he was here for a major bollocking, Jon was surprised by the mild tone of the Admiral's voice. 'Thank you Sir, that would be most welcome.' Once again Jon had a sore head and even if he was in trouble a coffee could only help.

The Admiral poured one for them both and joined Jon at the small table to one side of the main desk.

'I expect you think you're here for a major ticking off?' the Admiral asked smiling.

'Well, I did assault a journalist in front of a BBC TV crew Sir. I don't suppose that will have been well received.'

'We've had to do some string pulling but you will be glad to know you won't be on the six o'clock news tonight. Frankly, you only did what most of us have wanted to do at some time or another. I can't tell you the number of times I've read things in the papers where it was quite clear the author was either too lazy or too ignorant to tell the real story. In your case, there was severe provocation. As far as I'm concerned the matter is closed.'

'What about the journalist Sir? He was talking about pressing charges.'

'Don't worry about him. He's been convinced to keep quiet as well. I'll say no more. Now, more to the point, what about you?'

'Sorry Sir, what do you mean?'

'Jon, you've had an amazing career and there is no doubt that you could be destined for great things. I know it's early after the last week's events but I need to know what you want to do now.'

'Sorry Sir, I really haven't given it too much thought.'

'That's not surprising. Now look, I've spoken to the Naval Secretary and we've got a suggestion. I believe that you need a total break from everything you've been used to recently. Wipe the slate clean for a while.'

Jon smiled wanly. 'And get me out of the public eye, just in case a certain journalist decides to make waves?'

'That too. How's your Russian?'

Chapter 8

Jon had been given two weeks leave. He tried to suggest that he didn't want it and been told in no uncertain terms to take a break. It had been a dreadful time. With no better idea in mind, he had gone to stay with his parents but that hadn't really helped. He could understand why everyone wanted to give him sympathy but why couldn't they see that it only made things worse? His mother fussed around him and even his father seemed to want to treat him with kid gloves. He had taken to long walks in the surrounding country but all that did was remind him of his childhood. That had just made him feel more melancholy.

On one famous occasion, his mother had artlessly invited the local vicar around. It hadn't gone well. An old but upright man, who had been a soldier in the last war, he made the basic mistake of suggesting to Jon that everything was part of God's plan.

Jon had exploded and told the vicar in no uncertain terms what he thought of the so called plan. He went on angrily to say that he had no need of the emotional crutch of an imaginary friend in the sky to lean on when things were bad. The Vicar hadn't taken it well, especially when Jon went on to tell him, that as far as he was concerned, the Vicar's brand of organised religion was responsible for more misery and death in the world than just about anything else. Jon felt it was a success as he never saw the man again.

After a week, he could take no more and went home to his empty house in Cornwall. In some ways that was even worse. Brian had gone back to the ship and the house was full of echoing silence and memories.

On the last day before he went back to work, he went for a walk along the cliffs. The weather wasn't as bad as it had been. A brisk breeze was still blowing, the sky was full of scudding cumulus and the sun was still providing some warmth when the clouds allowed it to appear. He found a spot to sit at the edge of a steep cliff. He ruefully acknowledged to himself that his desire to jump over and join Helen had finally gone. He could just imagine what she would say to him if they met in some afterlife somewhere.

The last few days had also been involved in practicalities. Helen's estate wasn't large but she had left it all to Jon. The insurance company had made an offer for the value of the car. He was amazed at just how much it had been worth. He had given notice to the married quarter people and made arrangements to put his stuff into store. From what the Admiral had said there wouldn't be any need of permanent accommodation for a while. Looking out over the sea, he realised just how much he needed to get away from all this. He needed something to occupy his mind, so that maybe just occasionally, the pain in his soul could be forgotten. With a sigh, he knew it would never really be absent. He knew he was still in shock. Two days ago the Air Station padre had called. He was a very different character to the doddery old man who had spoken to him at his father's house. A fully qualified Royal Marine, Mike Brown was lean, fit and only thirty five years old. He was obviously used to dealing with personal loss in the military world and when he spoke to Jon, God wasn't mentioned once. The best thing that he had told him was to get on with his grieving and not to bottle it all in. He explained that there was a natural human process, that if allowed to go ahead would eventually lead to an acceptance and understanding. Trying to fight it would just make things worse. As Jon looked out at the distant horizon, he just hoped he was right because just at that moment he still couldn't really understand how his whole world could have been destroyed in such a fast and callous way.

So, it was with some relief that he finally boarded the night sleeper to London. Early the next morning, the train pulled in at Paddington and suddenly the bustle and smell of London assaulted his senses. At least the noise and crowds would make him feel less alone. He took the tube to Charing Cross and made his way towards Whitehall and the office of his appointer in the Old Admiralty building. He was on time and shown straight in.

Captain Henderson didn't beat about the bush. 'Jon welcome, I understand that FOF2 has already apprised you of our thinking, is that correct?'

'Yes Sir, I've been mulling it over and frankly can't think of anything else I'd rather do. My only concern is that I learned my Russian some years ago and although I got to a fair standard I haven't really used it since. Will it be good enough?'

'Good question and one we already have an answer for. Remember the family you stayed with in Edinburgh? Well, they've moved here to London now. We are going to billet you with them, while you do your various courses, of which there are quite a few. How does that sound?'

Jon grimaced. 'More hangovers that's for sure but I guess getting back into the Russian way of life is all part of what will be needed.'

'Good and has anyone told you who you will be working for?'

'No Sir, no detail was given.'

'I suspect this will please you as well but the Defence Attaché is Commodore Test. I believe you know him?'

Jon looked surprised but pleased. 'Yes Sir, he was my CO in Prometheus during the Falklands and also the Captain of Illustrious during a little foray into the Arctic soon after.'

'Yes, I know about that incident, not that we talk about in public. Anyway, you will be working directly for him as Assistant DA. There are also three other officers of half star rank for each other service. A Captain, Colonel and Group Captain but you'll get all the detail in due course.'

'And my role? What will be required of me?'

'The courses you will go on are designed to cover all that. The DA works directly to the Chief of the Defence Staff and has a directed letter from him setting out his duties. As his assistant, you will have the same responsibilities. However, you will also be accountable to the Ambassador for defence related issues as well as MI6 for certain other things. However, in your case, there is a little more.'

Jon raised an eyebrow in query.

'As I'm sure you know, the whole Soviet Empire is a mess at the moment and no one really knows which way it will go. Normally, there is no Assistant DA post in the Moscow Embassy but because of the turmoil there it has been decided to augment the staff. There are also more MI6 people being drafted in as well. We need to know which way the whole edifice goes when and if it collapses. You'll get a great deal more detail over the next few months.'

Jon mulled it over for a moment. 'Does that mean something more than normal duties Sir?'

Captain Henderson smiled. 'That's not for me to say Jon but I think you might just be in for an interesting time.'

The appointer's words proved to be more than true. Jon had over six months of courses and language training and they started with a knock on the door of a Kensington mews house.

The wife of his friend Victor, the ex KGB spy, answered the door.

'Hello Natasha, I think you might have been expecting me?'

With a cry of delight, Jon was enveloped in Natasha's large arms. She hugged him to her ample bosom and Jon reflected that she definitely hadn't lost any weight since he had seen her last.

'Jon come in, come in, it is so good to see you again. I'm sorry, Victor is not here and the children are at school but come in. I will show you to your room.'

Happy to let Natasha speak and anyway there didn't seem to be a chance of getting a word in edgewise, he followed her up two sets of stairs to a large airy bedroom on the top floor.

'Here we are Jon, this is all yours. You unpack and have a shower. The bathroom is through there. I expect that Victor will be home by then and we can all talk about old times.'

She was right and not only was Victor waiting for him when he came downstairs but so was the vodka bottle.

Chapter 9

Berlin 1945

The battered T34 tank ground to a halt and the hatch opened. Captain Vladmir Vorodov looked out at the total devastation that surrounded him. War weary to a degree that almost defied belief, he hardly took in the view. For years he had been fighting this war and seen every kind of devastation, every kind of atrocity. It has started when the Nazis had killed his family, pausing only to rape his mother and two sisters first. His youngest sister was only eleven. The bodies were left where they were dropped and Vladmir had found them some hours later when he had returned from the fields having miraculously escaped the ravaging soldier's attention. The long walk east had ended when he was able to enlist in the Red Army and he had joined a tank regiment. Such were their losses, especially early on, that within eighteen months he was a Captain and commanded twelve tanks.

During this last push into Berlin, three of his tanks had been destroyed and two more had broken down. He had even lost track of his remaining ones in the warren of streets but it no longer mattered. They had heard that Hitler had shot himself the day before in some hole in the ground and the city was theirs. He called down to Sergei his driver to pull over to one side and jumped to the ground, holding his rifle and looked up at the partially destroyed building in front of him. Some movement in one of the windows had caught his eye. He was joined by Mikhael his gunner.

'Seen something Captain?' Mikhael asked.

'Yes up there. Come with me.'

The two men were joined by Sergei and they cautiously approached the building. There was no door but the stairs in the ruined lobby appeared intact.

'What was it?' Mikhael asked in a whisper as they crept slowly in.

'Some relaxation,' Vladmir responded with a tired grin.

They climbed the stairs keeping a careful eye out all the time. The war might be almost over but there were plenty of pockets of resistance even now. The population knew what was likely to happen to them and some were still prepared to fight. As they reached the top, they all heard a noise from a door to the front of the building. Vladmir went to it and kicked hard. The door flew open and he saw into the remains of a once elegant living room. Dust and debris were everywhere and just as he had suspected there was a woman cowering behind the remains of a sofa.

The three of them marched across and Mikhael grabbed the clearly terrified female by the hair and pulled her to her feet. Before he could say anything, another much younger girl scrambled up from the floor behind the sofa and made a run for the door. Vladmir put out his foot and the girl tripped headlong. He reached down and pulled her up as well.

'Well what do we have here?' he asked, as he looked at the struggling girl. She was young, in her teens and was probably quite pretty under her coverings of dirt and ragged clothes. He looked over to the other woman and saw a distinct family resemblance.

'Well, we seem to have a mother and daughter here,' he laughed as the girl made yet another attempt to slip from his grasp. Tired with her struggles he backhanded her across the face and she abruptly stopped. The mother reacted violently and started shouting but Mikhael also had her in a firm grasp.

'Ask them if they have any food Sergei,' Vladmir ordered. His driver was the only one of them with any German. 'Tell them that if they have then they will be treated well.'

Sergei cocked a slightly disbelieving eye at his Captain but did as he was asked. The terrified woman pointed to a door and they all went into a kitchen. Mikhael released her and she opened a cupboard. There wasn't much in it but Vladmir saw there was enough for a better meal than they had enjoyed for many days. What was even better was that there were several bottles of wine and beer. Releasing the young girl, who immediately fled to her mother's side, Vladmir grabbed a bottle and opened it by simply knocking the head off with the bayonet of his rifle. Taking care not to cut his lips he poured some straight down his throat. It tasted like nectar.

An hour later, the women had given them a pretty fair meal and all three men were more than a little drunk. Mikhael belched contentedly and grabbed the older woman. He almost casually ripped the remains of her blouse off her, revealing a large pair of breasts. The other two men grinned. They knew what Mikhael liked. Vladmir had grabbed hold of the young girl when he saw what was about to happen.

Suddenly the young girl started shouting at her mother. The mother, while struggling, started desperately trying to talk to Sergei.

'Mikhael stop a second,' Sergei shouted. 'This sounds interesting.'

Mikhael paused while the woman talked although he continued to paw her breasts. When she stopped talking Sergei turned to the Captain. 'She says the building opposite was a bank and they never emptied the safe and that we would easily take it all.'

Vladmir laughed. 'What would we do with a load of old useless German Reich Marks?'

The woman must have understood something of what was being said because she started shouting one word. Sergei suddenly looked startled and started talking to the woman again.

He turned to Vladmir. 'She says that the bank has a vault full of gold. She says that we could use our gun to open it. She used to work there and can show you where it is.'

Vladmir snorted in amusement. 'Do you think the Nazis would be stupid enough to leave any gold behind? No, she's just trying to avoid our justice. These bastards raped and killed my family. Let's give them some Russian justice and maybe take a look later.' So saying he started to rip the clothes off the young girl.

An hour later, they grabbed the last few bottles of wine and the remaining food and left. The two women were huddled together naked in a corner clutching onto each other with a desperate look of despair on their faces. Mikhael levelled his pistol at them.

'No Mikhael,' Vladmir ordered. 'Leave them, maybe some of our comrades can enjoy them again and who knows maybe the Aryan race will have some fine Russian sons to look after soon.'

Mikhael laughed and holstered his pistol as he followed the other two out of the building. It was still quiet outside although the sound of fighting could be heard not far away.

'I suppose we had better go and find the others and get back into this war,' Vladmir said as he looked across the street. 'However, maybe the slut was talking some truth. You never know.'

So saying, he went over the street to the building opposite. It could have been a bank he realised. All the windows were blown out as was the roof but the walls were still standing. Kicking some debris away, he peered inside. In the gloom, he could see some sort of metal structure with a large wheel on the front. There must have been a wall in front of it at some time but that had long gone.

He called to his men. 'Sergei, start her up and Mikhael load with an armour piercing shell. There could be something here after all.'

The rumble of the tank's engine was followed by a whine as the turret spun around. Vladmir vaulted in through his hatch and took control of the final aiming. He pointed the barrel directly at where the vault was.

'Fire,' he ordered.

They were all used to the sharp explosion of the gun but their target was normally a great deal further away. Part of the front of the building collapsed and the whole street disappeared in a cloud of dust and smoke.

The three men jumped out, coughing in the dust and made their way across the street. As the visibility cleared, they could see that Vladmir's aim had been excellent. The vault could be clearly seen now as most of the building had been blown from around it by the explosion. The door was drunkenly hanging to one side and inside they could see something shining.

As they got to the door, Sergei hissed through his teeth with mounting excitement. 'The bitch was telling the truth. What do we do now Vladmir?'

Although the tank's shell had scattered much of the contents of the vault into random piles, they were clearly looking at a fortune in gold bars.

Several hours after the tank had left the mother and daughter crept out of the building. They had found some clothes and while both knew they should have stayed hidden, they had to see what the Russians had done. They had watched from their window as the soldiers loaded up their tank and then driven off. They clambered carefully over the rubble of the front wall of the bank. The mother had a fair idea how much gold was in the vault and knew the Russians wouldn't have been able to take it all. So she wasn't surprised to see several wooden crates still inside the vault.

'Help me girl, we need to get this hidden. Maybe some good will come from this after all.'

Forty five years later

The Dacha wasn't large but was clearly quite old. Set in amongst a pine forest, it was served by a long gravel drive that disappeared between the trees. Despite its age, it was very well maintained with a neat garden and large sloping lawn to the rear. It had been built in the previous century by a minor noble as a hunting lodge. Conveniently near to Moscow but far enough out to offer complete privacy. And those were the reasons why its occupant still valued it.

The country was in the grip of early winter and for this part of the world that meant snow and icy temperatures. Vladmir Vorodov didn't feel the cold as he stood outside looking over the snow covered lawn. Despite being over seventy, he could remember the cold of the plains as he manoeuvred his tanks into position to take on the Germans all those years ago. The temperature only served to make those memories stronger. These days, the memories often seemed more real than recent events. Or maybe it was because his mind shied away from the events of the last few years. When he had been commanding his tanks from the turret of his own T34 things had been simple. The Nazis had to be exterminated, his country had suffered enough. He had never expected to come out of the fight alive and he hadn't expected many of his men to do so either. The T34 was a simple tank, rugged agile and reliable. It had an excellent gun but was no match for the later German machines. What they did have was numbers. When Comrade Stalin had made the genius decision to move all production to the east of the Urals they had been able to churn them out in vast quantities and numbers were what was telling in this bloody, pounding war. Russian machines and men for that matter could be replaced. The Germans, so far from home, didn't have that luxury and were slowly being ground down.

In Berlin, the destruction was dreadful but no worse than the Nazis had inflicted on Stalingrad and he remembered that it had made him glad. What a contrast to nowadays, the bloody Germans had completely rebuilt the city that had recently been reunited when Gorbachev had let the wall come down. He remembered that moment when they had seen all that gold and at first didn't know what to do. However, the T34 may have not been the biggest tank in the world but it had enough room for what they had salvaged. They didn't take it far, just away from the city and prying eyes where it was reburied and then recovered later.

Vladmir loved communism, he loved the socialist system and for years revelled in the power of the Soviet Union. He was immensely proud of her armed forces, her space programme and the achievements of her mighty empire. None of that stopped him putting his windfall wealth to good use. Like any good Russian, he looked after himself and his family before the state. They had been such good times. As a successful officer, decorated by Stalin himself, he managed to avoid all the later purges. He carefully bought in to many state programs, particularly energy and raw materials. Despite the dogma of communism, trade had to carry on and he made many contacts with the west and his fortune grew. But even he had seen the writing on the wall.

On his few trips abroad, he had seen with his own eyes the cornucopia of the West. Shops bursting with produce, freedom to say things that would have got you a bullet in the head after a very lengthy and painful interrogation in Moscow. He knew exactly how much the economy of the USSR was stagnating. That bloody man Reagan had put the final nail in the coffin with his so called 'Star Wars' initiative. Vladmir knew there was no way his country would be able to keep up with that and he had been proved right. Reform had been necessary but this man Gorbachev had gone about it totally the wrong way. Perestroika and Glasnost were simply making the situation worse. What the Russian people always wanted was strong leadership. A strong and powerful father to tell them what to do, it was how it had been for centuries. Firstly under the Czars, then the benevolent hand of communism and it was what was needed now. With a start, he realised he was now thinking of things in terms of his country rather than that of the union itself. So many countries had been allowed to leave and more were sure to follow. What was that bloody man Gorbachev thinking? It could only lead to chaos and someone had to do something.

Just as the thought crossed his mind, there was a discreet cough behind him. Sergei was his right hand man even after all these years. They had stayed together ever since the war. It had been a good arrangement for both of them, especially after Mikhael had tried to take more than his fair share of the booty. Sergei had solved that problem with a pistol shot. The action had bound them together.

'They're all here now Vladmir.' Sergei announced quietly. 'Do you think they will agree?'

Vladmir sighed and answered without turning. 'We can only try old friend. What else can we do?'

The warmth of the house hit them in the face as they went into the high vaulted dining room of the Dacha. It was a large space, open to the rafters. A great fire was roaring at one end in a massive stone fireplace. The antlers of countless deer adorned the room's walls. All shot by the original owner. Vladmir and previous owners had left them in place. Along with the dark wood panelled walls, they gave the room atmosphere. The large dining table was covered in a green baize cloth and seated in ornate high back carved chairs were six people. Vladmir knew them all.

Three were industrialists like himself, two were very senior in the army and navy respectively and the final man was KGB. Vladmir was very confident of five of the men but this last person was more of an unknown quantity. If his plan was to have the slightest chance of success then the KGB would need to be involved. Delicate soundings over recent years had made him realise that if any organisation was inflexible and reactionary, it was the Secret Police. Discreet approaches had all been rebuffed. Then after the fall of Soviet Germany, this man had appeared. Although Russian, he had lived all his life in Germany and seemed far more amenable to realising that things could not continue as they were for much longer. If he was sound then they could go ahead soon, hopefully before it was too late.

'Gentlemen, thank you for attending.' Vladmir announced without preamble. 'I give you a toast.' And he reached for the tumbler of vodka in front of him. There was a similar one in front of each man. 'Mother Russia.'

All six men repeated the toast and tossed their drinks down in one. Vladmir looked at them all. The next part would not be so easy.

Chapter 10

'Jesus fucking Christ Sir, not so bloody fast,' there was a definite note of panic in the Sergeant's voice as he shouted across to Jon in the driver's seat.

The Ford Grenada was going flat out in reverse. Jon was grinning like a maniac as he looked over his shoulder down the long runway behind them. Just as the engine reached maximum revs and before the Sergeant could shout at him again, Jon did several things. He flung the steering wheel hard to the left as he lifted off the accelerator taking weight off the front wheels. He then put his foot on the clutch as he took the car out of reverse gear. Quickly letting the clutch out again as the car started to spin sideways he then put it down and selected first. With screeching tyres, the car was now almost facing the opposite direction, so he accelerated hard and wound off the steering lock. The car shot down the runway facing the way it was actually going.

There was a long moment's silence. Jon was just enjoying having pulled off a perfect, if rather fast, J turn. The Sergeant was deciding how to give this mad naval Commander yet another bollocking for grossly exceeding his instructions.

'Very good Sir but once again it was far too fast, please can you follow my direction?' The last was almost pleading.

Jon grinned at his instructor. 'Sorry Sergeant but I just got a bit carried away and you have to admit it went rather well.'

'Yes Sir but defensive driving isn't just about going as fast as you can. This course is designed to give you the techniques you need to save your life. It could be for real.'

Jon just grinned even more. 'Shouldn't stop it being bloody good fun though.'

The Sergeant gave up. All week he had been teaching the course to a group of senior officers destined for Embassy appointments overseas. It was given to everyone, even the wives if they wanted to participate and most of them did. But he had never had a pupil like this one. The bloody man almost seemed to have a death wish. Thank goodness it was now Friday and the course was just about over. He wasn't sure he could have taken much more, even if the Commander did seem to have some skill, as well as absolutely no sense of danger whatsoever.

For the first time since Helen had died Jon had been able to put her out of his mind, even if it was only for a few minutes at a time. The thrill of flinging these cars around on the old airfield at Leconfield required all his concentration and doing it fast helped although the Sergeant clearly didn't agree. In fact the whole week had been something of a revelation. There had been some classroom time but most of it involved being behind the wheel of a car for one reason or another. The skid pan had been fun and so had the cross country chases but the best had been the work on the airfield. With a sigh, Jon came down to earth. Another weekend with Victor loomed. Not that that was a bad thing, what it really meant was it was another week without Helen, like all future weekends would be.

He brought the car to a halt by the group of trainees and got out. The grin on his face fading as reality hit in yet again and the adrenalin slipped away.

He groaned inwardly as Group Captain Pearson approached. He knew exactly what the pompous twit was going to say long before he opened his mouth.

'Bit fast that Jon. Wasn't it?' The tall, thin, sandy haired Air Force officer queried in that irritating nasal tone he always used. Behind him was his infernal simpering wife who seemed to want to agree with everything her husband said and never seemed to have an opinion of her own.

Jon thought for a moment. It didn't help that he and the Group Captain were both destined for the same Embassy in Moscow, so he decided to keep a lid on any cutting remarks.

'Maybe Sir but the bad guys wouldn't have caught me.'

'Hmmph, well you really need to be more sensible.' The Group Captain turned away as if the remark was all that was needed to settle things and so didn't see the look of contempt on Jon's face although Marian his wife did. They had all met up several weeks ago at the start of the series of courses and Jon had taken an instant dislike to the two of them. It was made quite clear from the start that Jon was the junior officer and as he hadn't flown fixed wing jets he was almost beyond the pale. Jon was never in the mood to be patronised and he found that now he didn't really care what some senior Air Force officer felt about him. Jon may have only flown helicopters but he had managed to win an air to air fight with an Argentinian Pucara and shot it down. Which was almost certainly one hundred per cent more than the good Group Captain had managed. When Jon politely pointed this out, it hadn't gone down well and when they first met up in uniform and everyone saw the two DSO's on Jon's chest, the Group Captain appeared even more put out. However, Jon suspected that someone, probably Colonel, Mike Smart, who was also on the course and knew Jon from the past, had taken the man to one side and explained recent events. Soon after, their conversations had reduced considerably although the Group Captain clearly couldn't completely avoid the odd patronising or supercilious remark. Jon mentally shrugged to himself. Let the silly bugger think what he liked.

'Right ladies and gentlemen,' the Sergeant called out to the assembled students. 'That's it for the defensive driving course. I hope you all enjoyed it and learned from it. I know I did. Please remind me to ask that no more naval pilots be allowed to attend.'

Jon nodded to the man as a ripple of laughter ran around from the rest of the students.

Two hours later, Jon let himself in through the door to Victor's house. As usual, he was greeted like a long lost hero and had to tell the whole family about the course he had been on. After he had explained all, Victor took him to his study where the inevitable vodka was waiting. Much to his surprise, Victor turned on the television.

'Have you seen today's news Jon?' he asked as the set woke into life.

'Sorry, not had much of a chance, I was stuck on the M25 for ages.'

'Tis will interest you. You were in the Gulf last year weren't you?' He handed Jon a large glass of clear liquid.

The television screen showed a desert scene and the commentator was saying something about Kuwait. Jon listened intently as the tumblers fell into place. 'Oh the silly bastard, he's invaded hasn't he?'

'Well he's been threatening to for months now, claiming that Kuwait was undermining his economy by selling too much oil. Once again the western nations seem to have totally disregarded his concerns.'

'Spoken like a true Soviet, Victor,' Jon said as he took a swig of the vodka. 'The man's an idiot and a vicious one at that.'

'Maybe but he was the darling of the American and British governments until recently. Then, as soon as Iran was forced to the negotiating table, you dropped him. He's had no support from the West since.'

Jon considered the statement. Not long ago he would have launched into a vehement defence of his country's position. However, having been in the region and knowing a great deal about the situation on the ground, he found he actually had some sympathy with Victor's point of view.

'But to invade another sovereign country? Surely he realises that the West won't stand for it?'

'Maybe he hopes for help from elsewhere.'

'What from Russia, are you serious?'

Victor laughed mirthlessly. 'No Jon, not at the moment. There are enough problems for Russia to deal with a lot closer to home than any that Saddam could cause.'

'Yes, we've had some briefings already on that and of course there is quite a lot of speculation in the press. What's your take on what's really going on there? I assume you still have contacts in Moscow.'

Victor sighed and leant back in his armchair. 'Yes Jon you're right and I am still providing advice to your Foreign Office and MI6 as you well know. What do you understand about the situation?'

'Why don't you assume I know very little and tell me the story from your perspective. I'm sure it will be quite different from any that I get from our side.'

'Very well. On the one hand you could say it has all been caused by Mikhael Gorbachev. However, there is also an argument to say that what is happening is inevitable. Let's start with Mikhael. He is the first Soviet leader who didn't experience the war. He grew up on a collective farm and drove tractors. The fact that he managed to get into the central governmental apparatus at all is something of a miracle. And what has he been faced with since he got into power? I will tell you. Firstly, a failing economy that was still spending almost half its GDP on the military. Then there was the system that was providing the funds for that spending. It was and still is terribly corrupt and even worse it's terribly inefficient. He would have experienced much of that first hand. The problem with a system like that is that there is a great deal of vested interest to keep it going. Most of the people in the system are benefiting from the corruption. So, he introduced Perestroika or restructuring. His hope was to root out these problems. Unlike his predecessors, he was also prepared to look at other systems. Don't get me wrong, he is a socialist to the core but one with an open mind. As part of this policy, he introduced Glasnost or openness to try and make the system more accountable. He wanted people to have more freedom of speech and more democratic power. But here my friend is the contradiction. You know what's happened in Germany already and is going on in many of the old Soviet states. What Gorbachev and many of his people simply failed to understand, was that most of the people in the Soviet countries simply did not like Russian control and hated communism. It seems incredible but he honestly thought that given the freedom to reform, countries like Poland, Germany, the Baltic States even the Ukraine would still embrace Soviet style socialism. Of course that's not what they wanted. They could see what the West had had for years, despite all the propaganda to the contrary. Once they decided to move away, Gorbachev bound by his own policies was powerless and this process is continuing as we speak. And that is the inevitability that I spoke of. It is now a house of cards and it's falling around his ears. There is nothing he can do to stop it.'

'Nothing he can do, really?'

'It's crazy Jon, in March he managed to get himself elected as the first President of the Soviet Union. A typically Russian election, as he was the only candidate. The idea was to give him more power to drive through reform. The problem was that it was seen by many as yet another increase in his power base and drew a lot of open criticism. Glasnost remember?' Victor laughed and gulped some vodka. 'He is now in the position where his own reforms are biting him in the ass and that could be the real problem.'

'Why?'

'Well, because of the new open nature of his government, we can now assess just how much opposition there is to it. There are plenty of hardliners left and they are openly critical. I would not bet against some of them taking some form of action and soon. And that my friend could be a tragedy, both for the countries of the east and the west.'

Chapter 11

Once again, one of the many courses Jon was attending as part of his attaché training was diverting his sombre thoughts. However, this time he was having serious trouble stifling chortles. It didn't help that the bloody Colonel standing next to him was egging him on with sotto voce remarks.

The one day course they were on was meant to be a simple leveller. The wife of an ex Ambassador was taking them through the basics of etiquette and dining procedures. Once again, all the wives were in attendance as well as the men. The problem was that most people there were pretty familiar with the need to serve white wine with fish and how to lay out the knives and forks for a dinner. The only person who seemed fascinated and clearly wanted to learn more was the Group Captain's wife. Marian was in her element and even her husband had given up getting her to stop asking questions. Completely oblivious to the effect she was creating, she was even starting to annoy the Ambassadors wife with more and more trivial queries. However, it was when Colonel Mike Smart, who was standing at the back with Jon, started a muttered alternative set of answers to the woman's questions that Jon started to chuckle. He was desperately trying not to call attention to himself but every time he thought he had his mild hysteria under control, the Colonel would offer another, often quite crude alternative answer. Tears were starting to stream down his eyes when Marian asked yet another question about seating arrangements and who would take priority over who. Colonel Smart offered his solution which was totally based on the size of the person's wife's tits and Jon lost it. His only recourse was to start a fit of coughing and beg to be excused for a second to visit the toilets. The Colonel followed him out.

'You sodding bastard Colonel,' Jon managed to choke out once they were out of earshot. 'I've got to work with that Crab and his snob of a wife in a few month's time. You'll be alright, you're going to India.'

The Colonel was also a little red in the face and still chuckling. 'Sorry Jon but it had to be done. And to be frank, it's the first time I've seen you actually laugh since we met up for these courses.'

It was like having a bucket of cold water thrown over him. For a moment Jon didn't know how to react and then the truth of the remark hit home. 'You're right Mike. Shit, have I been that much of a misery?'

'If you really want to know, yes.' The Colonel was also now being serious. 'Apart from the times when you were trying to kill yourself on that driving course or seriously hungover from late nights with your KGB host, trying to get a laugh out of you has just about been impossible.'

'Christ Mike, you know why. I don't think I'll ever be really over her you know.'

'Yes but life does go on even if you don't see much point in it. I don't tell everyone this but I also lost my first wife. Not to an accident but to cancer. I know what you're going through, I really do.'

'Oh God, I didn't know that. I'm so sorry.'

'Look, it was some years ago now and I came out of it. And you will as well. Come and have dinner with us this weekend if you're not doing anything. Oh and you will be able to sit where you like, the wine may or may not match the food and I'm buggered if I know which knife or fork will be where but it'll be fun.'

It was. Mike Smart had a large house near Salisbury and with both his children away at University there was more than enough room. Jon already knew Cindy, his second wife from various courses over the last few months and so there was no awkwardness. However, what really threw him was that just after arriving another car drew up on the gravel drive and the smiling faces of Brain and Kathy Pearce appeared.

'I feel a conspiracy brewing,' Jon observed wryly as he saw who it was.

Cindy was standing behind him. 'Completely correct Jon. Mike did some digging and discovered that you and Brian go back a long way, so we thought we would invite them over.'

Jon suddenly realised that only a few weeks ago he would have resented being played like this but now he was simply grateful and said so.

The evening was a success much to the host's delight. Mike apologised to Jon for the subterfuge but in the end everyone enjoyed themselves, even Jon. It was the first time since Helen's death that he actually felt himself relax without a nagging feeling of guilt.

'So Brian, what has the appointer lined up for you now?' Jon asked. Brian had been selected for promotion on that summer's list but it would not be until Christmas that he actually took up the rank. Unless the system needed him earlier when he would get acting rank.

'Actually, they've asked me to go to HMS Dryad as an instructor. It seems the Maritime Tactical School think I may have learned a few things over the years, especially serving with a mad bastard like you and its time I passed some of it on.'

Jon laughed. 'Think they'll believe half of the stories?'

'Well I hardly do, so maybe they will take some convincing. But at least I start next week, so I get my brass hat early. So, as of Monday, I won't have to call you Sir ever again. Anyway, how have all your courses gone? You seem to have had shed loads of them.'

Jon sighed. 'Tell me about it. My language skills are all assessed as fine now, including military Russian. I can blame that mad ex KGB alcoholic for that. I've done the rounds of the Foreign and Commonwealth office till I'm blue in the face and then of course there have been some training I could tell you about but then I would have to shoot you. I've got all my uniforms up to scratch including all these fancy gold thingies I will have to wear. Frankly, I'll be glad to get to Moscow and do some real work.'

'Hmm and what is that work to be?'

'Good question and actually I haven't got a clue but I'm off to MI6 next week and hopefully I'll get some hint then.'

'As long as it doesn't involve going to the Arctic again,' Brian observed and then seeing blank looks around the dining table he continued. 'Oops, sorry everyone, shouldn't have mentioned that, please disregard.'

Kathy looked at her husband. 'One day Brian, I'm going to find out what the hell you two got up to that year.'

'Sorry Kathy, not just yet you aren't,' Brian replied with a twinkle in his eye knowing too well how much it annoyed his wife. She had been trying to prize out his secret for years without success.

The conversation drifted on over dinner and all too soon it was over. Brian and Kathy were also staying the night and it was no surprise when well after midnight the only two people left up were Jon and Brian. They were sitting slouched in two armchairs in the living room and both had a large scotch to hand.

'So Jon, how are you bearing up? It's been over six months now.'

Jon didn't answer for a while, just stared into his glass. Just as Brian was about to ask again in case his friend hadn't heard him, Jon replied. 'It's crazy Brian, I know life has to go on and the shock has worn off but every time I find myself ready to move on it makes me feel guilty. I feel that if I start to put her behind me then I'm letting her down. Does that make sense?'

Brian thought for a moment. 'I can understand that but how about this for a counter argument. What do you think Helen would want you to do? She loved you as much as you loved her and she was a bloody sensible girl. The last thing she would want is for you to be unhappy. She would want you to pull yourself together and carry on with life, wouldn't she?'

'I know, I've said the same thing to myself but it still doesn't solve the problem completely. I guess time is what is needed. Colonel Mike has told me all about when his first wife died and that has actually been a great help. But you know, no matter what happens in the future I will never ever love another woman as much as I loved Helen. There could only ever be one person like that in my life. In fact, I suspect that most people are not even as lucky as me in that regard, if that makes sense. And now I'm getting maudlin again, time for bed.'

Chapter 12

Vladmir turned to Sergei as the last of his guest's cars drove off with a swoosh over the snow covered gravel drive.

'What do you think old friend, do we have a conspiracy? Can we trust them?'

Sergei didn't answer for a moment. 'What choice do we have? All those comrades who died, all that devastation, was it for nothing? Do we just let it all drift away? No Vladmir, there is no choice, not if we still consider ourselves to be the men we were.'

'I'm tired Sergei. You can only fight for so long. Maybe we should just let things happen.'

'You don't mean that. I know you too well.'

The two men went inside out of the freezing temperatures. As they entered the main hall Vladmir stopped. 'Can we really trust that giant of a KGB man?'

'Yes, he is quite tall isn't he? Not the sort of man you would think of as a spy. He doesn't exactly blend into the crowd. Anyway, he's come from Germany but his father was a good Russian. Although the Stasi thought he was one of them completely, he was, in fact, working for us. Of course, as our goals were mutually compatible, then there was no conflict and it was why he was accepted back so quickly.'

'So, he was a spy working for the organisation he was spying on at the same time?'

'Yes but as I say there was no conflict in that, not until the country defected that is. So he is now a senior member of the organisation but completely clean with no baggage unlike most of his comrades.'

'And what do we know about his background, his family life?'

'He was born in 1945, so he's forty six years old. His mother was a German and his father a Russian diplomat who moved to Berlin as the war finished. Apparently, the woman had some money and was organising relief for the survivors. You know, soup kitchens and the like. They married and stayed on in Berlin but they sent the son to Russia for education where he came to the attention of the KGB. Because of his background, he was the perfect person to put into the Stasi as a sort of insurance policy I suppose.'

'And the parents?'

'The mother is dead. She died several years ago of cancer and the father is in a home outside Berlin. He won't last much longer. Oh and he's married to a woman who was also Stasi.'

'Well done Sergei, your contact in the Lubyanka has done us proud. And I agree with you. Your assessment seems to have been correct. He's definitely the missing link we needed. So now we are on track. The next few months should be interesting.'

Gunter Bukov sat back in the leather upholstery of his government supplied Zil limousine and reflected on the last few hours. He had been extremely surprised when the man had approached him several days previously. He was not used to being accosted on the street. However, as soon as the man had started to speak it, was clear he knew far too much about Gunter's past as well as his current employment. He remembered the slightly surreal conversation with the bald old man with the large moustache and shabby raincoat.

'Mr Bukov, I have someone who would like to speak to you and who I think you might want to listen to.'

Completely taken aback, Gunter hadn't immediately dismissed the man.

'I know you came from Berlin but you were not in fact working for your employers and that you are now back working for your real masters. No, hear me out please. We live in interesting times, would you not say?' Before Gunter could respond he carried on. 'There are some of us who have worked behind the scenes for many years and who have much wealth and personal investment in this country. We do not like the way things are going and believe we may be able to influence what is about to happen. We also believe that you might have similar views as you have not been part of our internal struggle for the last few years.'

Gunter had listened to the man for a few more minutes. He had some sympathy for what was being said. He made a decision and decided to attend the meeting the man invited him to but reserve judgement. He would need to know who he was dealing with and what their real agenda was. It would then put him in a position to go along with them or denounce them as he saw fit. Either way he would be secure.

The meeting had been a complete surprise. He had heard of Vladmir Vorodov but only as one of the more wealthy industrialists in the country and an ageing Hero of the Soviet Union for his time in the Red Army during the war. However, the other faces in the room were definitely not what he was expecting to see. Nor for that matter, was the content of the meeting. He quickly realised that here was a group of people with real power and influence. Just like them, he had hated what was happening to the country and now he realised he was in a position to do something about it. He also had a strong suspicion that he was a marked man and that if he didn't join in, his career or even his life might come to an abrupt end. So he had signed up without reservation. Of course, he still had misgivings but nothing would happen for several months and there were always ways of making an exit if he had to.

He wondered whether to confide in Beatrix his wife. They shared most things and had worked for the same organisation, even if it had come as a bit of a surprise when he told her of who his real masters had been all these years. She hadn't objected though when it had gained her the job she had always wanted. They shared most things and a second opinion would do no harm whatsoever.

As they lay in bed that night he told of the day's events. 'So, you see my dear I have agreed to go along with the idea.'

Bea was surprised. Her husband was normally very conservative and she said so.

'I'm afraid these are no longer conservative times my love. Whatever happens, we are going to be caught up in it. At least this way I might just be able to have some influence.'

'And this man, Vladmir Vorodov. What do you really know about him?'

'Not as much as I should nor the other men there, although I recognised them all.'

'So are you going to look into them?'

Gunter laughed. 'Well bearing in mind where I work that shouldn't be too difficult.'

Chapter 13

Jon stood outside the imposing stone building in Lambeth. It was a clear chilly Autumn day. It had rained hard the previous night but now the sun was out. The air was sharp and clean, and everything looked crystal clear. He hesitated before going in remembering Brian's story of how he had managed to gain access to the building and provide the information that had got him out of serious trouble a few years ago. Entering the imposing lobby, he went up to the reception desk and spoke to the pretty young girl manning it. She picked up a phone and after talking for a few moments turned a dazzling smile on to Jon. She asked him to take a seat. His escort would be down shortly.

Sitting in one of the chairs by the revolving doors, he looked around him. There was nothing to show that this was the headquarters of the British Secret Service but Jon knew how looks could be deceiving or in this case were meant to be deceiving. He had heard that they were building a massive new office on the south bank of the Thames. That would certainly put them more in the public eye. This current building could belong to any large organisation. His thoughts were interrupted by footsteps approaching from behind. He turned and without much surprise saw his old friend Rupert Thomas approaching.

'Jon, good to see you,' Rupert said offering his hand as Jon stood. 'I'm so sorry, I couldn't get to Helen's funeral but as you know I was out of the country.'

'That's alright Rupert, it's all done and dusted now. Why am I not surprised that they dug you out to do this briefing for me?'

Rupert looked into his friend's eyes and saw the pain was still raw but decided that there was no purpose in dwelling on it. 'Actually, because of that little fracas in Whitehall the other year, they put me in charge of a team doing the follow up. Our little spy was more than happy to tell us all and I've spent the intervening period making the best of it. Because it's all tied up with what is happening in Russia these days they've now assigned me to the Soviet desk. Anyway, more of that later. Come on up and have some coffee.'

He led Jon into a lift and up several floors into a large office crammed with desks and people pouring over large computer screens.

'The section has expanded a lot in the last year as you can imagine. We're bursting at the seams. The sooner we move into the new building the better.'

He led Jon into a small room to one side where a small desk had a coffee flask and cups laid out and indicated a chair for Jon to sit in.

'Now, you're going to be the Assistant Defence Attaché, is that correct?'

'Yes, although it's a new post and no one really knows what it means. Either that or they won't tell me.' Jon looked speculatively at his old colleague with an eyebrow raised in query.

Rupert laughed. 'It's a fair cop Jon and yes we want someone on the ground with certain skills.'

'Hang on a second. This isn't a repeat of the other year? I'm damned if I'm going to be a mole in my own organisation again.'

'No, nothing like that. Now look, what do you know about the situation over there at the moment?'

'When you live with a well-connected ex KGB agent you get to discuss that subject quite often. Put simply, it seems to me that Gorbachev has put in place a number of reforms and has started an avalanche which he's now stood in front of with and has no way of stopping it.'

'Not a bad assessment. Of course it's much more complicated than that and as I'm sure you can imagine there are factions within factions now fighting over the future of the Soviet Union or whatever it will become. One of the biggest questions is what will their military do? The KGB troops would seem to be the most loyal to current regime but the army seems to be dreadfully fragmented.'

'And their navy? I seem to remember it was them who started the last revolution.'

'Good point and that's one of the things we want you to concentrate on. With your background you will be well placed to make contacts and try to find out which way the wind is blowing. You've got the military expertise we need as well a previous experience in this sort of work.'

Jon snorted. 'Not much experience Rupert, apart from catching that idiot the other year. Why can't your people cover this?'

'Well of course they are doing so, as far as they can but you can look at things from a different angle. You may well be able to open doors or at least peek round them that my people can't. This is outside the remit of a normal attaché's role, so for the moment the only other people who will know about this will be the Ambassador himself, your boss the Commodore and the head of the Intelligence section.'

'So, how will I communicate what I discover? Do I liaise with your man? I can't believe that those two other august personages will want to get their hands dirty with this sort of thing.'

'Yes, I'll get you his details later and also I will be your contact back here. Obviously, you can keep your seniors appraised but as this is primarily an intelligence issue then MI6 will have the lead.'

'I'll do what I can old chap but I can't make any guarantees.'

'No, that's understood. Now, firstly you need to know a few facts that haven't made it this far west, at least in the public eye. In 1989, Gorbachev was still prepared to act and he sent paratroopers into Tbilisi in Georgia where there were similar protests to those in East Germany. It would seem he wasn't as convinced of his own policies as he wanted the West to believe. Twenty protestors were killed. The fall out with those who were involved and their hierarchy was not good, especially as nothing was done when the Berlin wall came down. As you know, there is unrest throughout the empire now. The west facing countries have either already broken their ties like Poland and East Germany or are on the way like the Baltic States. However, there is much more than that. Ukraine is starting to agitate for independence although that is even more complicated as it is actually made up of three separate internal states. The Crimea, for example, was always part of Russia. Remember our own war there last century? And of course it has a massive ice free port for the Russian fleet. God knows what could happen if that is taken away. The east of the country supplies a great deal of Russia's grain, so once again Moscow will be reluctant to let it go. Then there are the states that we never really think about like Chechnya and Azerbaijan, in fact, the whole of the Caucus states. I won't go on. After this chat, I will leave you with some briefing documents to study. You'll have to stay here to read them but there will be similar ones in Moscow so you can keep up to date.'

Jon grimaced as Rupert took out several fat folders from his briefcase. 'Seems I'll be here a while then.'

'Oh and then there is one more thing.'

Jon looked at Rupert. 'Why am I not surprised?'

'Sorry, it's a little nebulous at the moment but one of our men on the ground overheard a remark made by an ex Stasi officer who went to Moscow rather than stay in East Germany. For some reason, the Stasi aren't exactly popular there anymore.'

'I can understand that but we've heard little in the press about what's going on there nowadays.'

'What you have to understand Jon is that the East German Secret Police were everywhere, in all forms of life. They had set up such a culture of secrecy and informers even George Orwell would have been impressed. At one time, it was estimated that one person in ten was part of the system informing on their neighbours and even their own families. The Stasi themselves were pretty brutal but that was changing anyway. It seems that you can only push a population so far. Towards the end, they were turning to a more psychological approach. The amount of information they gathered on their own population was staggering. When the wall came down, they started to destroy as much as they could but their headquarters was attacked by a mob before they could get rid of most of it. There is now a great debate going on about what to do with it. Our assessment is that within months they will make it all public and then the shit will really hit the fan for any of the organisation still hanging around.'

'So, our guy got out as soon as he could?'

'Him and his wife.'

'And what was this big revelation?'

'It was at a reception in the Soviet Embassy. He let drop that he is involved in some sort of organisation that is planning to do something about the dissolution of the Soviet Empire. The conversation was meant to be private but one of our chaps managed to overhear it by chance. However, that was some months ago and since then we've been unable to find out anything more. That said, there may be a way of approaching him through his wife. The lady in question was a senior member of the Division of Garbage Analysis. Don't laugh, it's true. They were responsible for analysing garbage for any suspect western foods and materials. We knew about it of course and the Embassies were quite good at sowing disinformation by putting things into their rubbish. If it wasn't so ridiculous it would have been funny. However, her husband, Gunter, was a very senior member of the Main Coordinating Administration of the Ministry for State Security. That mouthful translates into the arm of the Stasi that coordinated with the Soviets and primarily the KGB. We think it's that connection that got them into Moscow quite quickly. As you can imagine, the West really wants to know what is being planned but we've had no other intelligence on the matter. If it is happening it shows just how careful these people are being.'

'So, where do I come in?' Jon asked with a puzzled frown. 'This is way outside my area of expertise.'

'Ah, not quite, you see the wife used to be a helicopter flight engineer in the East German Air Force before they were married and she took up garbage disposal. The husband must have quite some clout because she has got a job with the Kamov design bureau. I'm sure you know about them?'

'You mean the outfit that makes all those helicopters with double contra-rotating rotors like the Hormone. Yes, I've come across those a few times in my flying days. We used to see them on their warships quite regularly.'

'That's them. Now with the new openness in Russia these days these design bureaus are starting to operate more and more like conventional western companies. They are now making overtures to all sorts of countries for sales of their products, something that would have been unthinkable only a few years ago. The Kamov lot are touting a new attack helicopter, the KA 50.'

'Yes, I've seen pictures of that. NATO call it the Hokum. It looks quite clever. Apparently, it even has an ejection system for the pilot.'

'You probably know more about these things than me,' Rupert responded with a smile. 'Although I do know that the Soviets call it the Black Shark. It sounds a bit more exciting than Hokum. Anyway, the lady in question is now leading the Kamov sales team with their government's blessing and are even starting to sound out the West as to whether there might be any interest. So, with your Defence Attaché hat on and helicopter background you're the ideal person to make contact with her. There is even a good higher level excuse for you to pursue her. It's rumoured that Kamov have been developing a much more capable two seat version called the Alligator but have yet to come clean. Getting real intelligence on that will be valuable in its own right. If you start to make discreet enquiries about that then it should give you cover for your real purpose, which is to find out what on earth her husband is up to.'

'And why do you think she will talk to me?'

'From what we can gather she's a bit of an aviation nut and let's face it your face is quite well known. We deliberately let slip that you were coming to the Embassy and she's eager to meet you. Officially of course, it's because of the Kamov sales drive but we know that she will want to talk about all things aviation. Apparently, she mentioned how she would love to talk to the only helicopter pilot in the world with an air to air kill to their credit.'

Jon groaned. 'Oh Jesus, will no one ever let me forget about that? It was years ago anyway.'

'Sorry old friend but it's still a pretty unique achievement and it gives us just the excuse we need to see if there is any truth in the real story. So, here are a few briefing files for you to read. I'll leave you to get stuck in. Give me a shout when you've finished and we can finalise all the detail. Oh and one last thing, once we're finished here you will need some more technical background. Tomorrow, I want you to go down to Wiltshire and take a look at the Soviet Air Force.'

Chapter 14

The next day, with his head still reeling from all the information that Rupert had provided and the covert mission he was being asked to perform, Jon only had half a mind on his driving. Having had time to reflect on what Rupert had told him the day before he was becoming more and more convinced that most if not all of what he was being asked to do was simply an excuse to keep him occupied. A way of making him feel that he would be contributing. However, that didn't stop him from looking forward to the job and maybe something would come of it. Being in Moscow was certainly going to be fascinating.

He was in his old Ford as he made his way out of London and down the A303 to Amesbury. He wasn't concentrating when a flash of lights in his mirror and an angry horn snapped him back into reality. With a guilty shock, he pulled back into the inside lane and gave a half-hearted wave of apology to the angry driver who sped past him. *I really don't need an accident now*, he thought guiltily.

Within minutes, he had crested the hill that had inadvertently slowed him down and he could look down over the plain ahead. Off to the left, he could clearly see the large hangars of the Defence Research facility of Boscombe Down. Although he had never been there he had often seen it as he drove past over the years. He knew it was the home of the Empire Test Pilots School and where all important military flight testing was conducted. However, he was still in the dark as to why he needed to go there. Rupert had been very coy on the subject and Jon got the impression he didn't want to give the surprise away.

Five minutes later, he drew up in front of the main gates. A small car park was provided in front of the gate office and he parked up before climbing out and stretching. It had been quite a long drive out of London and an early start had been needed but looking at his watch he saw he was on time. He went into the security office and showed his MOD pass. The policeman behind the gate checked it and then looked at a list on a clipboard. Just as the policeman was about to speak, the door to one side opened and a naval Commander walked in. He immediately spotted Jon and came up with his hand outstretched.

'Jon, good to see you after all these years.'

For a second, Jon didn't recognise the smiling red haired man, then memory clicked into place. 'Bloody hell Simon, I didn't recognise you for a minute. When did we last meet?'

Simon Thompson laughed. '814 Squadron, when I was the deputy engineer and far too long ago.'

'Goodness, that brings back a few memories. We were on that States trip together I seem to remember.'

'Yes and we won't go there please. I seem to remember you misbehaving almost as badly as me.'

Jon did indeed remember a certain run ashore where most of the squadron had almost been arrested by the local police in a strip club. It had only been the fast talking of their Senior Pilot that had got them let off with a caution. Actually, they had both only heard about it afterwards as they had already made a hasty exit through a window in the men's toilet. That had only been the start of that evening's adventures. Jon smiled at the recollection of happier, more innocent times.

'So, what's this secret squirrel visit all about Simon? London were very cagey and I've no real idea why I'm here.'

Simon laughed. 'I think the best thing is for you to see for yourself if you don't mind waiting just a few more minutes. You can leave your car there and we can pop over to the other side of the airfield in mine.'

As they got into Simon's car, Jon saw something strange just past the main gate. 'Good God, what's that doing there?'

'Ah, that's the prototype Lightning fighter. They've mounted it on that plinth. Impressive isn't it? Of course they did all the testing on it here in the late fifties.'

'That's one machine I've always wanted to fly. It still outperforms much more modern machines.'

'Yup, one of the few aircraft that can accelerate beyond Mach one in a vertical climb. Mind you, they do have a nasty habit of catching fire now and then so they do have their problems. Absolute pigs to maintain as well by all accounts. Anyway, let's go see some more interesting things.'

Despite Jon's questions, Simon merely smiled and refused to answer as they drove to some traffic lights which then let them across the massive main runway to a number of large buildings on the other side.

'That's D Squadron were all the helicopters are tested,' Simon said, as he pointed out a large hangar and office block. 'But what we want is in that other hangar behind it.'

In a matter of minutes, they were parked by the mysterious hangar. Simon took a large key and opened an access door set into the massive main sliding doors. Indicating to Jon to wait, he briefly went inside and turned on the lights before motioning Jon to follow. Jon walked in and stopped dead.

'You have got to be fucking joking. Where the hell did you get these from?'

Arrayed in front of them were a number of fixed wing fighters and helicopters. They were all of Soviet design and all were current in-service types.

Pleased with his surprise Simon walked over to a massive helicopter. 'Glasnost Jon. These all belonged to countries that have decided that they no longer want to be a part of the Soviet Union. Getting some of them here was fun, as you might imagine but we've been able to evaluate most of them now.'

'But how the hell do you fly them without being seen? You're only a few miles away from a large town and a main trunk road.'

'Good question and actually most of the flying evaluation has been done abroad in whichever country has been helping us. They are then shipped here in bits or flown in at night.'

Jon looked at the massive machine in front of him. 'This is a Hind D, the attack helicopter that everyone has been talking about. Bloody impressive looking thing.'

'Maybe but it's not quite what you think it is. Now as I understand it you are off to Moscow soon and will be involved in aviation matters there?'

Jon realised that Simon would not have been given any details of his real task but the knowledge he could get here would be invaluable background. 'Yes Simon and the more you can tell me about these machines the better.'

'OK then, let's look at how they design their machines because their design philosophy is very different to ours. This Hind is a good example. Their crews call it a flying tank and that's pretty much what it is. They build the airframes extremely strongly and because that makes them heavy, they use bloody powerful engines. This monster has twin two thousand two hundred horsepower turbines. Compare that to a Sea King which only has fourteen hundred per engine and you see what I mean. This may make them rather cumbersome but it also makes them very rugged. Of course, this particular beast is also very fast although it's not that manoeuvrable. Did you hear the story about the Lynx and the Hind a few years ago?'

'Not that I recollect.'

'Well apparently an army Lynx came across one of these on the other side of the East German border and they ended up flying parallel to each other. As I'm sure you know army pilots make it up as they go along, so they started doing a few simple manoeuvres and the Hind started to copy them. In the end, the Lynx did quite an extreme torque turn which was a bit naughty as it's not actually cleared to do it but the Hind tried to copy them. They reckon he ran out of tail rotor control trying to stop the turn and ended up in a snotty heap in a field. If you look at the tail of this thing I think you can see it's quite small. The whole machine is actually based on an earlier machine, the Mil 8 Hip. Look, we've got one next to it.'

They walked over to the next machine and Simon suggested they get in and have a look at the cockpit.

'Nice colour,' Jon observed.

'Yes, for some reason the cockpits of all their machines, fixed and rotary wing, are all painted in this rather horrible greeny-blue colour. But anyway, just look at the switches and see if you can see a logic to them.'

Jon looked around carefully and soon realised what Simon was getting at. 'Bloody hell, they call a Sea King an ergonomic slum but this is ridiculous.'

'Yes, it does seem that they've stuck them randomly all over the place which is probably why this machine has a crew of three. This centre seat is occupied by a flight engineer. Can you imagine needing that in one of our Sea Kings? They are about the same size, this thing weighs in at about twenty five thousand pounds, so slightly heavier but it needs two, two thousand horsepower engines to make it fly. Mind you, it seems they are very simple to maintain. It's fascinating to see how a different set of minds have solved the same problem in different ways. And you really have to admire their engineering skills. That Mig 29 over there is apparently as good a dog fighting machine as anything in the West, yet there is no fly by wire or computers in it. Its all hydraulics and mechanical systems. Mind you the avionics are crap.'

'I don't suppose you've got a KA 50 hiding in here anywhere Simon?' Jon asked peering further into the hangar. It's one of the ones they are trying to sell these days and one I'm particularly interested in.'

'Sorry Jon. It's not in service yet, so none of the satellite countries have got hold of one. Still, where you are going you might get your hands on one before us. I'd love to have a look, especially at the ejection system. Apparently, it fires all the rotor blades off before the ejection seats fire. Can you imagine the damage that would cause if some maintainer pressed the wrong button in the hangar?'

Jon laughed. 'And of course that would always happen on a Friday afternoon just as everyone was about to go on weekend.'

They spent the rest of the day looking at the Russian machines. Simon introduced him to some of the pilots who had flown them and learned much about their flying characteristics as well as their design and build issues. One of them summed it up saying, 'once you are airborne, they fly just like any other helicopter with plenty of power but in general less manoeuvrability. However, understanding how to get them going and manage the systems is another matter. A simple example is the rotor brake. They all have them but unlike our machines, they all have an interlock to stop you starting the engines until the brake is released. We do exactly the opposite and start up with the rotors locked so we can accelerate them quickly once the engine is fully running. The trick is to understand the thought processes that went into the design or maybe in some cases the lack of a thought process.'

By the end of the day, Jon had plenty of food for thought and was grateful for the visit which had given him a tremendous insight into Soviet aviation.

Chapter 15

Despite all his preparations, Moscow still caught Jon out. None of the study, the briefings and the history books had prepared him for the scale and grandeur of the place. The flight out had started it all. He had been booked onto an Aeroflot flight from Heathrow. The aircraft was quite old and looked to Jon just like a British VC10 with twin engines on either side of the tail and high mounted tail plane. It may have been a copy of the British design but inside it was very different. Spartan would have been a polite description. That said, it seemed to fly quite well and the service was good as long as you liked vodka.

He was met by one of the Embassy staff at the airport and they took a taxi to the Embassy. They did a quick diversion to Red Square on the way and Jon was impressed not only by the grandeur of the architecture but also the cleanliness. He was so used to seeing everything about the place in black and white photographs he hadn't realised just how much colour there was. He was also amazed and not a little surprised to see that there were still lanes solely for the use of government vehicles. Not that there were many ordinary cars around anyway and most of them looked careworn.

The Embassy was quite an imposing building on the banks of the river. It was separated from the water by a busy road, only about a mile from Red Square and quite close to the Russian Parliament building known locally as the White House. Jon was dropped at the entrance and assured that his personal baggage had already arrived. So, it was with only a small suitcase that he mounted the steps. Inside, a tall imposing man in a dark suit greeted him.

'Commander Hunt, I'm Captain Sam Haywood, the Naval Attaché, welcome to Moscow.'

Jon shook the proffered hand and studied the man in front of him. Tall and with thinning hair, he was dressed in a smart business suit. The Captain noticed Jon looking at the suit. 'Yes, we don't normally wear uniform for daily business in the Embassy. Don't worry, you'll get plenty of opportunity to wear all those silly dangly things we are supplied with. Anyway, Commodore Test is waiting for a chat. Later on, I'll get someone to show you around and you will need to call on the Ambassador this afternoon.'

Jon realised this was a big building and of course it would have to be with all the staff living on the premises and was soon lost. The Captain

72

turned to Jon. 'Sorry, backstage it's a bit of a rabbit warren but don't worry, you'll soon start finding your way around. Ah, here we are.'

They had stopped in front of a large oak framed door. Captain Haywood knocked and went straight in. Sitting behind a large desk was Commodore Test, Jon's old Commanding Officer. Jon noted the increased grey in the Commodore's hair and the lines around his eyes but his welcoming smile was genuine.

'Jon, we meet again,' the Commodore said as he got up and shook Jon's hand warmly. 'I was very sorry to hear about your wife but I expect you've heard that too many times by now.'

'Thank you Sir, it's behind me now. Coming here is the clean break I need.'

'Right, well sit down and Sam please stay as well. There are a couple of things we need to talk about right away.'

The three men sat and it was clear that the Commodore was choosing his words carefully. 'Jon, you are joining as my deputy and don't think for one moment it's a ploy to keep your mind off recent events. There is a real job to do here. This is a very dangerous time in a very dangerous country. I'm sure you've been briefed to death but things take on a different perspective when you're actually in country. In some ways, the falling of the Berlin Wall and all that's happened since is a very good thing but it is also putting extreme pressure on the system here in Russia. There is no doubt that the whole edifice is coming down but where it lands is the real question. If the old hardliners prevail, we could end up with a smaller union but one that is just as much a threat to our interests as the old one. You only have to look at how many nuclear weapons they will still have under their control. Of course, democracy could break out and make the world a safer place. The problem is that we just don't know and more to the point there is very little we can do to influence things. The more people we have keeping a tab on what's going on the better. So you're going to be my right hand man and also my aviation expert.'

Jon nodded. 'How will I work with the Single Service attachés Sir? Won't I be in a rather difficult position?'

'No, just think of yourself as my Military Assistant, just like many senior officers have working for them. Now, if I am away the next most senior officer stands in for me. In this case that will be our new Group Captain, Dick Pearson, whom I believe you already know?'

'That's right Sir, we were on courses together. So, he's here already?'

'Yes, he arrived three weeks ago. How did you get on by the way?' Captain Haywood asked in an innocent tone.

It was Jon's turn to choose his words carefully. 'Fine Sir, although he does seem very single service oriented.'

The Commodore laughed. 'It's alright Jon, we're all dark blue here. The good Group Captain has already made it clear he's not that keen on aviators in the navy. Hopefully, we will keep him busy and out of your way. You've met this wife as well I take it?'

'Yes Sir, lovely lady.'

'Good tactful answer Jon,' Captain Haywood replied drily. 'We'll make a diplomat out of you yet. Anyway, I'll take you around the department this afternoon after you've called on the Ambassador and you can meet everyone.'

'That's good Sam,' the Commodore said. 'Now, if you wouldn't mind, I would like a few words with Jon in private we have some social to catch up on. I'll bring him along to your office when we've finished.'

'Aye aye Sir,' The Captain replied as he stood to go. 'See you later Jon.'

Once the door closed, the Commodore seemed to relax a little. 'So Jon, the last time we met it was rather colder.'

Jon chuckled. 'Yes Sir and I was in your sick bay in Illustrious I seem to remember.'

'You know, I was rather upset that we couldn't give you the recognition your actions deserved for that little mission of yours. But I made damned sure the right people heard about it.'

'Thank you Sir but I seem to get quite enough publicity as it is.'

'Yes you do, you've been pretty busy since eighty three including a rather spectacular right hook recently. I have to say that was well done in my view.'

'Oh God, did that make it all the way out here? I was rather hoping to live that down Sir.'

'Well, it didn't make the headline news but we still hear things. Don't worry, it's all in the past now. Anyway, let's talk a little about the latest little task that has been set you.'

'Which one Sir? I seem to have been given several.'

'The ferreting around the military bit is really part of all our jobs. However, you must liaise with Mark Speddings our tame spook over that. You're down to call on him later. As for the helicopter lady, we have something coming up soon which you may be able to use. There is going to be a reception here in ten days for the Queen's Birthday. I know her official one is in June but we also hold a smaller, more select one on the actual date. Madame Bukov will be invited as she heads this sales team which we are ostensibly interested in.'

'Not the husband then?'

'We try not to invite known KGB senior staff to our parties,' the Commodore said with a half-smile. 'If we did it would look decidedly odd. Anyway, I don't think you will have any trouble getting acquainted. She has already asked to meet you. I met her once and she seems to have only one topic of conversation.'

'I suppose I shouldn't ask but what does she look like? I've seen a couple of blurred photos but that's all.'

'Sorry Jon, you'll just have to wait. I'd hate to spoil the surprise.'

'Why does that sentence really worry me Sir?'

'Hah, patience Jon. Now, as I'm sure you know, the Ambassador myself and Mr Speddings are the only people who know about this part of your job here. As I said, you'll meet our MI6 head of section later. He will also show you where the secure line is for you to report back to London if necessary. But this is so sensitive and not part of a normal attaché's remit that it must be kept to our small group. If things come clearer then that might change but for the moment just us three only.'

'Understood Sir.'

'Right, so let me take you back to Sam's office and you can carry on. We have our own bar and dining facilities here and tend to eat together if nothing is going on, so see you there about seven?'

That evening, Jon managed to find the bar without getting lost. His accommodation wasn't far away and he would rather have had an early night but it was clear that he would be expected to socialise, especially as he was the new boy on the block. The three attachés were there along with many of the senior diplomatic staff, all with their wives. With a pang, Jon realised that he was one of the few single men present. He wondered what Helen would have made of this all. She would probably have disliked it as much as he was starting to. He was slowly coming to the conclusion that military attachés spent far too much time socialising. Still, if his briefings were anything to go by there would be plenty of trips away from the Embassy to look forward to in the coming months. The ability to explore the country that he had been brought up to fight was going to be fascinating. However, he still had a deep suspicion that, despite all the reassurances from everyone, his appointment here had been deliberately chosen to get him away from the public eye. The additional task to see if he could get information out of this German woman seemed a long shot at best.

His thoughts were interrupted by Group Captain Pearson and his tiresome spouse coming over to greet him. Putting on his best smile, he went to say hello.

Chapter 16

Gunter Bukov's office was near the top of the Lubyanka building with a fine view over the statue of the founder of the Cheka, the original Soviet Secret Police Force. They had 'liberated' the building after the revolution from its original owners, the All-Russia Insurance Company. Gunter wondered what Felix Dzerzhinsky would make of the current situation in his country. He remembered the old joke, that it was the tallest building in Russia even though it was only five storeys high, because 'Siberia could be seen from its basement'. He shuddered at the thought of what had gone on in those lower floors over the years. He then reminded himself that much the same had happened in East Berlin. Luckily, that had not been his direct responsibility although he has sent several people into the system. He prayed that what he was doing now would not result in him ending up there. Ironically, his new job was in the department responsible for suppressing internal dissent. He worked directly for the head of section. To be given such a responsibility was both flattering and a great concern. Although it aligned very much with his previous work, he was pretty sure it was a poisoned chalice. Glasnost was destroying the very foundations of the work the directorate should be doing. Every time they tried to move against a political agitator or subversive organisation they were told to leave them alone. He strongly suspected that no one else was prepared to take on the job, so it had gone to the naïve German newcomer from the sticks. Maybe that would backfire if things went as he hoped over the next few months. Of one thing he was certain, his boss was an old school communist.

There was a knock on the door and his secretary came in with the files he had asked for. They were all on paper even though these days they could have been put into the massive computer now installed in the basement. No one really trusted these new machines yet and anyway paper was still considered more secure.

'Thank you Kristina,' he said automatically as she put the files in the tray and turned to leave. As she did so, he admired her pretty rear. She was an absolute stunner, as were many of the girls working in the building. Rumour had it that when Beria ran the organisation the girls were chosen for their looks as well as their submissive nature. The place was a hot bed of sexual gratification for the senior staff and probably quite a lot of misery for the girls he reflected. However, the tradition of recruiting pretty females seemed to have been carried on even if the abuse had been stopped years ago.

Forcing his mind back to the job in hand, he reached for the first file. The three industrialists seemed to have fairly straightforward backgrounds. All had minor issues regarding misbehaviour of various sorts and it was strongly suspected that one of them was a homosexual but there was nothing to alarm Gunter. Likewise, the two service officers had relatively clean records. The Admiral had got into trouble as a young officer due to drunkenness. The incident wasn't recorded in any great detail but it must have been pretty spectacular as drunkenness amongst the military was almost compulsory in those days. The General seemed squeaky clean, although he had managed to get through three wives and his bank balance reflected the load.

However, when he came to Vladmir's files he started to concentrate. The man's later career was little different to the other civilians. He had invested heavily in exploiting raw materials and trade outside the country but it was all with governmental approval. His wife had died some years earlier and there were no children. The majority of the file was about his early years. A rapid series of field promotions had seen him end the war in Berlin as a Captain in a tank regiment. He had been decorated by Stalin personally a few months later. Soon after that, he left the army and started a small organisation. It couldn't really be called a company but it effectively owned several mines in the Urals. It was unclear where the money had come from to start up the venture. What was also odd was that there were several proposals to include his name on lists for purges and all had been turned down by very senior KGB officials. The man seemed to have a charmed life. At one point, Beria had hand written a note in the margins of one document saying to leave the man alone. 'He was a Hero of the Soviet Union and should not be harmed'. It was unprecedented. Despite a very careful study, Gunter could find no stated reason for this seemingly miraculous protection. That's not to say he didn't have a pretty fair idea of why it had occurred. If he was right then there would be no record of it anyway.

Sitting back in his chair he contemplated the view from his window once again. Did he need to look any further? There was nothing in the record to indicate that the man was anything other than he had said he was at the meeting at his Dacha. It was very clear he was heavily invested in the system, both financially and personally. There was something nagging at the back of his mind though and it wouldn't go away. He made a decision. He needed to find out more about his early years. It was clear he had come into significant amounts of money probably during the liberation of Germany. That in itself was not unusual. Looting the Reich had become the pastime of many soldiers. What was different was that whatever he had got his hands on was very substantial and he had spent it wisely. But there was something more. Those days, when Germany was collapsing from assaults on all sides, it had been total chaos. However, some records had survived back in Berlin and with his previous work there, he had an idea where to look. It might be nothing but he would send a request for one of their operatives still in Berlin to do a little more digging.

That evening, when he got home, Bea was getting dressed for an evening out. She seemed to spend a lot of time on these sorts of jaunt these days. He was wondering whether his idea to get her the job with a helicopter bureau had been such a good thing after all and said so.

She made a face at him and asked him to do up the back of her dress. 'This is all part of the job Gunter and you well know it. This country has never had more opportunity to sell outside its borders than now and we must make the most of it.'

'And where are you going tonight?'

'The British Embassy, I did tell you. You always seem to forget. The British are looking at a programme for a new attack helicopter soon and we want to be in the running.'

Gunter chuckled. 'And you really think that they will even consider a Russian machine? The Cold War may be just about over but that's a million miles away from being able to share military technology.'

Beatrix shrugged. 'You may be right but we have to start somewhere and it is very early days yet. We've been studying the specifications of the other likely contenders and think that we would have a chance, on performance grounds at least. The politics are another matter.'

'Well, I wish you the best of luck. Hang on a second, the British Embassy? So you will finally get to meet your hero, that naval pilot you mentioned.'

'What's wrong with that? And anyway if I can convince him we have something good it will certainly do no harm.'

Chapter 17

Jon looked at himself in the mirror and had to smile. As well as his row of medals, his simple black uniform was now adorned with an Aiguillette on his left shoulder. Made of gold lace and blue stitching he found it rather unsettling. For a second, he wondered what Helen would have made of it. She would either have laughed or been quietly impressed. He forcibly put the thought aside. The tailor who had supplied it had explained that they were originally part of medieval armour and were the lacing that held the metal plates together. Over the years, they had become purely ceremonial. In Jon's case, as part of the military attaché staff, it was an Aiguillette third class. Apparently, he had to be an Admiral or Aide to the Royal Family to move up to a higher class. He smiled to himself, neither option seemed likely. Finally happy that he was smart enough for his first formal reception, he made his way from his accommodation down to the ground floor reception area. As instructed, he was there a quarter of an hour earlier than the official start of the event and the Commodore was already waiting.

'Ah Jon, very smart. I expect all the extra gold lace feels a little odd?'

'Just a bit Sir but I'm sure I'll get used to it.'

'You wait and see what some of the other countries wear. You won't feel overdressed then. Now just a quick word. I know you've been briefed but you have to be careful at these do's. Everyone will be polite and even seem quite open in what they say but like us they will all have been carefully briefed as well. It's a bit like warfare with gin and tonic rather than guns. The worst are the Russians. They drink like bloody fish and will do everything they can to ensure that you do the same. So your aim is to let them drink but stay sober, well as much as you can anyway. You might just notice the large plant pots around the room. They can come in very handy believe me.'

Jon looked around and saw what the Commodore meant. 'I spent several months living with a Russian family before coming out here Sir. I've pretty much got the idea.'

'Good man and don't forget to have fun. If you get invited on somewhere afterwards that's fine but do remember to log out where you are going with the front desk. Now, we've got our lady from the Kamov Bureau in tonight. I'll leave it up to you how you deal with her but London will want to hear anything and everything as soon as you can.'

'Understood Sir, although I'm still not sure whether this is either a good idea or even feasible.'

'I tend to agree but you never know. Ah, here are all the others. We'll talk again in the morning.'

An hour later and the room was full. Music was playing quietly in the background, the hubbub of conversation was slowly getting louder as more guests arrived and more alcohol was consumed. Jon had started talking to a large Russian army officer and his even larger wife. He was amazed at how banal the conversation was and even more amazed at the amount of booze the two were consuming. He had been told that alcohol prices had shot up alarmingly in recent months and it would appear that these two were making up for lost time. He had just managed to make his excuse to continue circulating when the Commodore came over with a woman on his arm. She was wearing a simple red cocktail dress and had long blonde hair. It wasn't either of those that caught Jon's attention. This woman had presence. A Valkyrie was the first image that sprang to mind. A horned helmet and steel bra with braided hair would be far more suitable than a red cocktail dress. She was a good four inches taller than him and that was in flat heels. However, although she appeared large, she was also slim. He realised it was because her legs were so long. Her face was boyish with green eyes and laughter lines spreading out. He reckoned she must be in her mid-thirties. Realising he must be gaping, he thrust out his hand.

'I believe you must be Beatrix Bukov from the Kamov Bureau. Commodore Test said you would be coming tonight, welcome to the British Embassy,' he part stammered, trying to stop staring at her magnificent bosom as he spoke.

If she noticed his stare or his embarrassment she didn't acknowledge it. Her handshake was as firm as any man's but he found it very odd to be staring up into a pair of female smiling eyes. 'Commander Hunt, I have heard so much about you. It is a real privilege to meet you in person. For some years I was in the army and flew in helicopters and now I work for Kamov as you know. I would love to hear more about your experience in the Falklands.' She spoke Russian with a slight accent which Jon assumed was from East Germany.

The Commodore took his leave and gave Jon a conspiratorial look as he made his exit. Jon and Beatrix continued to make small talk. She had a deep voice but it wasn't in any way masculine. She also seemed to like her drink just like everyone else. It didn't take long for other guests to home in on them. Jon was amused to note that they were all men, several Russian officers as well as one from the West German Air Force. The conversation became quite technical at one point and while the other officers were deep into a discussion about the merits of different types of rotor design, Beatrix turned to Jon and spoke quietly. 'We will never have a chance to talk here Commander Hunt, maybe you would like to join me for dinner after the reception, we could talk privately then?'

Jon nodded. 'Beatrix, please call me Jon and yes that would be delightful.'

'Very good Jon and please call me Bea, all my friends do. We had better both circulate now. I will catch up with you when this is over.'

Two hours later, a slightly tipsy Jon was seated in a very plush restaurant with his new best friend. He had quickly changed out of his uniform finery into a jacket and tie after the reception had ended and joined Beatrix in the Embassy lobby. They had gone by taxi to a very unassuming building near Red Square. The interior was quite a revelation and would challenge anything in a western capital. Jon had decided not to comment. It was clearly another example of the privilege given to the few in this country. The menu was just as comprehensive as the décor but Jon decided to let Bea order. Many of the dishes were unfamiliar.

Once the waiter had opened and poured their champagne, he left with their order. Bea looked at Jon with an amused grin. 'Don't worry, my employer will be paying. I have a good expenses account.'

'Oh sorry, was I looking worried? No, it's just that I wasn't expecting quite such an opulent place in a Soviet country.'

'I think there is much we need to learn about each other's country's Jon,' she responded not appearing put out by his slightly tactless remark. 'I have been given a job leading a sales team to try and get business abroad. It is a job that no one in this country had ever tried to do before. Maybe you can give some advice?'

Jon laughed. 'I'm not sure you're asking the right person Bea. My job up until now has been to fly the things not to sell them but if I can help I will.'

'Thank you but one thing I would love to hear about is your adventures in the Falklands. Before I was married I was in the Air Force. They wouldn't let women be pilots but I managed to get the job as a Flight Engineer on the Mil 8, you know of it?'

Jon wasn't going to admit he had been sitting in one only a few weeks ago. 'Only by what we in NATO are told. It's a transport machine isn't it?'

'Yes but for troops as well as cargo. Although I was only the engineer they let me fly it when we were away from base and that is where I got my love of helicopters and flying from. When your story was published in the press I was amazed. Many of my colleagues refused to believe it was true.'

Jon realised he wasn't going to get away from recounting his exploits, so with good grace he told Bea the story. She listened raptly and only interrupted when she didn't understand something he said. When he had finished, she was silent for several minutes and as their food had arrived they ate in silence for a while.

'I never thought a helicopter could manoeuvre like that Jon,' she finally said. 'If we tried it in a Russian machine we would be dead.'

'We very nearly were but the Lynx is an amazing machine and also we were just a bit lucky.'

'I think some people make their own luck,' she replied. 'Our new machine, the Shark, is good but I'm not sure it could have rolled and attacked a fixed wing aircraft like that.'

Jon laughed. 'You wanted advice about how to sell an aircraft. Telling me it's not as good as the one I flew nine years ago is not a good place to start.'

She smiled back in return. 'You make a good point but of course ours is built for a different purpose.'

Remembering his cover story, Jon decided to try a little fishing. 'And any others that you might be working on?'

Bea gave him a sharp stare for a second. 'I'm sure you are well briefed Jon but I only head up the Shark team.'

'Fair enough Bea. Of course I am well briefed, as I am sure you are too?'

'Obviously and I'm sure you well know who my husband is and what he does.'

Jon decided that honesty was the best course. He got the distinct feeling that this formidable woman would stand for nothing less. 'Of course I do and I also know what you did after you were married and worked for your old government.' He looked her hard in the eyes as he said it.

She didn't flinch. 'Jon, I make no apologies for what I did or for that matter what my husband still does. We come from very different cultures. When you live in a system you have to make your way by its rules, whatever they are. Things are changing here very fast as you can see but what happened in the past is done now.'

'Sorry Bea,' Jon exclaimed. 'I understand and it's not really my business. How did we get on to this subject in the first place?'

'I think you were fishing for some of my company's secrets?'

'Yeah well, I guess I had to try. I'm pretty new to this game, rather like you. But I hope you don't mind me asking how on earth did you get the job of leading a sales team for a helicopter company? I wouldn't have thought your background was compatible, except for your time in the military of course.'

'I expect you know what division of the Stasi I worked for?' she raised an eyebrow in query.

Jon just nodded.

'It was only partly involved in sifting through rubbish bins, which is what I suspect you have been told. Mind you, that was more fun than you probably think. We knew much of what we were getting was deliberately placed there but that told us what you were trying to deceive us about and even that intelligence could be useful. Anyway, we had another section which I ran. We looked at all information that western military companies put out. Most of it came from things like trade shows. Of course we had more clandestine sources but we were staggered by how much information was put in the public domain. So, for many years I was able to see how these companies used marketing and sales promotions. This is something we have never done in the Soviet Union. We have never had to sell to our markets they are told to come to us. It may seem strange but I am probably more experienced in what is needed to start this new venture than anyone else in this country.'

'And your husband approves?'

'Why not? We all know that things have to change now and who knows, he might be out of a job soon.'

'Good point.'

She laughed her throaty laugh. 'Let's get on safer ground. Will you be attending the ERF in Italy next month? It will be our first time to take a sales team out of the country and I and some of my colleagues will be giving presentations.'

Jon looked confused. 'I'm sorry Bea, what is the ERF?'

'Surely you know of the European Rotorcraft Forum? It's the helicopter trade symposium for European manufacturers. It's held every year. This year it is at Lake Como in Italy in a few week's time.'

'I think I've heard of it but I'm not sure it's the sort of thing I would attend.' As he said it he realised it would be the perfect opportunity to get Bea in a neutral environment and try to find out more about the real issue. 'However, I will see what can be done. It sounds as though it might be fun.'

Chapter 18

Jon sat at his desk but stared into the distance. It was covered in files, all part of his reading in for the job. He hadn't realised just how much paperwork he was required to see each day. It was a far cry from the bridge of his Frigate or the cockpit of an aircraft. It reminded him of his short time in Whitehall and that hadn't been that much fun either. The slightly throbbing head and sore eyes probably didn't help he thought ruefully. More coffee was needed. His office had come with a coffee maker and he was putting it to good use. He was lucky to have his own office he reflected. He had half expected to be in some outer room to the Commodore as was common practice in Whitehall.

Without notice, the door opened and Group Captain Pearson appeared with a frown in his face. Something Jon was getting used to.

'Can I help Sir? Would you like a coffee? I'm just pouring,' Jon asked innocently. He had found it best to ignore the man's attitude. He didn't work for him after all.

'No thank you Hunt. Now, what's this all about?' He asked, waving a buff file at Jon.

'Er, not a clue Sir. I can't see what it is while you don't hold it still.'

'Don't get clever with me Commander. It's this application of yours to go to Italy next month. Do you think we have a budget so you can go half way across Europe just so you can go on some Jolly or other? I know what these trade symposiums are like and it will be a waste of your time and our money.'

'So you've been to some yourself then Sir?'

Jon immediately regretted the remark. The man looked about to explode. Then he seemed to reign himself in. 'Well, it's quite simple I am not approving it, so you had better get back to your proper work, whatever that is.'

Just then the Commodore who had been passing and had heard part of the exchange put his head around the door. 'That's alright Dick, I know you normally manage these things but if you look at the application it has been made directly to me and I want Jon to go, so be a good chap and sign it off.'

'But Sir, the cost, it'll make quite a big hole in the travel budget and I really don't see what value it will be.'

The Commodore stayed silent and just stared at the Group Captain until the man looked away. 'Right, that's sorted then. If you wouldn't mind Dick I need to talk to Jon in private.'

The door closed as the Group Captain stalked out and Jon let out a sigh but the Commodore spoke before he could. 'Don't worry, I'll have a word with him later. Now, what was your impression of the young lady?' He smiled conspiratorially as he asked the question.

Jon grinned back. 'Well, she's tall and blonde but I wouldn't want to meet her in a dark alley if she was in the mood for a fight.'

'Not your type then I take it?'

'It's not that Sir, no female is my type at the moment.'

'Sorry Jon, I do understand. On that note, how are you bearing up?'

Jon thought for a moment, his transient good mood rapidly evaporating. 'You might find this a bit odd Sir but I've accepted my loss of Helen. That is, as far as I ever will. I looked at coming here as part of making a break, which it certainly is. There's a big but though. Nearly all my career, I've been part of a team. Whether it's a squadron or a ship it's been clear where my part lies. Frankly, I'm not sure why I'm really here despite all the nebulous jobs I've been given and on top of that you all have your wives with you. I'm on my own. Sorry, I don't want to sound self-pitying but this isn't the navy I joined and I'm not sure it's something I want to be a part of.'

The Commodore didn't say anything but made his way to Jon's coffee maker and helped himself to a mug before sitting down. 'Jon, I'm going to be brutally honest about this. All of us encounter this situation in our careers. Unfortunately for you, it has come at a really bad time. You've just finished your first command and then lost your wife a few days later. Frankly, I'm surprised you've managed as well as you have.' He saw Jon was about to say something. 'No, let me finish. Your career to date has had far more than its normal share of excitement but you have to accept that it can't always be like that. There is more to the navy than flying aircraft and driving ships and that's a simple fact of life. If you decide that it's not for you, then like many others who reach this point in their lives, you can always apply to retire early. However, before you do that I recommend you look very carefully at what is available outside and also what the navy still has to offer you. I'm not going to say anymore. You're an intelligent man and any decision you make will be yours alone. Just do me the honour of thinking it through carefully. You are in a very good position here to be able to take your time and decide rationally. And for that matter, you are also in a position to witness what is probably the death of the Soviet Empire from first hand. All I'm asking is that you don't rush into anything.'

Jon recalled the last time a senior officer had given him a similar lecture in Whitehall. That had all been about fighting a war with paper rather than guns. The Commodore was being far more honest and Jon realised he was going to have to do exactly what was being suggested. He really had no idea what he wanted to do if he stayed in the navy and even less if he left. One thing he did accept was that, up until now, he had been in no fit frame of mind to make a rational decision. All the courses preparing him to come here had kept him sufficiently occupied, so that he didn't have to dwell on the future. The culture shock of coming to the Embassy had broken that catharsis and now he was going to have to think very carefully.

'Thank you Sir. I probably needed to be told that. Of course you're right, there are going to be momentous things happening here and I would hate to miss the opportunity to witness them whatever they are. But I honestly don't know what I want to do with the rest of my life. I'll give it time and think hard on it.'

The Commodore stood. 'I can't ask anything more than that Jon. Enjoy Italy when you go there.'

Lake Como was staggeringly beautiful. Calm and tranquil, it reflected an almost perfect mirror image of the clear blue sky, surrounding green hills and villas dotted amongst them. The weather had been perfect all week. Jon had never visited Italy before. At first, he wasn't impressed. The flight in an Air Italia aircraft had been full of smokers and screaming kids. The trip around Milan in the taxi had done little more to endear the place. It looked like the sprawling industrial maze you would find in any large European country. However, once they were clear of the city, the countryside asserted itself and by the time they had reached the lakes Jon was enchanted. He had been booked into a small hotel and his room had a balcony overlooking the lake from several hundred feet up. The view was simply staggering. The symposium itself had been fascinating. Every day there were a variety of lectures and demonstrations to attend. Most were given by the various European helicopter manufacturers although several nation's military also talked of their respective experiences. Although a European event, Jon was amused to see how many American companies had managed to gain attendance on the pretext that they supplied to European countries.

Although he knew very few people there, the evening receptions given by the various manufacturers were an ideal way of meeting people. Once again Jon's fame or maybe it was his notoriety meant that he didn't lack for company. The Westland Helicopter crowd in particular seemed to want to take him under their wing. Not surprisingly, as he was a walking advert for the quality of their product. The week had passed in a blur. Tonight was the final reception and then they would all go home the next day. In some ways Jon had sympathy with Group Captain Pearson's point of view. Yes it had been fun and he had learned some new things but you did have to wonder about the value of the whole exercise, especially for the companies present who seemed to spend an enormous amount of money for what seemed very little reward. He had made that point to one of the Westland salesmen whose answer was simple. Like many trade shows, you needed to be seen to be there. If you weren't, questions would be asked. Jon thought it a rather simplistic answer but he realised that this element of commercial life was new to him and maybe he should reserve judgement. After all he had been drinking their booze all week.

He looked at himself in the mirror. He hadn't worn his dinner jacket for some years and was pleased that it still fitted, even if it was just a little tight around the middle now. After a final check, he went down to the lobby. To his surprise, Bea was there. He had attended several of the Russian manufacturer's lectures and like many others had been surprised at how open they were being as well as how different their design philosophy was compared to western concepts. However, there had been less opportunity to talk to his prime target all week than he would have wanted. The Russians seemed to be in high demand. Maybe now would be his chance.

'Bea, what are you doing here? I thought your hotel was miles away?'

'Jon, good evening. Yes it is but we haven't had much time to get together this week and so I thought I would come and visit. I was just asking reception if you were in and here you are. And you do look smart.'

Jon looked at Bea who was as magnificent as ever. She was wearing a slightly longer dress than normal but it was made of fine wool that clung to her figure and once again showed off her long legs.

'Well, you look pretty good yourself. We can walk down to the villa together. I'm sorry but my Westland chums are hosting me tonight. Maybe we can get together afterwards?'

'Anyone would think you don't want to be seen with us evil Russians,' Bea teased.

'Actually, there is some truth in that Bea. I am in a rather sensitive position.'

'Sorry Jon, I do understand but you still haven't told me all about all your flying adventures and then there was that incident in the Mediterranean the other year that was in all the papers. I would love to hear about that.'

Jon sighed. He really didn't want to go over all that again, especially as Helen featured so heavily in that particular story. Still, if it got Bea to open up a bit and gave him the opportunity to find out more about her he would have to grin and bear it.

It was only a few minutes walk and they could see the lights of the villa ahead and a crowd of people out in the garden with drinks in their hands. Bea took her leave and went to mingle with Jon's promise to meet her afterwards.

The dinner was almost a success. Tables were set around the large ornate dining room in a random pattern and each seated twenty guests. The Russians were all seated not far from Jon and he was surprised when he saw that they had removed all the bottles of wine on their table and replaced them with vodka. He recognised the label on the bottles. He was even more surprised when later in the meal two of the Russians started to fight. To Jon's amazement, two bouncers appeared from nowhere and broke up the fracas very quickly. However, they then asked the rest of the Russian contingent to leave as well. Although Jon made his excuses to his hosts as soon as it was reasonable, when he went out, there was no sign of any of the Russians, including Bea.

Chapter 19

Gunter was home late and Bea was already there making supper. 'You're late darling,' she called from the kitchen as she heard the door to their flat close.

'Yes, sorry but something came up at the last moment.' He came into the kitchen and gave Bea an affectionate kiss on the back of her neck before heading into their bedroom to change. 'How was Italy then?' He called over his shoulder. 'Did you sell the evil West any helicopters?'

'I'll tell you over supper. It didn't go that well I'm afraid.'

Once they had settled in over the dinner table Bea recounted the week in Italy including the events of the final night.

Gunter snorted in derision when she told him about the last evening. 'What did you do when you were all thrown out?'

'I was furious, as you can imagine. Apparently, it all started when one of the guys from Mil said something rude about our designs. Can you imagine it? There we are at our first international trade symposium and two rival companies start fighting in public. I've sacked our man and I believe Mil will be doing the same to theirs. I just hope that we haven't done irreparable damage before we've even started.'

'I don't think so, these things are soon forgotten but I would suggest that vodka doesn't replace wine in the future. Oh and did you get together with your British boyfriend?'

She gave Gunter a stern look. 'He's not my boyfriend. That's your job remember? Anyway, yes we managed a few chats but because of my comrades propensity for fighting, I never got the time to have a proper talk. I would still love to know more about his Falklands stories and what really happened in that cruise ship in the Mediterranean. We're going to invite him to come and see our production facilities and the new Shark helicopter. We've got approval to take him there which is a bit of coup in its own right. So, I'll have plenty of time to talk then. Anyway, what's been going on in my absence? Any more developments with the Vladmir Vorodov issue?'

'Good question. I've just had a report back from one of our men still in Berlin. As you can imagine, information from that time is just about impossible to get hold of. The city was a bombed out shell and by the time our troops arrived it was total anarchy. However, we've been able to make an educated guess about the size of the sums that Vorodov must have acquired and the only currency that could have been available was gold. On that basis, we managed to look at financial records and we found one bank that was completely looted. Apparently, the vault was blown open by some form of artillery shell.'

'Maybe from a tank?'

'Exactly, and the timing is right for when he arrived, so there is a good chance that he was the culprit.'

'Is that information of any use?'

'Information is always useful my dear. Although, in this case, I can't see any immediate leverage to be gained. However, it does explain how he managed to avoid all the purges. Even in our perfect communist paradise, money has always been an effective tool.'

'And what of more recent events? Did your little cabal meet last week?'

'Yes, in a hotel this time, all very carefully arranged. I was quite impressed. However, there is one thing that they have suggested that I am having trouble with. It goes against all the principles that I have worked with for years but for all that it is also probably a very good idea.'

'Go on.'

'Before I tell you, let me explain the background. We have a good candidate now and Vladmir will be making an approach to offer him support. If he accepts, it will give us a leader although I do have some reservations about some aspects of his character. However, if what we suspect actually happens, we will need real time intelligence and my organisation will not be in a position to provide it for obvious reasons. So I've been asked to approach the West.'

'What? You're joking.'

'No, I'm not. After the KGB Alpha troop went into Lithuania in January and there was that bloodbath, everyone seems to be petrified of a repeat. The politicians are blaming us, at least in public but we know they approved. The net result is that nothing is happening. The organisation is like a rabbit staring into the headlights of a car and no one will make any decisions. Most of the hierarchy are old guard but they haven't a clue what to do so they're falling back on the tactic of just supporting the status quo.'

'Gunter, this could be extremely dangerous. What would happen if you were found out?'

He smiled mirthlessly. 'We wouldn't be the first Russians to defect if it came to that. I'm sure we can build in an exit strategy as the West call it. But look, the current situation can't last we both know that. At least I'm in a position now to try and help. To try and ensure that things don't end up in another bloodbath but with thousands involved rather than just a few. Whichever way things eventually turn out, we should be alright but if things go the way I hope, we will be in a tremendous position. For all those reasons I think the risk is worth it.'

Bea thought for a while. 'Are you asking for my approval Gunter?'

'Bea, actually I may be asking for a little more than that.'

She frowned. 'I'm not sure where this is going.'

'Look, when I said the West I meant either the Americans or the British. They're the only ones who are capable of gathering the intelligence that we need. I have some potential contacts with the Americans but you have your tame helicopter pilot. You've already told me that you will be travelling with him soon. Could you sound him out, carefully of course?'

'For goodness sake Gunter, he is a naval pilot, not a spy.'

'Don't you believe it. They're all given intelligence training. Just like we do with our own military staff. He may not be the right man for what we want but he will know the right people within their Embassy.'

Bea was taken aback by her husband's suggestion but she could understand why he had asked. She had been in the intelligence world herself but it also meant she knew the risks. She looked hard at her husband. He had never let her down and if anyone had a real understanding of what was going on in their mad world it was him. She decided she had to trust him.

'Very well Gunter, I'll see what I can do but I will need more detail of what you're proposing.'

'Explain our situation but only in general terms. Also, make it clear that we are only approaching him because he is a convenient point of contact. What we are looking for is real time information if and when things come to a head. If he looks in the least interested tell him we can supply telephone numbers and communication frequencies. Mind you. I suspect they already know most of them. Their place in Cheltenham is the world's best despite what the Americans might say. One final thing, give him this code word 'Triptych Blue' it's an old Cold War emergency code but will give them some idea of the credibility of what you are saying.'

'That's all fine Gunter but what can I say to convince him that this is in his government's best interest? After all, they might just want to lets us sort out our own problems.'

'Remind him of Lithuania and Georgia and what could happen if things go wrong. Nobody wants that on a bigger scale. They've been fighting this Cold War for years just like us and I'm sure will be ready to take any opportunity to stop it completely.'

'And what do I do if he says yes?'

'He won't, he can't straight away. But he will report it to his people and I expect we will get an answer pretty fast. They will probably bypass him then and appoint an expert. Then we can really get down to business.'

Their supper went cold as they spoke into the night. Eventually, they went to bed and made love in an almost frantic passion, affirming their trust in each other. As Gunter lay back waiting for sleep to come he reflected on the one thing he hadn't told Bea. The location of that old bank in war torn Berlin.

Chapter 20

Two days after returning from Italy Jon was back in his office. He had written up a short report of the visit, carefully leaving out all reference to his attempts to learn more from Beatrix Bukov and put it in a file for general circulation. He was just getting stuck into reading the latest intelligence digests when his phone rang and the Commodore's secretary asked him to call around straight away.

When Jon got there he saw the Commodore was reading his report. 'Jon, take a seat while I finish this.'

He did as instructed and looked out of the window at the river while his boss completed the file.

'Bloody hell Jon, so they all got fighting drunk?'

'They really did Sir. I don't think they've got the hang of the western commercial world just yet. It's a bloody shame though because I assume Bea had to go and sort them all out and I missed my opportunity.'

'Hmm, it may not be all bad. In fact, it may well play to our advantage. Have a look at this.' And he handed Jon a letter.

Jon read it with a surprised look on his face. It was an official invitation from the Kamov Bureau for Commander Hunt to visit their factory to see the KA 50 Shark helicopter.

Before he could speak the Commodore got in first. 'This is very unusual Jon. It's the first invitation to a western country to view a Soviet military factory. Whatever you did in Italy it's turned out in our favour.'

'But Sir, the Kamov Bureau is just outside Moscow. This letter is referring to visiting some city I've never heard of.'

'You're right, I had to ask the intelligence guys what that was all about. Apparently, their head office is here but their production centre is the other side of the Urals in city Seven Five. It seems they have several of these hidden cities tucked out of the way of western eyes until now. This one concentrates on the production of gas turbines and helicopters. Apparently, it all goes back to the war when Stalin moved wartime production into safe areas. The Ural Mountains are a formidable barrier and so it was much safer to hide behind them well out of range of Nazi aircraft. We've known about them but never managed to get anyone into one and the only pictures we have are from satellites.'

'So, do I get to go Sir? It sounds fascinating.'

'Hold your horses old chap. We'll need clearance from London for this and that may take a few days. I'll let you know. However, that doesn't mean you can't contact the Bukov woman and let her know we are considering it. I assume it's her initiative even if the letter is signed by the head of the bureau.'

Within twenty four hours, approval was received from London and Jon was given a very detailed briefing on what to do and what to look for. There had been some debate about whether to try and equip him with cameras or recording devices but in the end, they were disregarded as they would only upset their Russian hosts when they were discovered, which they almost certainly would be. The best he could do would be to take notes as he went along and to keep his eyes open. He was also given a list of questions to try and get answered and things to look out for. So it was with some trepidation that he was driven to Domodedovo airport some forty kilometres to the south of the city in one of the Embassy cars.

When they arrived at one of the departure halls Bea was there to meet him. Dressed in a business suit, Jon still thought she would look better in a breastplate and horned helmet but answered her wide greeting smile with one of his own.

'Jon, I am so glad you agreed to join us. Maybe, we will have time to talk this time.'

Jon laughed. 'As long as we all stay off the vodka Bea.'

She made a face at him. 'Believe me, that will never happen again. But I was so sorry I was not able to meet up with you that evening. As you can imagine, I had other things on my mind.'

'Yes, well let's put that behind us.' Jon replied. 'I have to say, I'm really looking forward to this trip. And both myself and my government would like to thank you for the opportunity. No one has even visited one of your production cities before.'

'Glasnost Jon. Things are changing fast,' she replied. 'Now let me introduce Yuri and Petter, my two colleagues.' She indicated the two large well-muscled dark suited men behind her. Jon shook their hands. He didn't think they looked like commercial employees, not the least because of the not so obvious bulges under their arms. He had been warned that he would almost certainly be closely escorted at all times and it seemed that the warning was correct. They were starting before they had even left Moscow.

He lifted an eyebrow at Bea but she either chose to ignore it or misinterpreted his meaning.

With typical Soviet efficiency for the privileged, they were quickly chaperoned through the airport system and onto their aircraft. As they walked up the steps, Jon studied it carefully. It was a Yak 42 which to Jon's eyes looked suspiciously like a British BAC 111 airliner but with an extra engine mounted in the tail fin. It also looked like it had seen better days. He had been warned about the quality of Soviet aircraft but it was another thing to realise he was about to fly a thousand miles over sparsely populated and unforgiving terrain in one of them. His only consolation was that he knew they were strongly built. When he climbed inside, he realised that they hadn't copied western interiors. The seats were flimsy and the carpets stained. There wasn't even anywhere to put his small overnight bag, so he jammed it under his seat as everyone else seemed to be doing. Looking around, he could only see a dozen or so other passengers and there were plenty of spare seats. That didn't stop Bea's two goons taking the seats directly behind them. However, like all commercial airliners all over the world, there was a safety brief which everyone except Jon totally ignored. This was partly because the stewardess giving it, much to his surprise, was remarkably attractive but mainly because he really did want to know what to do when the old crate burst into flames on take off.

It wasn't long before they were lined up on the runway and the engines throttled up. The acceleration was remarkably strong and Bea looked over at Jon who seemed to be tensing up quite a lot.

'Jon, you're not scared of flying, surely?' she asked.

'Two things Bea. Firstly I hate not being in the cockpit. It's rather like riding pillion on a motorbike. You get all the fear but none of the control and secondly and please don't take offense but this isn't the newest or best maintained aircraft I've ever seen.'

She laughed her throaty laugh as the wheels left the ground and they climbed steeply away. 'Don't worry, the forty two has a really good safety record.'

'Is that by your standards or the rest of the worlds? Sorry, just let me settle down.'

'That's alright, maybe this will help.' She reached under her seat and pulled out her bag. Inside it, there was the inevitable bottle of vodka and two shot glasses. Jon noticed that nearly all of the other passengers he could see were doing something similar.

'I take it there is no cabin service on this flight then?' He asked, as he took a brimming glass and then a large sip.

'This isn't the decadent West Jon, here we have to look after ourselves. But don't worry there will be some food later.'

'Oh good, let me guess it will be something to do with cabbage.'

'Ah, you are learning our ways at last,' Bea replied with a chuckle.

The flight lasted for two and half hours and after the second vodka, Jon decided that that was enough. He wanted his wits at least half awake when they landed, even if Bea seemed to have hollow legs. When Jon said so to her, he then had to explain what he meant and she laughed loudly at the explanation. She also managed to worm a few more stories about his time in the Falklands War out of him but when she turned to the hijack of the Uganda he told her firmly that he didn't want to discuss it. When she pressed him, he simply told her it reminded him of his wife too much and she immediately dropped the subject. It was clear she knew all about Helen and how sensitive the subject was to him.

With what felt more like a controlled crash, than a landing, the aircraft arrived at city Seven Five. It was even more disconcerting when all the other passengers, including Bea and the goons started clapping presumably with relief. Maybe they all hadn't been as sanguine as they seemed.

Bea saw the look on Jon's face. 'It's a tradition in Russia that's all Jon.'

Jon grimaced. 'But traditions are based on some truth and being relieved at surviving a commercial flight is hardly one to be proud of.'

'Don't be silly. Anyway, welcome to Vertoletgrad. We have much to see.'

'Hang on, I thought you called it city Seven Five, not 'helicopter town?'

'The number is the official name but with over a hundred thousand residents they weren't going to put up with that, so that is what the people who live here call it.'

Jon didn't reply but privately wondered at the incredible Russian lack of imagination. As he looked out of the window at the drab high rise buildings in the distance he then changed his mind. The name seemed almost romantic compared to what he could see.

Chapter 21

Gunter Bukov was sitting at his desk worrying. Despite what he had said to Bea the other night she had a far easier task than he did. Spending several days with a British military attaché was a relatively straightforward way of making contact. On the other hand, he wasn't sure how to go about the same task with the Americans. At one point, he was almost tempted to let her try first and see the result but that would halve their chances of success and time was running out.

His problem was that his role within the KGB gave him no excuse to be involved directly with any American agents. He was meant to focus on internal issues. Although foreign countries, particularly the Americans, had sometimes been involved in stirring up internal dissent it was something they had not done for many years now. *Probably because we are better off doing it for ourselves*, he thought wryly.

One thing was for sure, he couldn't just walk up to the US Embassy or even approach any of their men on the street, even if he knew who they were. He was going to have to be far more subtle than that. He had told Bea he had some potential contacts but those names were from the old days. What he needed was an excuse to get out of Moscow. In the end, it was ludicrously easy. He sent a written memo to his boss saying that now that Berlin was united again he wanted to make contact with some of his old sources of information. They would only talk to him, so he couldn't delegate the task. He explained that the purpose was to see how the German people were coping. To discover how much of what was reported in the western press was actually propaganda, whether there was still any support for the old regime and the Soviet Union, and if there was support, then how best to utilise it. His boss being an old hardliner wouldn't believe that everyone was happier under the new regime and within a day he had his answer. The memo was returned and signed with the word 'approved' scrawled over it.

Two days later, he drove across the border into his old country. The department had supplied him with an old VW beetle which would go unnoticed just about anywhere in Europe. He followed the Autobahn to Berlin. The first thing that hit him was the amount of traffic and it all consisted of cars he barely recognised. For the whole of the journey, he didn't see one Trabant. Only a few years ago they would have been about the only car he would have encountered. They were really dreadful machines he remembered but even so the absence of the ubiquitous little cars was a big surprise.

The surprises kept coming. When he reached the outskirts of his old city, he decided on a quick detour. Following the familiar roads that now seemed so alien with advertising hoards everywhere and crowds of happy looking people, he looked for the first sign of his childhood home to appear. The closer he got the more confused he became. Where were the tower blocks of flats that he remembered? Surely he couldn't have got lost? He turned a corner and pulled the car over to the kerb. In front of him was an open area of mud and machines. Of the four tall buildings he remembered, there was no sign. They had been demolished that was clear. This was where he had grown up with his mother and father. Their fifth floor apartment had been so much better than anything most people could aspire to. He had had a happy childhood. He remembered meeting Bea for the first time at the local school and how they had become teenage lovers before she was called up for national service and went off to her helicopters. Then he had been recruited directly into the Stasi. When she had finally left the military and they had married, they were given another flat in the adjoining building, all courtesy of the government. They had been happy here until everything changed and now it seemed the whole of his past had been wiped out. It was like a dagger to his heart.

He wound down his window as an old lady walked past.

'What's happened? There used to be people's homes here.' He called. 'What's going on?'

The lady stopped and looked at him. 'They knocked them down. They said they were getting dangerous but we all think it was because they were for the privileged and were a symbol of the old regime, may they all rot in hell. They're making the area a park now for the children to play in. We all think it's a wonderful idea. Why are you asking? You didn't use to live here did you?' There was a definite note of suspicion in her voice.

Gunter forced a laugh. 'No not me but I used to walk past here sometimes. I've only just returned. I've been abroad. Anyway, thank very much.' He put the car in gear and drove off before she could ask any more awkward questions.

He reflected on how things had changed. Only a few years ago an old lady like that would never have dared speak to a younger man in a decent car in such a tone. Everyone was scared of informers and the consequences of talking out of turn. He marvelled at how things had changed so fast.

Driving on, the road went past the Brandenburg gate which was now covered in scaffolding and clearly being repaired for the first time since the war. He was completely staggered. Already, you couldn't tell that the city had been divided. Yes, he had spotted the remains of the wall in a few places where they hadn't got round to tearing it down but his old drab East Berlin was transformed. The shops were all full. Everyone seemed happy and full of energy. Feeling strangely elated, he made his way to the small hotel he had booked into. It was just behind the Kurfürstendamm, one of the main thoroughfares of the city and full of shops, cafes and nightclubs. The hotel was tucked away in a backstreet. In another twist of irony, it had been used in the past as a safe refuge for Stasi agents operating across the wall. Its owners had been Stasi themselves but now they simply owned and operated the place on a commercial basis. Not wanting their past to become public knowledge had made it easy for Gunter to get a booking.

When he checked in at reception there was only a young girl on the desk. He was not surprised that the owners were nowhere to be seen and like them he would be happy to keep it that way. Once in his room, he unpacked his few things from his overnight bag and sat down to plan his next move.

Before leaving Moscow, he had done some careful research. One name, in particular, had come up. Several telephone calls later he left the hotel after asking the receptionist where to find a certain café. It was only a few hundred metres away and by the time he got there his man was waiting. It had been some years ago when they had last met and Gunter initially had trouble recognising him. When he had last seen Mike Miller he had been a bear of a man with dark hair and tanned skin. It was definitely Mike but the hair was almost completely grey now and he sat hunched over a beer staring into the distance.

Gunter sat himself down opposite his old contact. 'Hello Mike, it's been a long time.'

Mike looked up without any surprise on his face. In fact, it was almost devoid of any emotion. 'Heinrich,' was all he said.

For a second Gunter was confused but then he remembered that this man knew him under a different name.

'Yes, it's me, how are you?'

'You didn't ask me here to enquire after my health. Say what you have to. Then you can fuck off to hell.'

Gunter was taken aback by the anger in Mike's voice. But maybe he shouldn't be he reflected. The last time they had met, Gunter had basically blackmailed the man into passing over information he really shouldn't have. But he had also kept his side of the bargain and not allowed Mike's authorities to become aware of his predilection for young boys. Soon after, Gunter had been promoted and Mike had been sent back to the States.

'I didn't say anything you know. I kept your secret. Even in the Stasi we had some honour.'

Mike grunted. 'Your all fucking heart, you know that? Anyway, people like me are legal now. Well, as long as the boy is of legal age. So come on you old communist spy, what is this all about?'

'First of all Mike, why are you back here? I saw your name on the Embassy staff list but as we both know job descriptions for Embassy staff are often very far from the truth.'

'Sorry to disappoint you Heinrich but mine is accurate. I retired from active service several years ago but they kept me on in records. I'm afraid I really am the Embassy librarian. A tour to this new and united country seemed rather appropriate after all the shit I put up with when I was last here. And just look at the place. Do you live here still?'

Gunter smiled. He might as well tell the truth. It would have to come out fairly soon once he was talking to the right people. 'Mike, I was never Stasi. I was working for Moscow and that's where I am now. I only got into the city this afternoon.'

Mike grunted at the revelation. 'So, you've seen what they've done to the place since they kicked you bastards out then? Still believe in the Soviet Socialist paradise?'

'I never really did Mike but when you're in a system you can either fight it or go along with it and we never had the choice of anything else. There was a bloody great wall in the way remember? Now look, you know who to speak to on the secret service side?'

'Yes of course. I take it you want to make contact. Why?'

'Mike, I may still be KGB but I am also a patriot. I'm Russian and will serve whatever government is in power, just as you do, I might add. The problem is that the government may not be the same soon.'

'You mean because that idiot Gorbachev has started something he can't stop? Silly bastard, anyone with half a brain cell can see what's coming.'

'Maybe they can see that something is coming but what will it actually be? There's still enormous potential for it all to go wrong. I'm pretty sure your government will want to minimise the risk.'

'Stop right there Heinrich. I told you I was out of the department now and I am. I really don't want to know the details. I'll pass a message on that you want to make contact but that's all and don't hold out too much hope either. I'm sure they will know all about you and who you really are these days, so they can make a decision but knowing them it will take some time. Nothing happens quickly these days. Everything gets referred up the line. Give me a couple of weeks OK?'

'Fair enough but as a sweetener, please mention the code word 'Triptych Blue' will you? It's something from the past but it might just get their attention.'

'Ok, I'll see what I can do.'

Satisfied that he had done all he could, Gunter left leaving Mike to contemplate his beer.

Later that evening, Mike walked slowly back to his flat. He had a decision to make. He hadn't been exactly honest with Heinrich or whatever he was really called. Despite actually being the Embassy librarian, he wasn't retired and the job description covered more than looking after books and records. He was the senior analyst of that information. He also knew exactly what Triptych Blue meant. The other thing he had kept back from Heinrich was just how much he loathed the man. In a career going back decades, his slip up in Berlin had been his only mistake. He also knew how homophobic the Soviets were even to this day. All those years ago, he had vowed that given the chance, he would exact some form of revenge and now the opportunity had fallen straight into his lap. It would mean he couldn't pass on the message but so what? If the Soviet Union was collapsing and turning into a mess that was their own bloody fault. He had spent most of his adult life fighting the bastards one way or another. Why the hell should he do anything to help them? No, he wouldn't pass the message on, not in his lifetime.

Chapter 22

The hangar smelled like any the world over; a mixture of kerosene, hydraulic fluid and grease. Jon took a deep breath. It was almost like coming home. However, squatting in front of him wasn't a big green Sea King or sleek grey Lynx it was a matt black, vicious looking machine that bore little resemblance to anything he had ever seen before. It had a sharp nose and narrow glass cockpit with the bulbous intakes of two enormous engines either side of it. Further back, two large stub wings extended out with weapons hanging underneath. But the most striking difference to any other helicopter that Jon was used to were the two main rotors, one above the other. Although it had a large tail fin it also lacked the usual tail rotor. The overall impression was of a very capable, heavily armed and dangerous machine.

'Goodness Bea, it looks even more menacing in the flesh than the photos.'

She beamed back at him. 'Go and take a closer look Jon. We can answer most questions.'

He walked around the helicopter looking carefully at everything he could see and trying to mentally record it all. When he got to the cockpit, he looked enquiringly at Bea and the Kamov engineer who was escorting them.

'Go on Jon. Climb the ladder and jump in. The ejection system is safe.' As she said it she looked at the engineer who nodded in affirmation.

Tentatively Jon climbed in and eased himself into the seat. Unlike the machines he had examined at Boscombe Down, this cockpit, although painted in the standard Russian duck egg blue, looked far more modern and logically laid out although he didn't have a clue what all the switches did. It would be the same if a Russian climbed into a Lynx of course. However, what was the same were the flying controls and basic flying instruments. There was a collective lever by his left hand side and a cyclic control that fell naturally to his right hand. His feet landed on conventional rudder pedals. He wondered how they worked with no tail rotor. Presumably, they altered the torque of each main rotor somehow. He made a mental note to ask when he got the opportunity. The flight instruments were even in the familiar 'T' pattern he was used to. If the engines and rotors were going he was pretty sure he would be able to fly it. Somehow, he didn't expect they would let him.

One thing he had never seen in a helicopter before was the large red double D shaped handle protruding up between his legs.

'I assume that this is the 'get out of trouble free' handle,' he called to Bea who had also climbed up and was looking over his shoulder.

'Yes, if you pull that there are explosive bolts in the root of each rotor blade. The centrifugal force simultaneously gets rid of all the blades extremely fast and then if you look behind you that large container has a rocket and long flexible rope. The idea is the rocket shatters the canopy and flies up. When the rope is taut it smoothly pulls the seat, with you in it, free of the machine.'

'Oh, so it's not like a conventional ejection seat with a rocket pack in the bottom?'

'No, it gives a far less violent ride but is almost as fast as a conventional seat. With the need for the time delay to shed the rotors this was the best compromise. You will still be clear of the machine in less than a second and it works from zero altitude and airspeed.'

Jon had to think about that. In all his flying career in helicopters he had never once thought of the possibility of actually bailing out of the machine. On one occasion during training, he had worn a parachute when they flew a Wessex up to ten thousand feet but even on that trip the consensus was that it would be better to stay with the helicopter if something went wrong. Helicopters had their own in-built parachute with their rotors. Of course, this machine was designed to fight in a low level hostile environment, so maybe the ability to get out quickly was actually a very good safety feature.

'I suppose that with just one pilot it's not a bad idea Bea. All the machines I've flown have at least two crew and often four. I can't see such a system working in a Sea King for example.'

'Yes I agree but for this helicopter we think it will be essential, a unique feature. Now come, we have another demonstration for you.'

Jon climbed out and was led out of the rear door of the hangar. There, sitting on the tarmac was another Shark. This one was manned and on seeing them come out of the building the pilot immediately started the engines. Bea and Jon were handed large cloth helmets with ear covers to keep out the noise. In a remarkably quick time the machine's rotors were up to speed and suddenly it leapt into the air and dropped its nose at least thirty five degrees before accelerating away into the distance.

As the noise dwindled Bea turned to Jon. 'Twin, two thousand two hundred horsepower engines, so it can fly the whole envelope on one if need be. Well spaced apart to minimise damage. Its maximum weight is twenty four thousand pounds which is more than one of your Sea Kings. It cruises at one hundred and forty five and can achieve one hundred and seventy flat out, so it is faster than anything you have.'

Jon was impressed and looked it. Of course he already knew the figures from his intelligence briefing. However, it was reassuring to know that they had got it right.

In the distance, the Shark had banked hard and was coming back towards them at very high speed. It shot over their heads at what Jon assumed was its maximum speed and then pulled up and executed a series of very impressive manoeuvres. Torque turns, wingovers and vertical climbs. It didn't attempt any extreme rolling manoeuvres he noted and it seemed to him that the twin rotors got awfully close to each other at times. However, he kept his counsel. There was no need to criticise.

Soon, the helicopter landed in front of them and the engines and rotors wound down. Bea gave a cheerful wave to the pilot and turned and escorted Jon back to the office they had started out from that morning. Coffee was waiting for them.

'So Jon, what do you think? Could we enter such a machine in your forthcoming search for a new army attack helicopter?'

Jon thought hard. He had spent quite some time on the telephone back to London talking to the Operational Requirements and Procurement staff there. He had quite a good understanding of what they were looking for.

'Bea, its early days for that programme. They haven't even formalised the requirement yet. So I expect you would have to redesign certain elements to be compliant, particularly with the weapon systems. Also, there will be a great deal of emphasis on maintenance workload and spares costs. Don't underestimate how much importance that is given. When we assess costs it is based on everything including how much support the machines will need throughout their life.'

Bea didn't look at all put out by his remarks. 'Of course Jon, we understand that. We have been doing research on your procurement procedures. But from what you have seen do you think the Shark could be considered?'

'Considered, yes of course. We have an open policy to allow anyone to bid. However, don't get your hopes up. There's some serious competition out there. The American Apache and the new Eurocopter Tiger will be prime candidates. And then there are the politics, which I'm afraid is way above my pay grade.'

'And mine but I was given this job and irrespective of what the politicians say I will do it to the best of my ability.'

'Fair enough.'

That evening Jon met Bea in the lobby of their hotel. They had finally got rid of their two goon escorts who must have decided that he had seen all he could by now. His whole experience of a Russian closed city had been almost surreal. The hotel was modern by nineteen fifties standards. It was like entering a time warp. Everything was clean and well looked after. It was just that it seemed to be part of another world.

The bar was simple and seemed to only serve a local lager and of course vodka. Bea bought him a beer and a vodka for herself. It seemed to be the only thing she ever drank. They sat down at one of the Formica topped tables. After the Shark demonstration, Jon had been given a limited tour of the production facilities. He was well aware that there was probably a great deal of the city he would not be allowed to see.

'So Jon, what do you think of the city in general?' Bea asked.

'Strange Bea. It's not like anything I have experienced before.' He knew he would have to choose his words carefully because it seemed as drab and introspective as the hotel but he didn't want to upset his host. 'But what do the population think? I've seen guard posts on the exits. Surely you don't force people to stay here?'

She laughed. 'Jon those checkpoints are to stop people coming in. These cities may be closed societies but there is everything here that the people need. Schools, hospitals there's even a fun fair. You remember seeing it as we drove in from the airport? No, these cities are very popular. They get good food and conditions have always been excellent.'

'And access to the outside world? Can they travel or see western media?' Jon knew he was getting on dangerous ground but it was one of the things he had been asked to discover.

'These places are called 'letter box' cities Jon because you can't write directly to anyone in them. But things are changing. Glasnost is starting to be felt even here on the far side of the Urals. These things take time and it's just the start.'

Jon recognised evasion when he heard it but Bea's answer was pretty much the confirmation he was looking for. He wondered what would happen to such a closed society once the reigns were loosened, especially for the young.

'So, we're back to Moscow tomorrow? Unless you have something even more exciting to show me Bea?'

'Sorry Jon, nothing more but I'm sure you've seen and learned a lot. Now, how about you tell me more about your flying in the Royal Navy?'

Chapter 23

The outside of Vladmir's Dacha had undergone a transformation. The snow had melted long ago and under the hand of Sergei, the garden was a riot of colour. The air was scented by flowers and the tall stand of pines to the rear. The two old men were sitting together on a bench overlooking the rear lawn enjoying the late spring sunshine. A small table with the inevitable bottle of vodka lay to hand.

'I love this time of year Sergei,' Vladmir remarked. 'For some strange reason it reminds me of our days in Berlin. And that's odd because I don't recall seeing one flower there, only destruction and misery.'

'It's probably because that's what you were wanting to see. We had survived but only just. It was all in your mind.' Sergei replied. 'I remember the same things but also recall the camaraderie and the feeling of victory. I also enjoyed seeing the bloody Germans smashed to the ground. After what they did to us they all deserved it. They brought our revenge on themselves. Remember Breslau?'

'Yes and thank God we didn't stay for the siege. They only surrendered two days before the war actually ended. But that was the worst time. Those anti-tank grenade launchers, what where they called?'

'Panzerfaust. They did a lot of damage to our tanks until we got the infantry to clear the ground ahead of us. Oh God, there was that little girl, remember? She took out Dimitri's tank and then we shot her. But what else could we do? You know Vladmir, when I was walking east to join up I came across a village, well a small town actually. It was completely deserted. Little was touched and I managed to get some good supplies to keep going. But as I left, the smell hit me. The Nazis had rounded up the whole town and shot them all, men women even little children and dumped them in a pit. They hadn't even bothered to cover them up. And to this day I can't see why they did it. The town wasn't important and the people there were just people. Once they had been slaughtered the Germans just moved on. And as you well know that is just one story out of thousands. I have no regrets about how we behaved once we reached Berlin. There were no innocents in that city.'

'Just like there were no Nazis in the whole of Germany that summer.' Vladmir snorted cynically. 'But do you know what really annoys me about Germany?' He carried on answering his own question. 'We broke them, brought the whole country to its knees. We stole most of their wealth, what was left of it and most of their science. And look at the respective countries now. Germany got major support from the West and is now one of the wealthiest countries in the world and God knows what will happen now they've been reunified. Look at Russia and I don't mean the blessed Union of Soviet Republics, I mean our country, mother Russia. We had a moment of glory in the sixties with Gagarin and then what happens? The Americans beat us to the moon by a few months, so we tear it all up and deny we were ever even trying. Since then, we spend more and more on defence that we don't need and the country slowly falls apart. Where is the justice?'

Sergei had heard it all before, he kept silent.

Vladmir carried on. 'And now this bloody man Gorbachev is tearing up what is left. Has he never visited the West? Has he never seen what life can be like when you don't spend half your income on military toys? Surely, he realised that by lifting all restrictions, countries would leave us in droves?'

'Ah, I take it you haven't heard then?'

'Oh God, what is the idiot planning now?'

'He's drafting a new bill of Union for the remaining fifteen republics. It will give them more autonomy. I assume the thinking is that if they are given more power they will be grateful and the union will stay together.'

'Oh, for goodness sake. Surely he knows how the old guard will react? They've been teetering on the edge for months now. Surely this will push them over?'

'That's my guess too but one has to ask why he's really doing it. You don't get to move up from tractor driver to the only President of the Soviet Union by accident. He's no fool.'

'So you're saying that he's playing some form of double game here?' Vladmir looked perplexed. 'What's he trying to do, flush out the dissent? That is a very dangerous game my friend.'

'But that's what we Russians have called it for centuries now isn't it? The Great Game is a Russian pastime after all. Vladmir when did you last go into the city?'

'You know me Sergei. I like my home comforts too much these days. I don't think I've set foot in Moscow for over a year.'

'Well, you really ought to go because there is a very strange atmosphere there these days. The bars and cafes are all full of young people. The media is reporting things that would have had them shut down and their editors visiting the Lubyanka only a few years ago. There is an almost desperate air of hope but you get the feeling that many don't believe it will last. It's a powder keg Vladmir and the pressure is rising. At some point, something is going to have to give.'

'Maybe that's what Gorbachev is planning on Sergei. Hmm, I wonder. When is this bill of Union going to be signed?'

'No one is quite sure. It takes time to go through the motions of government. A couple of months no more. So that would be sometime late summer.'

'And what news from our KGB man, have we made contact yet?' Vladmir looked worried.

'Yes, he went to Berlin the other day and says he did but he's worried that the Americans might take some time making a decision. So he is also trying an approach to the British but hasn't said how he's going to do that. I just hope we can get something set up soon. Time is clearly running out.'

'And our man, Gorbachev's old protégé, what news there?'

'Apart from him trying to support the Russian vodka industry all on his own?'

'Come on Sergei, we all like a drink. What's this on the table here?' Vladmir said pointing to the bottle and two empty glasses.

'I know but I just hope it doesn't cause us a problem when we don't need it. Anyway, as you know, in two weeks there will be an election for the President of the Russian Soviet Federative Socialist Republic. The latest polls suggest he is expected to win it easily. It's one election Gorbachev can't rig even though he has his own candidate running.'

'So basically, we will end up with two Presidents, one of the Russian Empire and one of the Russian state. Both of whom hate each other. How on earth is that supposed to work?' Vladmir sighed in exasperation.

'I think most people realise that it's crazy. Maybe it's something to do with what Gorbachev is up to with his Union bill.'

'Well, it certainly emphasises the need to get real time intelligence as soon as we can. There are going to be a great deal of conversations going on behind closed doors that we need to know about. And if people react in the wrong way, particularly the military, there could be real problems despite having our own people on the inside.'

Chapter 24

The car taking Jon and Bea to the airport was quiet. Both back seat passengers were more than a little hungover. After meeting in the bar, Bea had taken Jon back to the Kamov main offices where there was a cafeteria and they had dinner with members of the staff. It had been a little awkward at first as everyone seemed keen to get Jon to agree that their helicopter was a serious contender for a programme that wasn't even in place yet. He had fended off as much as he could discovering levels of tact he didn't realise he had. However, soon the conversation had become more general as the booze flowed. Bea had severely embarrassed him at one point by recounting some of his Falkland War stories. He hadn't asked her to keep them to herself but he hadn't expected her to broadcast them so widely either. But even that passed and the evening ended up in a series of toasts to their respective countries.

When they got back to their hotel, there had been a moment of awkwardness as they said their goodnights. Jon wasn't sure whether he was expected to make a pass at Bea and he was pretty sure that she wasn't sure either. In the end, they parted in the corridor and that was that.

Bea was mentally kicking herself. She still hadn't passed Gunter's message to Jon with that odd code word. She knew she had been putting the moment off. She had no idea how he would react and she really didn't want to alienate him now by making him think this whole trip had been purely a cover for that. Her last chance would come on the flight back and that would have to do.

As he sat back in the cheap plastic seat of the car, Jon looked sideways at his host. He was also kicking himself for the same reason as Bea. He still hadn't tried to sound her out about the possible conspiracy her husband was involved in. But he was confused. He was having trouble sorting out his feelings for her. That she was attractive wasn't in doubt, as was the fact that she had made it clear she was happily married. The problem was that he had never met a female who was so intimidating and yet so much fun. In a strange way, she reminded him of Brian Pearce. They were about the same height and shared a similar wicked sense of humour. Bea always seemed to be on the point of laughing at something yet could be serious at the same time. Her smile lit up her face. But strangely, Jon felt absolutely no physical attraction towards her at all. In almost every way she was different to Helen which might be the reason. However, he realised that while not attracted to her as a female, he was starting to like her very much as a human being. He had never had a relationship with a pretty girl of any sort that hadn't either ended up in bed or at least with him wishing it would. On top of that, she was an ex Secret Police woman married to a senior member of the KGB, effectively still the enemy of his country.

He was saved from any further introspection by the car pulling up at the rather dilapidated terminal building of the small airport. Jon looked around and noticed that the aircraft they were meant to be flying out on, the Yak 42, was nowhere to be seen.

'Looks like things are running late Bea,' he remarked as they pulled their bags out of the boot of the car.

Bea looked around as well. 'I'll check once we get inside.'

Jon remembered the terminal from when they had arrived. It was unlike any other he had been in, no adverts, virtually no facilities and just one desk which was currently unmanned.

'Just wait here a minute Jon, I'll go and see if anyone knows what the delay is.' So saying, Bea went through a small side door with a determined look on her face.

It wasn't long before she returned with an even more dour expression 'The flight has been cancelled apparently. As we were the only passengers they decided it wasn't worth it and they didn't bother to think of to tell us.'

'What you need around here Bea is a revolution. Oh no hang on you did that a few years ago didn't you?' Jon responded with a smile.

'Very funny Jon and far too near the truth. The next scheduled flight is in three days.'

'Shit, so what do we do? I don't suppose we could get a car and drive it?'

'Over a thousand miles and across mountains with some of the worst roads in the country? Even the bloody Germans couldn't get here. There used to be a train but that stopped several years ago because of the so called reliable air links. So, we either go back to the hotel or see if there are any other aircraft leaving today. The control tower is just over there. I'll go and ask if there are any other planned movements.'

Jon sat down again while Bea strode purposely out of the terminal to the small glass topped building a few yards away. Once again, it didn't take long before she reappeared but this time she looked happier.

'Some luck Jon, there's a freight flight going to Moscow in a couple of hours. It's a twin turbo prop Antanov 24 and apparently has a couple of jump seats we can use. It will take twice as long to do the trip and won't be as comfortable but at least we'll get home tonight. It's that or three more days here kicking our heels.'

'And destroying our livers. Let's go for it Bea,' Jon replied in a relieved tone. The trip had been fascinating but three more days with nothing more to do and little to see would have him climbing the walls.

By now, their car had disappeared, so there was nothing else to do but wait in the terminal. The only facility apart from a very rudimentary toilet was an old vending machine. Jon spent a happy five minutes kicking and swearing at it until it eventually produced two paper cups of a fairly warm brown liquid.

He handed one to Bea. 'There you are but don't ask me what it is. It's the only selection I could get to work and the label on the machine has fallen off.'

'Tea,' Bea replied as she took a sip.

Simultaneously Jon did the same but he said, 'coffee.'

They both burst out laughing.

Two hours later, Jon was doing anything but laugh. In fact, he was berating himself for being a complete idiot. The Antanov 24 they were flying was well past its sell by date. As they had climbed, in he had noticed that there was rust on the leading edge of the wings and there were oil streaks weeping out of just about every panel on both turbo prop engine pods. The inside wasn't much better, it stank of some unknown mixture of oil, fuel and presumably whatever their cargo was. The cargo itself was contained in large wooden containers held down with old nets clipped to the floor and didn't look too secure.

When he mentioned his misgiving to Bea she laughed. 'Come on Jon, this machine has done the trip every week for years, it's quite safe. The AN 24 has a tremendous reputation for strength and safety.'

He really did want to get back to Moscow, so he reluctantly let himself be persuaded that it was alright. A member of the ground crew had shown them to two very uncomfortable looking seats at the rear of the cargo area. In fact, the take off had been remarkably smooth. The machine clearly had plenty of power. After half an hour, a young man in a white shirt that could have done with a wash, with two gold bars on the shoulders and a dreadful case of acne had appeared and asked if they wanted to come up to the flight deck. With little else to do in the noisy and uncomfortable cabin, they eagerly agreed. There was plenty of room to stand behind the two pilots and they were both handed headphones so they could speak. Jon wasn't impressed here either. The cockpit looked as scruffy and tired as the outside of the aircraft.

The lad with the acne introduced himself as Bogdan the co-pilot. Albert sitting in the other seat was the Captain. As far as Jon could see both of them were barely out of school but they seemed to be able to handle the aircraft reasonably professionally, so he merely smiled. Bea, on the other hand, introduced him as the famous British aviator and once again Jon had to stop her recounting all his Falklands exploits in lurid detail.

The aircraft was flying quite low and the Ural Mountains were rising in the distance to meet them. The view was quite stunning although the terrain looked far from inviting. Vast swathes of forest were interrupted by rocky outcrops. There was absolutely no sign of habitation anywhere.

Jon looked at the altimeter and did a quick conversion from metres in his head. They were flying at about ten thousand feet. 'Hey guys, why are we so low? Can we get over the mountains at this height?'

There was an embarrassed silence for a few seconds and then Bogdan answered. 'We have a problem with the cabin pressurisation I'm afraid and so we are limited to this height. Don't worry we've done this trip several times already. There is plenty of clearance over the mountains in certain places. One of the reasons for going to Moscow today is that the spares we need have arrived and so we should be able to fix the system when we get there.' He turned and gave Jon what he thought was a reassuring smile. It did the exact opposite. Jon had flown in mountains many times in Norway and knew just how dangerous it could be without the right experience and preparation.

'And the weather forecast?' he asked innocently.

'Oh, that's good all day,' was the glib reply. Jon wasn't so sure. He could see cloud streaming off the tops of the peaks ahead of them which always indicated moisture in the atmosphere.

The flight droned on for a while and they exchanged inconsequential chat with the two pilots. Jon was reluctantly persuaded to recount his encounter with the Argentinian Pucara but all the while he was watching the approaching peaks with increasing trepidation.

'Just where is this pass we are heading for?' he asked as he looked out at the rapidly rising terrain.

Albert answered as he pointed out just to the left of the front of the aircraft. 'See the big peak there in front of us with snow on it that looks like an old man's face?'

Jon looked and saw the mountain top. 'Yes, I see that and it's higher than us, so where is the pass? There's cloud cover all to the left of it.'

'Ah, well, what we do is just keep that peak passing close down our right hand side when we get there and then we know we are in the pass. Even if there is cloud we know there is plenty of height clearance so we just hold our heading and within a few minutes we'll be on the windward side and past all the danger.'

Jon didn't say anything because he was appalled by what he had just been told. These two bloody cowboys were planning to fly through a narrow mountain pass, in probably zero visibility, on the basis that they knew roughly how far away they were from a mountain several thousand feet higher than they were. He decided to put his foot down.

'Sorry guys but I've got to insist. This is crazy and far too dangerous. You need to turn around and wait for better weather or you get the pressurisation system fixed.'

'Hey, it's alright, we've done this before you know.'

'Just because you're not dead doesn't mean it's safe,' Jon was starting to get angry now and the mountains were getting ever closer. 'Bea, if they won't listen to me, maybe you can convince them. You know all about my flying experience, believe me, this is a really bad idea.'

Before Bea could reply, Bogdan spoke. 'Actually Mister Hunt, we don't have any choice. You see we don't have enough fuel to turn around and get back to the airfield.'

'What? We've only been flying just over an hour. That means we can't make Moscow either. What on earth are you two clowns doing?'

'Relax, we will be landing at a small strip to refuel once we're over the mountains and we'll also be offloading some of our stores. Then we'll be able to take on enough fuel to get to Moscow.'

'For fuck's sake, so we're low on fuel and committed to flying through a blind mountain pass with no navigation aids except seeing a mountain peak and a bloody compass?'

'It'll be fine, as we said we've done it before several times. Why don't you go back and strap in if you're so worried.' Albert was starting to sound upset at being criticised.

Jon realised he had no choice and motioned to Bea that they needed to do exactly what had the two pilots suggested. There was no option. They just had to pray that they would get through safely.

As they shut the door behind them, Bogdan turned to Albert. 'I wonder what he would have said if we told him that the radar altimeter has failed as well?'

Chapter 25

There was a knock on Captain Haywood's door and the Commodore put his head round. 'Sam, have you seen Jon Hunt this morning?'

'Sorry Sir, I was looking for him myself. He should have been back yesterday afternoon but he hasn't checked back in yet. There haven't been any messages either. Do you want me to contact the Kamov people and ask?'

'Yes, good idea and let me know what they say.'

Half an hour later, the Captain knocked on the Commodore's door and went in. 'Something's very odd Sir,' he announced.

The Commodore indicated a seat. 'What do you mean by odd?'

'Well, the Moscow Kamov people rang their counterparts in the city they had gone to visit and they say that the scheduled flight that Jon should have been on was cancelled but he and the Bukov woman checked out of their hotel and haven't been seen since.'

'Were there any other flights that day?'

'No passenger flights although there was one routine freight flight. They are trying to contact the airport now and see if they got on that.'

'What else could they have done I wonder?'

'Well Sir, there are apparently no rail links and the road has to go over the Urals. But anyway there are no cars missing. So, all I can think of is that they got on that flight. We should know fairly soon.'

'Hang on Sam, if that flight was delayed or didn't arrive, surely Moscow air traffic would know?'

'Good point Sir, I'll chase that up as well. As soon as I find out anything I'll let you know.'

When the door closed, the Commodore sat back and looked out of the window, a worried look on his face. What on earth was going on?'

Jon opened his eyes and immediately wished he hadn't. The only time he had felt pain like this was when he came to after crashing his Sea King in Beirut some years back. As his thought processes started functioning again, he tried to recall where the hell he was. Nothing, it was a complete blank. It was also very dark and very cold. Where the hell was he? He suddenly felt nauseous and rolled onto one side and was violently sick. The stomach spasms made his head hurt even worse and everything went black.

Sometime later, he came round again to the stench of vomit and if anything it was even colder. He had no idea of how much time had passed. He felt the back of his head and his hand came away sticky with what he assumed was blood. 'Jesus what the hell happened?' he muttered to himself. He realised that we was lying semi-prone, so he tried to get up. His head throbbed and the whole of his back hurt but he managed to get to his knees. Suddenly he could see a little. There was a faint light coming from something narrow off to his left. He half crawled towards it. Something sharp bit into his hand. Looking down he could just make out a jagged edge of metal in the faint light. Looking further, he realised he was seeing stars in a black sky.

Suddenly, memory returned. They had been flying and he and Bea had gone to the rear of the aircraft and strapped in. He had no recollection of anything after that. Shit, he was right. Those two cowboys flying the plane hadn't got over the mountains. They must have crashed. Shit, Bea, where was Bea?

He turned from what he realised was a gash in the fuselage and called her name. There was no response. Back on his hands and knees, he went back to where he had regained consciousness. If the aircraft had hit something, their seats must have failed and they had impacted the crates in the cabin as they were all thrown forward. She must be around here somewhere. He groped around with his hands in the blackness frantically calling out her name. His hands encountered one of the jump seats or what was left of it. He suddenly realised the smell that had been in the aircraft all along was now much stronger. His fingers encountered what felt like splintered wood and then something smooth and soft. For a moment he thought it was Bea but then he realised it was something completely different, a fur coat or something similar. Pushing it aside, he found what he had been looking for. It was a human foot. His hand travelled up the leg he realised he must have found Bea. Desperately pulling aside more of the fur, he managed to get access to her head. He quickly found that she was breathing but like him must have been knocked out cold. He also realised that his head was spinning again with all his exertions but whatever was in the crate that had broken open was amazing insulation. He gathered as much of it as he could around him and Bea and lay back for a minute to gather his thoughts and at least get warm for a minute. Ten seconds later he passed out again.

The Commodore was holding an emergency meeting in his office. All the attaché's were there as well as Mark Speddings the head of intelligence.

'Gentlemen, we have a problem,' the Commodore announced. 'Jon Hunt and his escort from the Kamov Bureau have gone missing. We know that the scheduled flight that was due to bring them back to Moscow yesterday was cancelled although no one is telling us why. We have also established that they boarded a freight flight in an Antanov 24 instead and that left mid-afternoon. It hasn't been seen or heard of since. Moscow air traffic have no flight plan for the aircraft but apparently that was not unusual. In fact, they weren't even concerned that it never turned up as its movements are quite irregular. I am even having trouble convincing anyone that there is actually a problem. However, if Jon had landed elsewhere for whatever reason, he knows that he has to ring in and tell us. Of course they may be somewhere where there are no phones but even in this backward country that's hard to believe.'

'So what do we do Sir?' Group Captain Pearson asked. 'As you know, I spoke to Moscow air traffic and as you say, they don't seem in the slightest worried. They told me that as the aircraft was known to have taken off, then if there was no sign of it in a few days, they would take appropriate measures, whatever that means. When I tried to insist that they take it more seriously they simply hung up on me.'

The Commodore looked over at Mark Speddings. 'Mark, this woman's husband is a fairly senior member of the KGB is he not?'

'Yes he is and I know what you are about to suggest. He's deputy to the department for internal security, so if anyone can light a fire under the civil authorities it will be him. I take it you want to contact him straight away.'

'Yes please, I've already cleared it with the Ambassador, so see what you can do.'

Jon came to again because he was getting uncomfortably hot. He also realised that he could now see. Daylight was filtering in through the gash in the aircraft's skin and what appeared to be snow was drifting in. He pushed away the thick layer covering him realising that it was the fur pelt of some black haired animal. Putting that to the back of his mind, he looked over the where Bea had been. She had gone.

Groaning, he staggered to his feet, suddenly realising how dreadfully thirsty he was. It was bitterly cold now he was out of the insulation of the fur pelts. He turned to see if he could grab one to keep him warm but quickly realised they were individually too small to wear. Making his way to the rear of what was left of the cabin, he looked out through the tear in the fuselage wall. All he could see was a stand of trees about ten

120

yards away and various bits of aircraft scattered around. There were foot prints leading away from the wreck in the light snow covering heading off to the left. He squeezed out of the tear and followed them. As soon as he was clear, he could see what had happened to the aircraft. The wing on his side had been sheared off. Looking back, he could see the remains of it in the trees along with a trail of damage to the trees themselves. Forward, the fuselage had split in two. The rear section was reasonably intact but the section ahead of the wings had broken off and appeared to be embedded in a small rock cliff. The whole cockpit area seemed to have been crushed.

He caught sight of movement up by the nose section. Bea was frantically dragging something.

'Hold on, Bea let me help,' he called as he hurried towards her. He soon saw what she was doing and also that it was a complete waste of time.

'Leave him Bea. He's not with us anymore.' The body she was pulling out of the remains of the cockpit was one of the two pilots although there was no way to tell which one.

He went and grabbed her putting his arms around her. The body was half out of a broken window but Jon could see the reason Bea hadn't been able to move him was that his lower body was crushed inside the wreckage. There was no sign of the other pilot but that wasn't surprising as that whole side of the aircraft was smashed flat against the rocks.

Bea turned and hugged Jon back. 'Sorry Jon, I didn't know what I was doing. She pushed him back slightly. 'Are you alright? When I woke up you were breathing, so I went to see if I could help here.'

'I'm fine, just a little concussed I think. I've got a terrible head ache. How about you?'

'Me too,' she turned her head and he could see a livid bruise all down the left hand side of her head.

'Look, we must leave the pilots for a minute. There's no way the other one could have survived and this guy is gone. Come back inside, we must take stock.'

'But what about the wreck? Surely there's a danger that it could catch fire and explode?'

Jon laughed even though it hurt. 'Bea, you've been watching too many films. If it was going to do that it would have gone up long ago. We can do a proper check when we're better organised but it's safe I'm sure. Now come on let's get out of the cold and sort ourselves out.'

Gunter Bukov was surprised to receive a call directly from the British Embassy. He was even more surprised when he the station head of MI6 came on the line and told him his wife was missing. He listened in silence as the man told him what he knew. He thanked him and promised to look into it. As soon as he had finished he started calling various people. He wasn't too worried. There were a thousand good reasons why they hadn't turned up yet. However, he wasn't going to take any chances. If there had been an accident of some sort then the longer things waited the worse things could become.

Once he had finished lighting fires under the backsides of the air traffic people, he sat back and contemplated what to do next. Yes, he was worried about Bea but he was also worried about the Americans. There had been no response to his visit to Berlin and events seemed to be speeding up. Maybe this dialogue with the British would be the opportunity he needed.

Chapter 26

'Protection, location, water, food,' Jon looked at Bea as he said it. They were back in the rear fuselage. Bea had found several bottles of water which had been a blessing for them both.

'What do you mean Jon?' Bea asked as she drank heavily from her bottle.

'I've done several survival courses and those are always the priorities. We need protection to survive as the first. There's no point at all trying to do anything else unless we can protect ourselves. Once that's done, we need to do all we can to ensure we can be found. That means anything from having signal fires ready to light, to finding things like flares or even radios we can use. After that, we need water and finally food. We can probably go several days without water and even several weeks without food.'

'God, how long do you think it will take them to find us?'

'I've no idea. The weather is pretty shitty here. I've no idea if this is typical or whether it will clear.'

'Why is it so cold? It's almost July after all,' Bea asked as she looked out at the light snow that was still falling.

'Well, we're probably up at eight to ten thousand feet here. The temperature drops about two degrees for each thousand feet. So even if it's twenty degrees down on the plains it's going to be near freezing up here and that's in daytime. At night it's going to get much colder.'

'I see what you mean about needing protection but surely we won't have to wait too long?' Bea was looking more worried by the minute and starting to shiver.

'Did they file any sort of flight plan? That might make a difference.'

'I've no idea but it was a regular weekly flight so they must be expected in Moscow.'

'Good point, so hopefully we're already missed. So let's think about protection. Frankly, this bit of fuselage seems pretty good for keeping us out of the elements. What on earth are all these pelts doing here?'

'Ah, I think I can explain that. They're Sable pelts. There is a big market for them in Russia and abroad.'

'Where did they get them from I wonder?'

'There are many hunters in the mountains and they're even starting to farm them these days. However, I think our two pilots may well have been doing some illegal smuggling. These crates are all marked with the Kamov stamp which means they should contain helicopter parts. I suspect that our planned stop before Moscow was to unload the pelts. It might also explain why they were so keen to press on.'

'Well, illegal or not they're going to help save our lives. We need to do a quick inventory but it seems there are enough for us to make a coat each and also have enough for bedding.'

Despite his enthusiasm, Bea could see Jon was still hurting. 'Before we do any of that I need to look at the back of your head. Come here and let me see.'

Jon turned his back and Bea probed his head carefully. She took out a handkerchief and damped it down with water from one of the bottles. Carefully wiping away the crusted blood she could see a lump the size of an egg with skin split over it.

'That's a nasty bump Jon and there is a small wound, we need to find a first aid kit to put a dressing on it.'

'I'm afraid if there is one anywhere it's going to be up front in the cockpit area. Can you make a dressing out of one of my shirts for the moment? Our bags seem to have survived over there.'

'I'll see what I can do.'

'Ok, then I'm going to check you out as well.'

Half an hour later, they both looked like pirates with strips of Jon's shirts turned into bandages for both of them. They had ransacked their bags and put on as many extra clothes as they could. Until they could work out a way of stitching some pelts together, they had only been able to pad out their clothing which although giving them good insulation also made them look even more ridiculous.

Suddenly, Jon felt faint and was forced to lie back to catch his breath and started shaking. Bea looked at him with concern. 'Jon, that's a nasty head wound. You've got to take it easy. Look, we've survived and we can keep warm. There's snow on the ground outside so we should be alright for water. Let's just rest up a while before we do anything else.' So saying she sat herself down next to him in a pile of the soft pelts. 'You never know they might find us soon.'

They didn't. After a few hours, Jon started to feel slightly better and the feeling of disconnection with reality was fading. Intellectually, he knew that the effects of the shock of the accident, coupled with a concussion were going to be bad but knowing it and doing something about it were two different things. Lying in the pile of pelts he felt warm and safe and the temptation to stay there and just wait was starting to become overwhelming. It was Bea who made the first move.

She levered herself up from the pile of fur. 'Come on Jon, we need to do some basic things just like you said earlier. Why don't you go and look in the cockpit area for anything we might be able to use particularly a first aid kit. I'll check through the cargo here and try and see what we've got.'

For a moment, Jon thought about arguing but he knew she was right. It was just that he was so warm where he was. He forced himself upright and staggering slightly, went outside into the daylight. It had stopped snowing and the cloud cover had broken. At least that was a good sign. The rear of the cockpit section was high up in the air and there was no way to climb in that way. His only option was to go in through one of the front windows. With only the front right hand side of the cockpit accessible, he was going to have trouble getting inside especially as the body of the pilot was still half hanging out of the broken window. His only option was to push the body back in and clamber over the corpse. The exertion was far harder than he imagined and several times he had to stop and catch his breath. When he finally managed to get in, he saw the remains of what must have been Albert the Captain in the left hand seat. It was like looking into an abattoir. Scarcely anything was recognisable as a human being. He felt his gorge rising and without anywhere to go was violently sick over the cockpit.

Suddenly frantic to get out of the place, he looked desperately around for anything of use. The radios were all smashed and anyway how would they power them? He looked behind the seats to the area where they had been standing only the day before. There was clear sky behind. Nothing there. Then he glanced down at the back of the left hand pilot's seat. A flare pistol was pushed into some form of holster. He grabbed it and pulled it out. Although of Russian manufacture, it was obvious how it worked. He opened it up and found one cartridge already loaded. Looking at the holster, he could see two more cartridges which he grabbed and stuffed into a pocket. There was nothing else of any use. With an enormous gasp of relief he half climbed, half fell, back on to the ground outside. He had to sit for several minutes to stop his vision swimming and his breath to get back to normal.

When he felt recovered enough, he made his way back to the rear of the fuselage. Bea was just clambering back over the crushed wooden crates. 'Did you find anything Jon?'

He waved the pistol. 'Just this with three cartridges but that's better than nothing. How about you?'

'There's one more crate of the pelts. The others are what they say. They're just helicopter spares. There's nothing we can use.'

'Any sign of any food or medical supplies?'

'No sorry, nothing. What do we do now Jon?' Bea was starting to look very upset and Jon went and hugged her.

'Listen Bea, we've got an excellent shelter and several bottles of water left. We can use all the wood from these crates to start a fire, so we can melt snow and there's plenty of wood outside. The pelts are more than we need to keep warm. So come on, we're not done yet, not by a long way.'

They both sat down and Jon drank some more of their diminishing water supply. Despite his brave words, he knew they were in deep trouble. Lighting a fire wasn't going to be easy and with no food and the cold temperatures they would start needing calories much sooner than he had suggested earlier. He forced himself to calm down.

'Let's see if we can get a fire started. It will help with our second priority as it will help anyone looking for us day and night and the psychological effect is always good. Look, you get some of that wood from some of the broken crates and bring it outside and I'll go and see if I can find anything for kindling.'

Two hours later, the light was starting to fade and they still had no fire. Jon had bent the metal of the split in the fuselage so they had a more useable entrance and Bea had made a good pile of broken wood. They had also shifted some of the intact crates to create a wall giving them a completely enclosed space to live in. On all the survival courses Jon had gone on they had been provided with some sort of device for at least making a spark. Neither he nor Bea smoked and so they had nothing at all to start a fire with. In desperation, Jon had gone back up to front of the wreck looking for an intact battery so maybe he could spark the terminals but there was no sign of any and he had no real idea of where to look anyway.

He came back and looked morosely at the pile of wood and smaller pile of bark he had stripped from one of the trees for kindling. 'Any ideas Bea? There's no sign of any batteries, I'm running out of ideas. Maybe we should just wrap ourselves in the pelts and sleep it out.'

Suddenly, Bea remembered something. 'I hate to suggest it Jon but I saw one of the pilots smoking before we took off. There may well be a lighter in one of their pockets.'

'Oh God. Alright just wait here.' Jon trudged along what was becoming a well-worn path to the cockpit. Because of the tilted angle of the nose he could reach into the corpse without having to climb completely in. He felt in the pockets of the trousers. With an exclamation of relief, his fingers found the small shape of a cheap plastic lighter along with what was clearly a packet of cigarettes. Praying that he wouldn't drop it, he carefully extracted the lighter from the man's trousers.

Half an hour later, there was a roaring fire on the ground in front of the entrance to their survival shelter. Both their spirits had picked up as soon as the first flames had appeared.

'Isn't it amazing how a fire can cheer you up,' Bea said as she squatted on the ground staring into the flames. 'What do we do now Jon?'

'We really ought to have someone awake all night to keep it going. It's going to be the best beacon we can have if anyone comes looking for us. How are you feeling?'

'Tired, scared and hungry but you look awful. I'm quite happy to stay awake for a while. Why don't you get some sleep. I'll wake you when I've had enough.'

Jon realised he was too exhausted to argue. The pain in his head hadn't gone away and having lost so much of his stomach's contents throughout the day he was feeling weak and dizzy. 'If you don't mind Bea, that sounds a really good idea.'

She smiled at him. 'Go on Jon, get some rest, you need it.'

He went into the fuselage and fell on to the bed they had made out of pelts. Within seconds he was asleep.

Some indeterminate time later he opened his eyes. It was dark and the fire had obviously burned down. He still felt groggy but better than before. He was about to call out to Bea when the howling started.

Chapter 27

The room in the interior ministry could have been in any government building just about anywhere in the world. A green baize covered table was surrounded by uncomfortable metal framed chairs. The walls were plain and the lighting harsh. It was also full of tobacco smoke. It seemed the message about the dangers of smoking was taking its time filtering through to Russia.

A large map was taped to an easel at the front of the room. Several lines had been drawn on it in red pen and also several large square areas had been shaded in. Suddenly, the far door opened and rotund man in a standard black Russian business suit came in flanked by two other similarly dressed men. The Commodore immediately recognised the Minister for the Interior.

The Minister sat down at the head of the table and immediately began to speak. 'Gentlemen we are here because we appear to have a missing flight with a British Naval Officer on board as well as a senior member of the Kamov Bureau, who also happens to be married to a senior member of our interior police. This is not a good situation and I want it sorted out as soon as possible. However, first I must ask what on earth was a British Military Officer doing visiting a closed Russian facility?'

There was a stunned silence around the room. The Minister was looking pointedly at Commodore Test and as no one else was speaking, he decided to reply. 'Minister I can only answer that by saying that it was your ministry that gave permission after a request by Kamov themselves. As I'm sure you know they, along with many other industrial organisations in Russia, are trying to open up new markets. It's all part of your policy of Glasnost I understand.'

The Commodore knew he was being provocative with his last remark. The Minister was well known as an old school communist but if the man was so ignorant of his own ministry's workings it wasn't his fault. It also looked like a standard politicians trick to deflect the blame and he definitely wasn't having that either.

One of the Minister's aids leant close and whispered something. The man seemed to deflate slightly. 'Yes, of course, please accept my apologies Commodore. It must have slipped my mind. I'm a busy man these days as you can imagine.' The sharp look in the Minister's eyes belied his apologetic words. Commodore Test inclined his head in wry acknowledgement.

Group Captain Pearson leaned close to the Commodore and muttered quietly, 'seems their ministry is as bad at internal communications as ours.'

'Very well, will the military please update the meeting on what has been going on,' the Minister said looking at the man sitting next to the large map.

The ruddy faced Air Force Colonel stood and went to the front of the room. 'Gentlemen, we have confirmation that the AN 24 took off at fourteen thirty two days ago. It was outside civilian radar coverage after half an hour. The last radio call was normal. There were no distress calls made after that. We have checked the local air defence radar system for the same time. The flight was noted by the operator but not tracked as it was an internal flight. So if it did crash, we cannot say when the radar lost contact. On that basis, we have two possible routes that it would have taken. They're shown on this map and follow the designated airways across the mountains. We have had search aircraft looking along these corridors. From the last radio call, we can estimate where the aircraft would have been and then search from that datum. To date, nothing has been found. I have to stress that the terrain we are searching over is heavily forested and it is quite possible for an aircraft to crash and be virtually impossible to see from the air. There are very few people living there, and so the chances of anyone witnessing a crash are minimal.'

Group Captain Pearson nudged the Commodore. 'May I ask a question?' he asked quietly.

'Go ahead Dick, that's why I brought you along.'

He put up his hand. 'Colonel, I am Group Captain Pearson, Air Attaché at the British Embassy. Can I ask a couple of questions please?'

'Of course Group Captain, go ahead.'

'Firstly, you keep talking about the aircraft crashing but isn't there anywhere it could have landed? There must be airfields around. Maybe it just had radio failure.'

'Good point and it's one we considered, especially when we first started looking. However, there are only five airfields the aircraft could have got to and they are all to the west of the mountains. We have spoken to them all. There has been no sign of it and no radio contact. Once clear of the mountains, there are many places it could have successfully force landed but we have good satellite coverage and there is no sign anywhere. Also, if it had managed to clear the mountains, the

Moscow air defence radars would have seen it which they didn't. You had another question?'

'Yes, do we know what height it was flying at? I only ask because I note that the airways you mention have different base levels and of course there is always the possibility that it was flying low level.'

'I'm afraid we don't know. When they last checked in on the radio they said they were passing three thousand metres. We have to assume they were climbing to normal cruising altitude of about nine thousand metres. So, all the information we have, suggests that at some point before crossing the mountains something happened to the aircraft. Now, before anyone asks, we intend to keep looking for several more days yet but we have to be realistic. It is quite possible that we will not find anything. At least not until a human being stumbles across a wreck and that could take years. It has happened before. I'm not saying we should give up hope merely that we must be realistic. This is a vast area to search and the trees can swallow aircraft whole.'

Silence greeted the Colonel's final remark. The Minister levered himself to his feet. 'Gentlemen, thank you all for attending, I'm sure that along with me you are grateful for the Air Force's continuing efforts. We will keep everyone informed if and when we find something.' Turning, he left the room with his two aides.

A muttering of conversation broke out as the other attendees also stood. The Commodore was turning towards the door when a man blocked his way. He looked gaunt and tired. He was also very tall and towered over the Commodore who had a pretty good idea who he was.

'Commodore, I am Gunter Bukov. I am the husband of the lady your Commander was travelling with.'

The Commodore put out his hand and had it half crushed by the giant. 'I guessed who you might be Mr Bukov. May I offer you our sympathies.'

'Of course but there is hope and I really believe they will be found. But Commodore although this is a bad time, I would like to speak to you on a different matter. I'm sure you know what my job is. It would normally be impossible for us to meet openly so I am taking this opportunity. Could you relay a message to your intelligence people for me? Could you please tell them I need to act under code word 'Triptych Blue'. They will understand. Now I must go and thank you for your time.' He left, leaving the Commodore wondering what on earth had just happened.

'Wasn't that the woman's husband?' Group Captain Pearson asked as he came up. 'What did he want?'

'Do you know Dick, I have absolutely no idea.'

'Alright everyone, settle down,' Jock Spalding, head of the Soviet section of MI6 in London called to his people. 'Are we all here?' he asked as he looked around the room and then answered his own question as he saw that they all were. 'Ok now, we've had an urgent communication from the Embassy in Moscow. It seems there may have been an aircraft accident and one of our military attachés has gone missing but that's not the issue at hand. Our man was travelling with the wife a senior KGB operative by the name of Gunter Bukov. I'm sure that some of you in the room will know exactly who he is. For those of you who don't, he is the deputy head of their department for internal dissent. His wife is working for a helicopter company and was taking our man to visit some facility or other. However, that's incidental. Bukov approached the Defence Attaché at a meeting to talk about the crash and made a rather odd remark.' He looked down at a piece of paper he was holding. 'I'll read it out verbatim. He said and I quote, 'I need to act under code word Triptych Blue'. We've dug around everywhere and there is no record of that code word in any reference material we can find. He seems to be sending us a message but we haven't a clue what it is. Does anyone here know what it means?'

Rupert Thomas felt like someone had thrown a bucket of cold water over his head when he heard the words Triptych Blue. He knew exactly what they meant but he also knew that there was no way they could apply to what was going on in Russia now.

Chapter 28

He had never heard a sound like it but it awoke a primeval fear in Jon that had him leaping for the entrance without conscious thought. Bea was just getting to her feet as he joined her.

'What the hell is that Bea?' he gasped as he tried to regain his breath.

'I'm not sure Jon but it sounds like wolves.'

'What? Jesus, you still have wolves around here?'

'This isn't tame Western Europe Jon. We need to get the fire going hard again. I'm sorry I must have dozed off.'

Jon looked at the fire. A few embers were still red. He grabbed some of the stacked wood and started breaking it into small pieces. Bea pushed him out of the way. 'I'll do that Jon. See if you can find something we can use as a weapon.'

The howling was getting closer. The hairs on the back of his neck were standing up. He hated to leave Bea outside but he also understood she was right. They didn't have much time. He desperately searched for the flare gun but in the darkness he couldn't find it. The only other thing he could think of was to rip one of the long slats off the side of one of the remaining intact crates. It was about six feet long. With a strength, amplified by the fear caused by the almost continual howling now coming from outside, he wrenched the wooden plank free. He ran back outside just in time to see several pairs of eyes glowing in the weak light of the fire which Bea was desperately blowing into.

Without any other idea, Jon took a step forward and started shouting. At the same time, he started to swing the plank from side to side. There were three wolves he could see now. They took a pace backwards but lowered the snouts and started snarling at him. The one in the middle was the biggest. It was a shaggy grey and looked just like Jon imagined a wolf would look like except it was twice the size and twice as terrifying. Behind him, he heard a crackling sound and the light improved. Bea must have got some wood to catch. The wolves took another pace backwards but then stood their ground. With no other thought, he took another pace forward, continuing to swing the plank and shout. It was a mistake.

With no notice at all, the middle animal simply leapt at Jon while making a blood curdling half snarl half howl. Its mouth was wide open and Jon could see the savage rows of blackened teeth quite clearly. His first thought was to turn tail and run but immediately realised that would mean almost certain death for both of them. He had two choices. He could swing the plank at the animal and hope to clout in on the head but it looked far too big for that to be effective. He did the only thing he could think of and dropped to one knee, planting one end of the plank into the ground. As the wolf landed, the end of the plank hit it in the neck and the wood promptly snapped in half. Several hundred pounds of howling animal landed on top of Jon smashing him to the ground. The wolf's face slammed into Jon's and stinking saliva sprayed everywhere. For a second he expected to die. The animal was thrashing about and then suddenly it was silent. He pushed it clear with his feet. He was covered in blood but it wasn't his.

Before he could react any further, Bea ran past him with a burning piece of wood, brandishing it wildly at the surviving two animals who suddenly turned tail and ran off into the night. Jon looked at the one that had attacked him. Embedded deep in the wolf's throat was the broken piece of plank. When it shattered, the animal's momentum must have carried it straight on to the jagged wood. Shaking with reaction, he realised just how lucky he had been.

Bea walked backwards to him still waving the burning branch. 'Come on Jon, let's get the fire really going, they won't come near that.'

Fifteen minutes later, the fire was a roaring inferno and Jon was still shaking with reaction. The wolves were nowhere near but they could still hear them.

'Oh Jesus, they must be up at the cockpit. Can't we stop them?' he said as he realised just what the pack of animals were feeding on.

'How Jon? There's nothing we can do. I'm sorry I should have thought of this. We should have buried them when we had the chance.'

'Don't be silly Bea, we had other things to do and anyway who would have thought this might happen.'

They spent the rest of the night by the fire. The wolves didn't bother them anymore and when daylight came they had gone. Still shaking with fatigue and reaction, Jon walked up to the cockpit area. There was absolutely no sign of the bodies not even any bones. He felt a curious sense of relief. Walking back to their camp, he contemplated the shaggy grey corpse. Grabbing one hind leg, he pulled it off to one side, marvelling at just how heavy it was and also how incredibly lucky he had been.

Bea appeared out of the fuselage as he dumped it clear. 'We'll need to bury it or take it far away Jon. We don't want them coming back.'

'Actually Bea, I have a far better idea. He wanted to eat me, so I think it only fair that we return the complement.'

'What? Eat a wolf? You are joking aren't you?'

'I can't see any other form of protein around here can you? Look Bea, this is survival. Did you know that Amundsen ate half his Huskies when they were making for the South Pole? A husky and a wolf are cousins. Bea, let's be realistic, we're going to have to manage on the basis that it may take some time for anyone to find us. We're going to have to rely on anything we can find and that bloody great lump of meat just might make all the difference.'

'Why don't we rest for a few days, get our strength back and then try to walk out?'

'Absolutely not, the first rule of survival is to stay put. They will be looking for an aircraft crash and if we move away they'll never find us. On top of that, there are wolves out there and God knows what else. How would we cope with them? We have no weapons. No, for the foreseeable future we stay here.'

'Alright but I'm completely spent and you still look awful. We both need some sleep before we tackle that monster.'

Jon suddenly realised how exhausted he felt and he had managed several hours sleep before the wolf attack. Bea would be in even worse shape. 'No Bea, you go and get some rest. I'm going to see if I can find anything sharp to cut up the wolf and also I've got an idea of how we can cook it.' He could see she was about to argue. 'No, I insist. I'll be fine go and get some sleep.'

Several hours later Bea reappeared looking slightly better. There was no sign of Jon but over the fire was a large conical container held up with a series of what looked like metal poles. She suddenly recognised one of the aircraft's propeller cowls. In the improvised cook pot, she could see water, presumably from melted snow.

'Jon, where are you?' she called.

A voice answered from somewhere up front. 'Over here Bea, under the port wing.'

She made her way forward and round the other side of the fuselage where the port wing was still attached. Jon was underneath it covered in blood.

'Oh my God, are you all right?' she asked.

Jon heard her tone of voice and managed a weak laugh. 'You try skinning a wolf with a bit of aluminium, without getting covered in blood. Here, you can take this. We can have a nice wolfy stew with it.' He held out an unrecognisable haunch of meat.

Later that morning, they had filled up all their plastic bottles with water from melted snow and then put the haunch of meat in to simmer. The smell was driving Jon wild with hunger. He had lost all the contents of his stomach the day before. It may have been a haunch of stringy wild animal but he didn't care. Finally, unable to wait any longer he pulled it out and they set to with their fingers. It wasn't properly cooked, it was tough and stringy but it tasted marvellous. With some degree of hunger sated, he started to feel slightly more human and to think to the future.

'We've had almost permanent cloud cover all the time that we've been here Bea. That's not good for anyone looking for us but we must plan on making sure they can see us when the cloud breaks. Later on we'll gather lots of firewood but also lots of those pine branches with leaves on. If we hear an aircraft during the day we can throw them on the fire and make smoke. It's the best way of being seen. We need that flare pistol to hand as well. I couldn't find the bloody thing last night when I needed it so we'll hang it up by the entrance.'

'And as I said earlier Jon, we need to hang something else up, either that or bury it.'

'What?'

'That wolf carcass. Because it will attract more predators if we leave it on the ground.'

'You mean like more wolves?'

'That or bears.'

'Oh Jesus, there are bears here as well?'

'Sorry Jon, this area is vast and unpopulated. There might even be tigers but they are very rare.'

'You know, when I did my aircrew and Arctic survival training it was all about evading humans or surviving long enough to be rescued. No one ever mentioned bloody tigers, bears or wolves. Ok, I'll get another piece of aircraft skin and you can help me cut off the rest of the meat then we'll have to find something to dig a hole with.'

It took most of the rest of the day to finish the butchering and then dig a hole deep enough. By the time they had finished, they were both exhausted but there was enough meat stored inside the aircraft to keep them going for some time.

Jon was starting to feel literally dizzy with fatigue and Bea insisted that it was his turn to get some sleep. He didn't argue.

Chapter 29

Rupert Thomas knocked on the door of his head of section.

'Come in,' a voice called.

'Sorry to bother you Jock but I need to tell you what Triptych Blue means because we might have a really serious problem on our hands.'

'How come you didn't own up at the meeting just now Rupert?'

'Sorry Jock but I think you will want to hear about this in private.'

'Go on, grab a seat and tell me what it's all about then.'

'It's a long story and could possibly get some people into trouble, including me but if it's been invoked that's not important. We'll have to act.'

His boss frowned. 'Spill it Rupert.'

'This goes back to the seventies when I joined the department. I think I'm the only current member of the Soviet section who was also there in those times which explains why no one else knows. I had just joined MI6 and was a junior desk officer but we were all indoctrinated. You see, this was never official. You might even call it a conspiracy although for all the right reasons.'

'Now you're really starting to get me worried, go on.'

'You have to understand the paranoia about the Soviets going all the way back to the fifties. Their leadership was even worse than ours. Old men who had mostly fought in a terrible war, faced with a technologically and financially superior potential foe. Not only that but their ideology was completely at odds with ours. However, below that level of leadership there were plenty of sensible human beings who really didn't want a confrontation and some of them worked for the KGB. There was a surprising amount of dialogue between them, ourselves and the Americans in those days. More so than now in fact. I don't actually know how it all started. It was before my time but there was an agreed system for the three intelligence agencies to let their counterparts know if things were going seriously wrong at senior levels. Not just the Russians but ours and the American governments.'

'What, you're saying that one of our people would warn the Soviets about our government's intentions? That's treason Rupert.'

'Put like that yes, it would have been but many people thought that would be better than nuclear annihilation.'

'So what does it mean?'

'There were three code words, one for each country. The Soviets were Triptych, we were Trinity and the Americans were Tribune. Along with the code words you probably won't be surprised to know that there were three levels of alert; yellow, blue and red. Yellow meant that something had happened that meant that contingency plans were being readied. Blue meant that there was a serious risk that the relevant government was considering action within three months and Red meant there was a real risk of confrontation within seven days. The whole point was that this wasn't anything to do with the military or their alert levels. It was all based on what the individual government was thinking. As I said, it was unofficial so there will be no record.'

'So why didn't we get an alert in nineteen eighty three when the Soviets thought we were about to attack them?'

'Now, that's a good question. Oh hang on. I think I can answer that. Andropov had just taken over as General Secretary and prior to that he was head of the KGB and he'd been leading the investigations into American belligerence. It's not likely he would alert us over his own preparations. And of course he got no word from us, so maybe that helped stay his hand. Look Jock, the real question is why the hell invoke a blue alert now?'

'Do you think Gorbachev is about to do a Galtieri on the West to take the pressure off his home politics?'

'I wouldn't have thought so. The man's in trouble but it's of his own making. Threatening the West would hardly help although he may try something in one of the republics but then why warn us?'

Jock sat back deep in thought. 'It could also mean something else. We all know how factionalised their government is becoming. Could this be one of those factions warning us of some form of internal ruckus about to take place? You say the blue alert means something happening within three months?'

'That was the original meaning yes.'

'Well Rupert, it sounds to me as though we should keep this in house for the moment until we know what's really going on. Someone is going to have to go and talk to this man and as its only you and me in the know, guess who that's going to be?'

Twenty four hours later Rupert was ensconced with the intelligence staff in the Moscow Embassy. He had been appalled to discover that it was his friend Jon who was the subject of the searches going on in the Urals. Not only that but he had been travelling with the wife of the KGB operative who had passed on the emergency code word. He forced himself to concentrate. There was nothing he could do about it. The matter in hand was just far too important. It had been agreed that the senior Embassy staff could be brought in on the affair but as Rupert was a new and unknown face he would do the necessary field work.

Despite long discussions about what the message really meant no one could really give a definitive answer. There was only one way to take it forward and Rupert had the job.

Later that evening, he was strolling along a cracked pavement outside a large block of flats. He spotted the car and adjusted his pace accordingly, so that when the man got out of the back seat, he was walking past. There was no doubt that he had the right man, he was head and shoulders taller than anyone else around. As the car drew away Rupert stumbled into him.

'Triptych Blue,' he said. To anyone looking it would appear that he was apologising for his stumble.

The man hesitated and then turned to Rupert. He had clearly caught on quickly and answered as though he was replying to the apology, except what he actually said was an address and a time. Rupert nodded and went on his way.

Back at the Embassy, the senior intelligence staff studied the information that the address had given them.

Rupert had put a map up on an easel. 'This is the Dacha of a Mister Vladmir Vorodov,' He said pointing to a spot well clear of the city. It's a popular area for the rich to have their country houses with several prominent politicians and businessmen in the area. He's been on our radar a little because he is a very successful businessman. One of the many that hide behind the curtain of socialism but behave very much like capitalists. However, there is no record of him being linked directly to any governmental group. Up until now he seems to have been content to stay in the background. The fact that he has made contact through a senior member of the KGB is extremely interesting. Of course Gunter Bukov isn't your normal mainstream KGB man. Until recently he was working in East Berlin and a member of the Stasi. Maybe he has a different outlook to his Russian counterparts. Anyway, going back to Vorodov, we know a little about his past. He was a tank commander in the war and took part in the liberation of Berlin. He acquired money from somewhere and has invested heavily over the years. If you ask me, any move of Russia towards a less socialist government would be a good thing for him. However, as a decorated Hero of the Soviet Union, we can't rule out that he is actually a hardliner and desperate to maintain the status quo. And then there's the other question. What is our policy here and how far can I go if I go to this rendezvous?'

Mark Speddings answered. 'As of today, Her Majesty's Government's position is that we do not interfere with the legal government of another country and that includes the Soviet Union or Russia.'

There was a ripple of amusement from those in the room.

'Fair enough,' Mark acknowledged. 'The get out of jail free card for this is that we are also charged with maintaining the security of our own country. So, if we see an opportunity to weaken the Soviet Union which for years has offered a direct threat to the security of our country then of course we can act. So in principle, if our man Vorodov is asking for our help and it is in our interests to give it then there is no question. Rupert, go to the meeting, keep your cards close to your chest. If it's clear that this is something to do with an internal threat to the stability of the Soviet Union that could jeopardize our security then I am authorising you to make a preliminary agreement. However, if it is anything to do with propping up the old guard, make whatever noises you think necessary and get the hell out.'

Rupert nodded.

That evening his unprepossessing and tattered old Lada drew up in front of the imposing house set back in the pine forests north of Moscow. As he got out, a bald headed man with a rather imposing moustache appeared.

'Triptych Blue?' the man queried. Rupert noted the bulge under the left arm of his suit and nodded. 'My name is Smith, from the Embassy.'

'Of course it is Mister Smith, please come with me.'

They entered a large wood panelled hall and then through a set of doors into a grand room with antlers on the wall. There was a large table and several men standing next to an unlit open fire. One of the men stepped forward. The man with the moustache announced. 'Mister Smith from the Embassy, Vladmir. He has the code.'

Rupert looked at the assembled men. Three he didn't recognise but Gunter Bukov was there and the man who greeted him was clearly Vorodov. He recognised the tall thin faced man with the iron grey hair straight away.

The thin man put out his hand to be shaken. He had a surprisingly strong grip for such a frail looking man. 'Mister Smith, as I expect you already know, I am Vladmir Vorodov. Let me introduce my comrades.'

Rupert shook all their hands managing to keep the surprise out of his expression when he realised just who they were. He was then invited to sit and offered a small glass of vodka. Once they had all had a drink, they got down to business.

Chapter 30

The weather had turned warmer and all the snow had gone. It was proving to be even worse than the cold dry snowy weather. The crash site was now almost permanently shrouded in fog and rain as the wind blew from the west forcing moist air up over the mountains and turning it to cloud. The ground was turning to mud and Jon was slowly sinking into despair. The chances of being found in this weather were almost zero. There was no way an air search could find them in these conditions. It was now the fifth day since the crash and nearly all of his optimism had evaporated. Despite his earlier certainty, he was starting to consider that the only way they could survive was to try and walk out. They were almost out of food. The wolves hadn't been back but nor had any other living thing and even if it had they had no way of killing it. He had tried some rudimentary traps with absolutely no result. If you didn't know what you were trying to trap it was always going to be hard to make something that would actually work. On top of that, the wound on the back of his head wasn't healing and Bea was starting to get worried about it. Despite knowing what was happening to him, he was slowly lapsing into a sort of somnolent despair.

They had carefully searched around the local area. It was a long valley with peaks on either side. Only a few hundred feet above them they could see the end of the tree line. Two days previously, they had struggled up there to see if they could get a better idea of the topography. Unfortunately, the visibility was so poor that they could make out very little apart from rocks. Jon wasn't even sure of their altitude. The tree line on mountains could vary from as little as five to over twelve thousand feet depending on local conditions.

Now that the snow had melted they were even having trouble getting enough water. Bea had found a small trickle out of the rocks some distance away but they both had to go and fill up their bottles. With the ever present risk of wolves or worse, they had decided it wasn't safe to go alone and they took the flare gun as their primary and only defence. Jon had kept on meaning to rig up some form of rain collector but never seemed to find the time.

Keeping the fire going was also proving more and more difficult as they had used up nearly all of the wood from the crates in the aircraft and everything they could gather was now soaking wet. They had dragged as much as they could inside the fuselage to keep it dry after leaving it close to the fire to at least get the worst of the moisture off.

However, the almost ceaseless toil, just to stay warm and get water, was inexorably sapping their strength. The only saving grace was the 'nest' they had made inside the fuselage out of the Sable pelts. They had set it up as close to the entrance as they could, so that the heat of the fire reflected in. However, even that was now turning damp.

Jon was slowly realising that it was now Bea who was in charge. Her survival instinct seemed much stronger than his despite all the training he had undergone. It was one thing to study survival in a classroom and then try it out in the field but when you knew it was an exercise it was totally different to the real thing.

He was lying down on the pelts and starting to shiver when Bea came in with an armful of wood. She took one look at him and dropped the load.

She put her hand on his forehead. 'You're starting a temperature Jon. How do you feel?'

'Hot one minute, cold the next. Sorry Bea.'

'Don't be silly Jon. It's not your fault. Let me get you some water. Then I'm going to wrap you up and keep you warm.'

It was starting to get dark, so Bea stoked up the fire as much as she could and then sat with Jon. They still had some meat left and their makeshift cauldron was full of a sort of broth but Jon wouldn't eat. One minute his teeth were chattering with cold, the next he was sweating. She just prayed that the wound on his head wasn't the cause because the nearest anti-biotic was probably thousands of miles away.

Despite Jon's fever, he couldn't sleep and Bea knew she had to stay awake as well. So they talked. She told him about her childhood, about growing up in a closed society that was nevertheless happy and fun. There were always helicopters flying over their house and so how she wanted the impossible, to learn how to fly, which wasn't allowed in her Germany under the communists. The closest she had managed was when she was called up for national service and got the flight engineers job in the Air Force.

Jon asked her how she had met Gunter.

'We knew each other from our teenage days. We grew up in adjacent flats but first met at school. We were both so much taller than our friends, so I suppose we were always going to be attracted to each other. Then I went off to national service and managed to get the job I really wanted with the Air Force. We sort of grew apart because of that. Then something strange happened. We were tasked to fly some police out to a small village. I never got to find out why. One of them was Gunter but we didn't really have the chance to talk.' She laughed at the recollection. 'A couple of days later some flowers arrived. We've been together ever since. You probably have a very stilted view of what life was like in East Germany then. Believe it or not, we still knew how to have fun and Gunter was very good at it. Of course being with the Stasi, he had access to more things than much of the population but who was I to argue. He then pulled some strings and got me a job in his organisation once my national service was over. But we've always been happy. I couldn't imagine life without him.'

She saw a wave of pain go across Jon's face and realised it wasn't from his illness. She decided to distract him. 'So Jon, tell me about your life. Did you always want to fly, like me?'

'You may find this a little odd but no, it wasn't a dream of mine. My parents had sent me away to private school and when my father suggested I go for an interview for the navy, I took it, as it got me away from the school for three days.'

'You didn't like your school then?'

'I hated it, believe me if I ever have children I'll never inflict that on them.'

'So why did your parents do it to you if you hated it so much?'

'Well, my father was in the oil industry and always moving about. Mother followed him, so by sending me to a boarding school I got continuity and anyway it was the done thing in those days.'

Bea grimaced. 'And to think of all the criticism my system has had over the years. So you joined the navy?'

'Yes, straight out of school. Moving from one institution to another.' he chuckled. 'At the college, they had a small squadron of Chipmunk aircraft based near Plymouth. We were able to fly them at weekends. They were lovely little machines and I found out I was quite good at flying them. So when we had to decide on which career specialism to choose, I volunteered for the Fleet Air Arm. During training, we had spent a little time in a submarine and it scared the hell out of me. I guess I'm a little claustrophobic. The surface fleet seemed all work and no play. So flying was the obvious thing.'

'And you never looked back after that?'

'I suppose so. The training programme was pretty hard and coming straight after general training it seemed to take forever. I'm on a career commission, so I had to do all that seamanship stuff first. But you're right. I've loved every minute since.'

Bea could see he was about to go on but had stopped himself.

'You were going to say something else Jon?'

'No, it doesn't matter.'

She decided to take the bull by the horns. 'You lost your wife last year didn't you? Please, would you tell me about her? She must have been a fantastic girl, to keep up with you.'

'Put up with me more like,' Jon responded almost automatically. Suddenly he found himself telling Bea all about Helen. How they had first met and he had made an ass of himself and then how he tried to suppress his feelings when she had come to work for him as the Staff Officer on his squadron. The fantastic wedding they had enjoyed and then the enormous pride he had felt for her when she did so well in training having joined the navy properly. The separations and joys of getting together again while she learned to fly and he was given his first sea command. How she went on to become the navy's first qualified female helicopter pilot.

'The last time I spoke to her was over the radio from the bridge of my ship. She had just pulled off a remarkable rescue and was finally heading home to safety. And then some drunken fucking farmer decided to kill her and the child she was carrying.'

He suddenly stopped talking and Bea could see all the pain and rage was still there, bottled up inside him. He was also starting to shake. She pulled him closer and put her arms around him. He was hot but she realised the shaking wasn't because of his fever.

'Cry for her Jon. You've never really done that have you?'

He didn't answer but she pulled her head back and could see the tears streaming down his face. For long minutes they just lay there while Jon let it all out.

Finally, he calmed down. In a subdued voice, he spoke to her. 'Thank you Bea. I don't know whether we are going to get out of this but thank you. Why is it I can talk to you?'

'Because we're friends Jon, that's all.'

He didn't answer. She realised he had finally fallen asleep.

Hours later, Jon woke up. It was just starting to get light and Bea was snoring loudly. The fire had burned down very low and needed banking up. His head was throbbing horribly and he felt light headed and woozy. His mouth was dry and he desperately needed a pee. Gently disentangling himself from Bea and the soggy mass of pelts, he managed to get to his feet. He felt so dizzy that he had to grab onto the side of the aircraft for support until his head cleared enough that he felt capable of walking. Stumbling outside, the cold damp air caught in his throat and he doubled over coughing. As his head came up, all thoughts of water or stoking the fire fled. He looked in fear at the edge of the trees fifty yards away. Bea had warned him about the danger of bears but had always intimated that they were solitary. He could see four of them advancing menacingly towards their refuge.

Looking at the fire, he realised that there was nothing he could grab and brandish at the approaching creatures. His eye was caught by the sight of the flare gun hanging by the entrance. With shaking fingers, he grabbed it and tried to wrestle it out of its holster. He also started to shout for Bea but his parched throat only allowed him to croak.

Finally wrenching the flare gun free, he cocked the hammer back and turned towards the approaching bears. He was amazed to see how close they had managed to get in such a short time. The flare gun felt like lead in his hands and he was having trouble focusing and pointing it. Bea was suddenly at his side and saying something to him but he couldn't make out any words. The damned bears were roaring now just as his knees gave way and he collapsed. Everything went black.

Chapter 31

Rupert put the secure telephone back in its cradle and looked over at Mark Speddings. 'London says they are up for it and want the list of names.'

'I'll get them sent over in the diplomatic bag today, Rupert,' Mark answered.

'Why can't we just fax them or even pass them over the phone Mark? It's not a long list.'

'If we were short of time I would agree but the bag is by far the most secure system and I really don't want to take any risks with this. GCHQ will have the details within twenty four hours.'

'Fair enough I suppose. However, we also need to establish a secure communications link to Vorodov as well. Can we use a land line to his Dacha?' Rupert looked thoughtful.

'This is Russia Rupert, there's no such thing as a totally secure land line. That's why all our links are by narrow beam satellite radio these days. You used something similar during the Falklands I believe?'

'Not me but we gave one to our French engineer. It seemcd to work pretty well.'

'Things have moved on a great deal these days. The kit is a great deal simpler and easy to use. We have several of the new units in store. I'll get one of our chaps to update you and then you can deliver one to our new best friends.'

Later that day, Rupert drove his tattered old car back to the Dacha. Sergei was waiting for him and helped him unload the suitcase from the boot of the car.

Once inside, Sergei turned to Rupert. 'It's good to see you again Mister Smith. Only Vladmir and I are here today. I hope that's not a problem?'

'Actually, that's fine Sergei. We should keep the number of people who know how to use this equipment to a minimum.'

Just then Vladmir walked in and after saying hello, Rupert opened the case to show them the radio system. 'We used to have a great big antenna for these things but now we can do the same with this smaller aerial.' He showed them the little black device, shaped like a saucer. 'We want it to be directional towards the satellite. That way it's almost impossible for someone to intercept it. That means you need to know how to line it up. The best place would high up and looking out of a south facing window.'

'We have several on the top floor that face south,' Sergei replied. 'That would also keep everything out of sight. They're the old servant's quarters up there and they don't get used these days.'

'Excellent, can we go and see?' Rupert asked.

Vladmir broke in. 'If you're going up there then count me out. My old bones don't like all those narrow stairs and Sergei is more than capable of operating a radio without my help.'

Four storeys up, they found an attic room with a good view in the right direction.

'This looks excellent,' Rupert commented peering through a grimy window and lining up a small compass. 'The only problem seems to be a lack of electricity. Can you run a wire up here? The radio works on batteries or the mains but a continued supply would be best.'

Sergei nodded. 'No problem, I can get an extension wire later on.'

Half an hour later, Rupert was happy that Sergei knew how to operate the set and they had made a test transmission to confirm that all was well. Suddenly, there was a creak of floorboards behind them and Rupert was surprised to see Vladmir in the doorway.

'I know I said I wouldn't come up but I've just had the most surprising telephone call.' Vladmir announced with an odd expression on his face. 'Mister Smith, I'm sure you know that one of our team member's wife has been missing for some time along with one of your Embassy staff. Something very surprising has happened. You may not know it but I operate several mines in the area of the Urals. This morning, a small team of miners who were out on a hunting expedition, found the remains of an aircraft and two survivors. It seems the survivors are the two people everyone has been searching for.'

Jon slowly came to and for an unknowable time lay back trying to remember what had happened. His head still hurt but nothing like as much as it had. His feverish shivers seem to have gone as well, although he still felt weak. Even the bed of sable pelts felt different. Suddenly, with a start, he remembered the attack by the bears and tried to sit up. Something constrained him. He opened his eyes and was immediately confused. He was in a white room and in a normal bed. He realised it was the sheets that were holding him down.

Suddenly Bea's face swam into view. 'Hello Jon, you're back with us at last.' Her cheerful voice flooded him with relief. Whatever was going on it must be alright if she was there. He tried to speak but it only came out as a croak.

'Hold on, I'll get you some water.' She quickly came back with a glass which she helped him sip carefully. He wanted to gulp it all down but she held it back. 'Slowly Jon, we don't want you to choke. How do you feel now?'

He lay back on the pillow and thought about the answer. 'Better than yesterday,' he managed to croak.

Bea laughed. 'I think you mean two days ago Jon. You've been out of it for quite a while.'

'But what about the bears? And where the hell are we?' His voice sounded stronger the more he used it.

'Bears? What on earth are you talking about?' Then she laughed. 'Jon those weren't bears they were a hunting party taking time out from a mine about twenty miles away. They smelled our smoke and came to investigate. That's where we are now. They have a small infirmary with a resident doctor and luckily a good supply of antibiotics.'

'Oh God, I was trying to shoot them with the flare gun. I didn't, did I?'

'Jon, you couldn't have hit a barn door with a shotgun the way you were. Now, I'll go and get the doctor. Oh and they're sending a helicopter today to take us out as long as the doctor says you're fit enough to travel.'

As Bea left, Jon lay back and wondered at their good fortune. His memory of their last few days was pretty hazy but he realised just how close they had come to not making it. He also realised the debt of gratitude he owed Bea. It was her spirit that had kept them going. He also remembered their conversations of that last night. Suddenly, he felt as if a large weight had been lifted from his soul.

A small grey haired man came in with Bea. He prodded Jon, took his pulse and examined the back of his head.

'I don't see any reason why you shouldn't leave us today.' He announced. 'You realise just how lucky you were of course? That head wound was a bad one. Luckily it seems you have a pretty thick skull because there is no sign of a fracture but it will take some time to heal. When you get back to Moscow you will need several weeks to fully recuperate. I'll get some food sent in and we expect the helicopter this afternoon.' Without waiting for an answer he bustled out.

Jon took Bea's hand. 'Bea I can't thank you enough. I don't think I would have made it without you.'

She looked startled for a second. 'No Jon, I would say the opposite. It was your knowledge and skill that made the difference. That and your unique method of killing wolves.'

'Christ but we were lucky weren't we?' He looked at her seeing the lines of strain and fatigue still on her face. 'I want to thank you for something else.'

'Oh, what could that be?'

'Ever since Helen died, I've felt like I was living in a bad dream. Every day has merely been something to endure. You've made me realise that life can go on and I don't have to spend every moment in mourning. I'm sorry if that sounds a bit of a cliché but I really mean it. I can remember every word we spoke that last night and also the sense of relief that I was able to fully confide in someone at last. So thank you for saving my life in more ways than one.'

Bea was completely at a loss. She squeezed his hand and realised that tears were forming in her eyes just as they were in Jon's.

Suddenly the door opened and a man in an apron came in with a tray of food. Bea helped Jon sit up before getting the man to put it down in front of him.

'Bloody hell, Bea we almost made fools of ourselves in front of the natives.' Jon remarked looking at the man's retreating back.

She leant over and kissed him on the forehead. 'No we didn't Jon but we will stay friends forever.'

Chapter 32

Jon lay in another bed, this time in the Embassy infirmary. The doctor had just left but given him the welcome news that he would be discharged the next day. He was restricted to light duties only but it would be a welcome return to normal life nonetheless. The tedium of the infirmary was slowly driving him mad. He was just reaching for his paperback on the bedside table when the door opened again and he was surprised to see the smiling face of his old friend and colleague, Rupert Thomas.

'Bloody hell Rupert, what on earth are you doing here?'

'And hello to you Jon and nice to see you too.' Rupert's grin belied his slightly sarcastic words.

'Well I would get up and give you a bloody great hug but the doctor says I have to stay here for another day.'

'Safest place for you frankly, because as we both well know, wherever you go there's bound to be some bloody great furore and I was right. I just had to come over and see what the hell you've been up to now.'

'Oh yes, why don't I believe that? I've seen that look on your face before.' Jon propped himself up against his pillows. 'So come on what's up?'

Rupert pulled up a bedside chair. 'I'll give you the full picture in a minute but first I want to go over your antics of the last few weeks. I know you gave a pretty full debrief when you got back here but I was away on a little task.' Rupert saw the question forming on Jon's face. 'And before you ask, I'll tell you everything, just be patient.'

Jon repeated his story to Rupert. The only thing he left out was the last night with Bea. That was personal and he had no intention of telling anyone about it.

Rupert listened in silence until Jon finished. 'Bloody hell Jon, you killed a real wolf with a plank of wood? That must have been terrifying.'

'Tell me about it but frankly I had no choice and there was one good thing.'

'Oh what?'

'He tasted pretty good. But don't ask me to repeat the exercise. I'll never look at a dog the same way again.'

'Unless you visit South Korea of course.' Rupert replied and they both chuckled.

'So come on Mister Thomas, what the hell are you really doing here? Last time we met you were in London and seemed firmly ensconced behind a desk.'

'Before I answer that, one more question if you don't mind. Remember the task we asked you to perform before you came out here? Did your lady companion ever mention a code word? It's an odd one called Triptych Blue.'

Jon looked puzzled. 'No, sorry Rupert, she never said a word. I tried on several occasions to get her to talk about things other than helicopters and she was always very evasive and I never really had the chance to confront her. What on earth does it mean?'

It was Rupert's turn to talk and he briefed Jon on the whole situation. How Bea's husband had made contact at the meeting to discuss the search for the missing aircraft and the subsequent contact with Vorodov and his people.

'So Bea's husband is part of this conspiracy? That confirms what you told me in London before I came out.' Jon remarked. 'From what Bea has told me he's pretty progressive in his thinking. I wonder why he didn't approach the Yanks though.'

'Good question and it appears that he did but they've taken so long to get back to him he's given up.'

'That seems odd, So have we told them what we're up to?'

'Not yet,' Rupert grinned. 'If they want to sit on their arses that's up to them. I'm sure someone higher up will let them know in due course but in the meantime this is our operation.'

'And what of the overall political situation Rupert? Presumably, we think that supporting these people is the right thing to do but has anything actually happened?'

'Another good question. A few days ago Boris Yeltsin was elected as the President of Russia and Gorbachev remains the President of the Soviet Union. Most of us think this is unsustainable and something will have to give and soon. The mood on the streets is weird. With all this Glasnost about, people seem almost to be competing to say what they feel while at the same time looking over their shoulders in case someone is listening in. I think that just like us, they want more change especially if it gives them more freedom. They've seen how quickly things in East Germany have improved. However, they are still at least in part under the thrall of the old system and are terrified it will come back. We are also pretty sure that the whole place is just about bankrupt. The whole Soviet bureaucracy system is turning into a joke. It's so inefficient it's completely lost track of its expenditure. Gorbachev went cap in hand to the G7 asking to join and when they refused him, he then also refused an offer of aid. It seems that was just too much like accepting charity. His only friend these days seems to be the German Chancellor, Helmut Kohl, which is pretty ironic seeing the history between the two countries. Kohl seems to hate Yeltsin almost as much as Gorbachev does. Interesting days my friend.'

'But we support Yeltsin I take it? That's what this Triptych Blue thing is really all about?'

'I guess you could say we are covering our bets at the moment. We've agreed to help out the Vorodov faction by supplying information but of course we control that supply. Basically, if the dam breaks then we are in a position to do something but that doesn't mean we have to. It gives us just that much more flexibility.'

'Do we know if there are any likely timelines for things now? As you said this situation can't last.'

'The only hard date is the twentieth of August. In just over a month, Gorbachev is planning to sign this new act of Union with the fifteen Soviet Republics. That's causing a great deal of concern. However, nobody seems to be taking any overt action at the moment.'

Jon looked at Rupert. 'I take it I can just concentrate on my day job now? You haven't got any more sneaky little tasks for me in the sidelines?'

'Not for the moment old chap but knowing you, you'll find a way to get into trouble sooner or later.'

'Not me, I'm for the quiet life from now on. Stabbing wolves and attempting to shoot at bears, even if they weren't really bears, has been enough excitement for a while.'

Rupert lifted one eyebrow. 'I'll believe that when it happens. Anyway, I've been ordered to stay here now for the duration to head up this new development, so I will be able to keep an eye on you.'

They chatted a little more and then Rupert took his leave. Despite his words, Jon realised that his job was likely to be more than a little interesting over the summer months to come.

Bea was sitting at her desk in the Moscow office. She had been cleared fit two days previously but was having trouble concentrating.

Her reunion with Gunter had been very mixed. He had been delighted to see her but wanted to know all the details of their accident. When she had explained how the aircraft was almost certainly involved in the illegal smuggling of fur he had contacted the local police to take the necessary steps. He had quizzed her hard about Jon and what they had got up to. Eventually, she had lost her temper and told him to back off. The tension was still simmering and she was glad to be away from him for a while. However, he had confided in her about the contact he made with British intelligence. In some ways that had come as something of a relief as she had had to confess that she hadn't managed to broach the subject. Now she didn't know whether to be cross with him because of his obvious jealousy or worried for him for the risks he was taking. Either way, she was sure things would settle down, at least for a while and she could concentrate on her real job.

Gunter was also sitting at his desk, thinking about Bea and the events of recent weeks. His relief at her rescue was tempered by the on-going worry about his involvement with the Vorodov conspiracy as he was calling it in his mind.

He forced himself to get back to the present. He had just come out of a rather extraordinary meeting with his boss and Vladmir Kryuchkov the head of the KGB. In front of him was a handwritten list of names. The meeting had been to discuss contingency plans in case anything happened over the next few months. Gunter saw it as ironic that he was being entrusted with this information for exactly the same reasons that Vladmir had recruited him all those months ago. As a 'new' member of the KGB administration and therefore untainted with the prejudices and inertia of most of the old guard, he was seen as a safe pair of hands. After all, he and his wife had fled East Germany and returned to Moscow. Even now, most people in the system refused to accept that anyone would not want to be part of the Soviet utopia. Presumably, his boss still thought there hadn't been enough time for him to become ensnared in one of the many factions developing around him. Either way, the information in front of him could be critical. The list included some very senior people in most of the Soviet countries and all would need to be warned off or recruited if things came to a head. His job was to set up lines of communication to them, so that they could be contacted quickly if and when necessary.

Scanning the list, he looked for one name. There it was nearly at the end where he expected it to be. Taking a pen he carefully crossed it out before calling for his secretary to take it away for typing.

Chapter 33

Jon was sitting at his desk reading yet another intelligence digest. His coffee had grown cold. Things were moving fast in the Soviet Union or what was left of it. Mark Speddings had co-opted just about everyone to bolster Rupert's team and try and keep tabs on what was going on. Picking up his cup and realising the content was now undrinkable, he was about to go for a refill, when his door opened.

Commodore Test put his head round. 'Morning Jon, all staff in the briefing room now please.' Before Jon could respond he was gone.

Curious and with all thoughts of coffee fled, Jon went out into the corridor to be met with a stream of people all heading in the same direction. He found a seat near the back of the first floor room used for internal mass briefings and meetings. Just about everyone from the military, trade and intelligence sections were there. Suddenly, the Ambassador and Mark Speddings accompanied by Rupert walked in. Everyone stood but the Ambassador waved them to sit.

As he reached the front of the room he motioned for the doors to be closed. 'Gentlemen, we have received some remarkable intelligence only a few hours ago and you all need to know about it. As of nine this morning, President Gorbachev is no longer in Moscow. He left by plane for Foros on the Black Sea where he has a holiday villa.'

Jon was taken aback by the announcement. So what? Everyone went on holiday this time of year presumably even the President of the Soviet Union. Then the penny dropped.

Before he could think it through further, Rupert took over. 'In case anyone here thinks that's not important consider this. In sixteen day's time he is due to sign the new Union Treaty that's got all the hardliners really worked up, yet he considers it sensible to abandon his power base in the weeks leading up to it. Something's up. We need everyone to keep their eyes and ears open. If anyone gets any intelligence of any sort, please report it to me or my team immediately. Any questions?'

There were but in the end it was all speculation. No one could come up with a sensible reason for the President to leave the capital at such a sensitive time. As the meeting wound down, Rupert motioned to Jon.

'Jon, are you still in contact with the Bukov woman? Making contact with her husband could be very tricky at such a sensitive time but you have a legitimate reason for speaking to her still. Maybe she can tell us what's actually going on.'

'I'll try Rupert. In fact, I was going to talk to you about seeing her again anyway and ask what I would be cleared to say to her. I guess you've just answered the question. But surely the intercepts that GCHQ are making will tell us what we need to know and we can talk to Vorodov and his people over that link can't we?'

'Maybe but her husband works in Moscow and has to be extremely careful now. He probably can't get to Vorodov that easily at the moment. You can never have enough intelligence and who knows what's said that doesn't get transmitted over wires or the radio.'

'Fine, I'll get in touch. By the way, does the Commodore know you're asking me to do this?'

'Not yet but he will. Don't worry I'll clear it with him.'

Later that day, Jon managed to get a call through to Bea and they arranged to meet at a pavement restaurant near Red Square. Jon arrived first and was enjoying a beer in the almost festive atmosphere of the city. The sun was shining and it was proving to be a very warm summer. Every month since he had arrived, there seemed to be more people about and more smiles on faces. He was pretty sure it was nothing to do with the improving weather.

Bea joined him. She was wearing a light yellow summer dress and looked happy and relaxed, unlike the last time they had been together. He ordered a beer for her as well.

'So, how are you Bea? The last time I saw you was when they were hauling me out of that rattly old helicopter.'

'Oh, I'm fine now. They took me to a Moscow clinic for a few more checks but I was back at home the next day.'

'Hah, they kept me in bed for ages in the Embassy. I was going stir crazy by the time they let me loose.'

'That was a nasty head wound Jon. I'm not surprised.'

'Well, I'm fine now, although I'm told there will be a scar. As I can't actually see it, I can't really worry about it. How was Gunter when you got home?'

She gave Jon an odd look. 'He was fine but I must get you two to meet. No husband likes to think of his wife with another man in such intimate circumstances even if they were so extreme. I'm sure if you two got together he would see what a really nice man you are.'

'I'm flattered but I'm sorry if I've made him jealous. We both know there's no reason for it. Now look Bea let's put our cards on the table. This is one of those 'I know, that you know, that I know', situations. In other words we both know that Gunter has been in touch with my people and I'm sure he's told you all about it. Am I right?'

She nodded. 'Yes, as I told you after the crash, we share everything.'

'Right and I'm now briefed fully on what's going on as well. You know, I was meant to try to find a few things out from you before we had the crash but never really worked out how. After that it wasn't exactly my top priority.'

Bea laughed. 'And I was supposed to do the same Jon. You could almost say the accident was a good thing because it gave Gunter the opportunity he needed to make contact. If they had waited for us to bite the bullet they would still be waiting now.'

He laughed with her. 'You're right but crashing and nearly dying isn't my preferred way of opening up lines of communication.'

'Nor mine. But I'm guessing there's something more you want to know.'

'Spot on. Contacting Gunter directly is felt to be too dangerous, particularly at the moment but nobody is going to be surprised if we meet. We have a professional relationship through your work but also we just spent over a week in the mountains surviving an aircraft crash. Getting together won't be suspicious, at least if we don't do it too often.'

'Or maybe people will think we have a different relationship now.' She grinned at him.

'That's true but don't let your husband hear that. I know how big he is.'

'He's a pussycat really but come on Jon. What's this all about?'

He looked at Bea in the eye. 'Gorbachev Bea, he's gone on holiday and we can't work out why. His power base has never been so weak and with this Union Treaty about to be signed, he's pissed off just about all his normal supporters. Why leave Moscow now?'

'You're not the only person wondering that Jon. It seems almost ripe for what some call a Khrushchev moment.'

Jon looked blank.

Bea continued. 'In sixty four, Khrushchev was in a Dacha on holiday and the rest of the Politburo met in his absence and decided to oust him. He was recalled to Moscow to find the whole lot of them, led by Brezhnev, waiting and demanding his resignation. He gave it, he had no choice. His absence had been enough to allow sufficient debate to get everyone to line up against him. Gunter and I talked about it this morning and he hasn't a clue what Gorbachev is up to either, although there is a rumour going around that he's very tired and worn down.

Maybe he really does need a break or maybe he's just too arrogant to think anything can happen to him. Look, if I hear anything I'll let you know. But we can't meet like this too often. If I need to get in contact, I'll call you at the Embassy and leave a message about the Shark. Let me think, I know I'll ask if you want to visit our Moscow facility to see some upgrades. That will work because we can actually meet there and talk freely.'

'That's a really good idea Bea. I'll make sure our reception knows to get hold of me no matter where I am. Now, we had better chat some more and maybe stoke the rumours about our non-relationship. '

An hour later, in a mellow mood after several large beers, Jon made his way up the steps into the Embassy. As soon as the receptionist saw him she called over. 'Sir, I've been asked to tell you that you need to go and see Captain Haywood as soon as you get back. He will probably be in the bar at the moment.'

Thanking the receptionist, Jon went to the bar where the Captain was sharing a drink with his wife. As soon as he saw Jon come in, he excused himself and came over. 'Jon glad you're back, some bad news I'm afraid. Commodore Test was taken ill this afternoon with suspected heart problems. They're sending him home straight away. In fact, he'll be on the plane by now.'

'Oh, that is bad news, How serious is it?'

'No one's quite sure. It might have even been a mild heart attack. He's alright though. He was quite lucid. However, it's felt he will get much better treatment at home. Of course you know what else this means?'

'Oh bollocks yes. The good Group Captain is in charge now.'

'Yup and you're now his deputy, good luck.'

Chapter 34

14 August 1991

The next ten days were a nightmare. Group Captain Pearson was a very different person to his predecessor not that Jon needed any notice on that score. On more than one occasion Jon was about to tell the man exactly what he thought of him but managed to bite his tongue. Unlike the Commodore, who let Jon get on with things and gave him minimal supervision, the Group Captain was a 'long screwdriver' person and interfered in just about anything Jon was doing. Luckily, the extra intelligence tasks that Rupert was asking the staff to perform gave Jon the excuse to be away from his desk as much as possible.

He had developed a habit of going out to lunch. He had acquired a taste for Russian cuisine and one particular café served Pirozhki, a sort of cross between a Cornish pasty and a pie depending on the filling. He was slowly working his way through their extensive menu of fillings. There were several other new bistros operating nearby as well and they were starting to become crowded at lunchtimes. He was looking forward to the gastronomic journey through all of them over the next few weeks. Unless wolf was on the menu of course. Although they were proving popular with the staff of the various Embassies nearby, they also attracted a good smattering of locals. Sitting and enjoying a beer and a Pirozhki offered the opportunity to eavesdrop on conversations. At the same time, it had the added benefit of keeping him out of sight of the Group Captain.

With a sigh of reluctance, Jon realised he really couldn't dally at his table any longer. It was time to go back to the office. Maybe he would hear from Bea today. They had had no contact since their last meeting and although Rupert kept asking, Jon trusted her enough to leave her alone. When there was something to know she would pass it on.

He managed to sneak past the Group Captain's office without the long hand of the RAF reaching out and grabbing him and settled in behind his desk. Someone had filled up his in-tray in his absence and he was just about to reach for the first file when his phone rang.

'Switchboard here Sir, I've got a lady called Bukov on the line, do you want to take it?'

'Yes, of course,' Jon replied.

Bea's voice came on the line. 'Commander Hunt, hello again this is Bea Bukov. I was wondering if we could arrange a visit for you to our Moscow facility. We've got a few upgrades in the pipeline you might be interested in.'

'Hang on, I'll check my diary. Actually, I'm free this afternoon, would that be too soon?'

'No, that's fine. I'll come over by car. Would two thirty be too early?'

Slightly surprised that she was coming herself, he agreed and then picked up the internal phone to the intelligence section.

'Rupert, I've had Bea Bukov on the phone with the agreed message. She's coming herself to pick me up in half an hour.'

'That wasn't quite what you agreed,' Rupert replied. 'Did she sound her normal self?'

'I think so, will you tail us?'

'Yes, just as a precaution. Good luck.'

Jon packed his desk away and was just about to leave when Group Captain Pearson walked in unannounced.

'Ah, Hunt, I've got a small job for you if you don't mind.' he said in his normal arrogant tone.

'Sorry Sir, got to dash, something has just come up.' Jon walked swiftly passed the man before he could respond further. He almost made it to the stairs at the end of the corridor before an angry shout reached him. He ignored it and shot off down the stairs two at a time.

To his surprise, a car with Bea in the driving seat was already waiting. He realised that she must have been very close when she phoned. He jumped in and Bea promptly drove off into the traffic without looking behind her. She didn't seem to notice the angry horn being sounded behind them or the flashing headlights.

'Jesus Bea, drive carefully. We survived an aircraft wreck let's not have a car crash,' Jon exclaimed.

'Oh shut up Jon, I've been driving for years.' She replied cheerfully as she changed lanes again without looking behind or indicating.

Jon made sure his seat belt was well fastened and made a conscious effort to pull his foot up off the imaginary brake. 'So what's come up Bea?'

She was silent for a moment then answered. 'Actually, it's your help we need Jon. Gunter feels it's too dangerous for either of us to go to the Dacha. Apparently, there are all sorts of things going on at the Lubyanka but he is only party to a few of them. It's enough to get him worried but he can't find out exactly what's going on. What he does know is that it's going to happen soon. He was tasked to ensure a number of key people in various governments were contactable in an emergency and has now been told to be ready for the eighteenth. That's only four days time. Can you check with your people and let us know if you've intercepted anything?'

'Yes, of course I can ask. However, one thought does occur to me. What are Mister Yeltsin's movement over the next few days, do you know? It sounds to me as if it would be better for him if he was out of the country.'

'You may be right Jon but you will need to get that message directly to Vladmir via your radio link. As I said, Gunter and I daren't be seen doing anything suspicious and that definitely includes calling the Dacha or even going out to it. You are effectively our only link.'

'Understood, we had better go out to your offices just to make sure this conversation looks normal. As soon as I get back to the Embassy I'll see what I can find out. However, it does look like we're going to need a better method of communication than this. Let me talk to our people and see what we can arrange. They're the experts after all.'

Three hours later, Bea dropped Jon back at the Embassy. He had survived the drive in both directions but still wasn't quite sure how. There again, just about everyone with a private car in Moscow seemed to drive like Bea, so maybe it all cancelled itself out.

The receptionist called to him as he entered the lobby. 'Sir, Group Captain Pearson wants to see you straight away. He told me to tell you the moment you returned.'

Jon nodded his acknowledgement and ignored the summons. Instead, he went straight to the intelligence section. Rupert was in his office despite the lateness of the day.

'How did it go Jon?' he asked as soon as Jon appeared at the door.

Jon plumped himself down on a chair. 'Fine, the first thing you need to know is that something is about to happen and the critical date seems to be the eighteenth. Gunter reports that the KGB are all gearing up for something but he's not sure what.'

'Actually, we've a pretty good idea what,' Rupert replied. 'They're going to mount some sort of coup. What we don't know is how they intend to do it. That date ties in with the intelligence we've been getting from GCHQ.'

'What about Yeltsin? Has he been warned?'

'Yes and he had a trip to Kazakhstan planned, so he's going a day early. Was there anything else?'

'Yes,' Jon replied thoughtfully. 'We seem to have a bit of role reversal going on. Bea says that her husband is tied up in the Lubyanka and with all the turmoil there its far too dangerous for him to go anywhere near Vorodov's place or even to call him. He needs to be kept in the loop and Bea seems to be our only conduit to him. He asked her to ask us if we have any information about what's going on, which is a bit ironic really.'

'Hmm, he's probably right. We've got a good link working to Vorodov and therefore to Yeltsin but being able to maintain a secure communication path into the KGB is probably going to be just as important.'

'Do you have any ideas about that Rupert? I did a few courses before coming out here but that sort of thing is starting to be way outside any limited expertise I might have.'

'That's alright Jon. We'll set up a dead letter drop system. You'll have to arrange one more meeting with the lady to brief her on what to do. Then we'll have a secure channel to pass on what we know and for them to communicate with us. It won't be instantaneous but it will be safe. As you've been her handler for want of a better word I would like to keep you in that role if that's OK with you?'

'That's an interesting phrase. I don't think I'll explain my role to her in those terms if you don't mind,' Jon replied with a grin. 'However, there is one more issue that needs to be resolved. Have you briefed Group Captain Pearson about all this and my role in it?'

'Oh bugger, I spoke to the Commodore but of course he left in a bit of a hurry. There's going to be a problem though. Unlike you, the man isn't cleared for this level. It seems that your previous exploits have raised your clearances way above his.'

'Maybe the best thing to do is to get the Ambassador to temporarily assign me full time to your section. That way I can stay out of his way, at least until this is all resolved.'

'Good idea Jon, leave it with me.'

Chapter 35

15 August 1991

'Is it working?' Vladmir asked Sergei as he put the old Bakelite receiver down in its cradle.

'Yes Vladmir,' Sergei replied. 'Good old fashioned Second World War field telephone technology. Sound powered and very simple. It couldn't be more different to that machine in the loft but it works just as well. Running the wire over to Boris's Dacha wasn't hard except for crossing the main road but we managed to string it up high between two trees. We now have a totally secure landline. We can pass anything we get from the British over there straight away and without any risk of it being intercepted.'

'Good and of course it means Boris can deny any contact with outside agencies.'

'Well, if someone found the wire they could follow it back to here but it's very well concealed. Even over the road we have two trees that almost touch so it's totally invisible.'

'So, where are we now with what we think is going on?'

'The Eighteenth is the critical date. We're pretty sure of that. We know that the head of the KGB and Gennady Yanayev, the Soviet Vice President, are the main instigators and that there are several other conspirators maybe up to a further six. There is going to be massive attempt to contact all the Soviet Republic heads of state and other senior politicians over the next few days. But our man in the KGB has managed to keep the name Yeltsin off the list. He is now in Kazakhstan but intends to return here on the evening of the eighteenth. If anything is going to happen, he wants to be on hand but at a distance if that makes sense.'

'Yes it does. It will allow him the flexibility to act as he sees fit. What do we think the conspirators expect of him?'

'They know he hates Gorbachev, so I expect that if this is a coup they will hope he will support them.'

'They're in for an unpleasant surprise then,' Vladmir laughed mirthlessly. 'And the military? How are they going to react?'

'They will have to respond to an order to deploy. There's nothing we can do about that but our people have been recruiting quietly and I would be extremely surprised if any shots are fired.'

'We can only pray Sergei. Once things become chaotic anything could happen. It only takes one idiot to fire a gun and everything could change. Then all our good intentions will have been for nothing.'

'I know Vladmir but we're doing the best we can.'

Jon stood in front of Group Captain Pearson's desk like a naughty school child in front of the headmaster. In years gone by he would probably have blown his top already. Now he tried to just let the words wash over him.

'I'll have you know I was flying fast jets before you were wet behind the ears and I won't stand for any more insubordination, is that clear?'

Glad that he was at last about to get a word in edgeways, Jon was trying to reconcile what flying jets had to do with anything, when the Group Captain decided that his silence was yet another mark of disrespect.

'Did you hear me?' he was almost shouting now.

Jon had had enough. 'Yes Group Captain, I'm not deaf.'

'Don't you dare speak to me like that Commander. I'm your senior officer and you speak to me with respect.'

That did it. 'Why?'

'What? What do you mean why? I outrank you, that's why.'

Jon looked at the man behind the desk with total contempt. He spoke quietly. 'Firstly I only respect people who have earned it.' He could see another explosion coming but got in first this time. 'Sir, I don't give a fucking toss about what you've flown and how many hours you've got. And if you want to use that as an argument for superiority of some sort then I've got almost as many as you and they may not be in your bloody Phantoms but I managed to shoot down an enemy aircraft unlike you or any other RAF officer since the last war unless you count the two of your own that you shot down by mistake.' The Group Captain was starting to look apoplectic. Jon ploughed on. 'I've also commanded a squadron and in doing so brought a ship hijacking to an end. Not only have I flown in combat, I've commanded a warship of over two hundred people in action against a very determined enemy. If you think for one moment that your bluster and threats compares to any of that you are completely mistaken. Yes, you have one more cloth stripe on your arm more than me and yes you can try to use that to intimidate me but it won't bloody well work.' Jon leant across the Group Captain's desk and looked him hard in the eye. 'I don't bow down to paper tigers and bullies, is that clear?'

Group Captain Pearson looked shocked. Jon realised that he had probably never been spoken to like that before. He almost wished he had managed to keep his anger under control but knew in his heart that this would have happened sooner or later. At least it was all out in the open now. The bloody man probably had grounds for a serious complaint against him, probably enough for a court martial even if it would be Jon's word against his. Jon realised he couldn't care less.

'Right, well, that's enough of that,' the Group Captain blustered. 'I think I've made my point clear now Commander.'

Jon was staggered. The man was backing down. Maybe there was something to be said for blowing your top once in a while.

'Now, I've had a chat with Mark Speddings and you are seconded to his section with this Mister Thomas for the foreseeable future. He won't tell me why but I'm sure it's important. So off you go.'

Just like that, Jon was dismissed. Deciding that saying another word would be a really bad idea, Jon nodded and left the room. Five minutes later, he was back in the intelligence section for a briefing with Rupert about the contact system he needed to establish with Bea.

'Ah Jon, there you are,' Rupert said as Jon entered. 'Sorted things out with the Group Captain then?' he asked innocently.

Jon caught on when he saw the look on his friend's face. 'Oh shit, did you hear what was said?'

'Me and about half the Embassy I'm afraid. If you're going to shout at senior officers, take a tip from me and close the door.'

'Oh bugger, so everyone will know?'

'Within minutes would be my guess but don't worry, there's not one person who isn't on your side. It might just get that arrogant prig to come down a notch or two. But Jon be careful, he could make a great deal of trouble for you if he wanted to. I didn't make that last remark by the way.'

'What remark?' Jon said innocently. Surprised and gratified by Rupert's support.

Later that day Bea, let herself back into their apartment. To her surprise, Gunter was already home.

She gave him her ritual peck on the cheek. 'You're home early darling. I thought everyone was working late these days?'

'No, it's suddenly all gone quiet. The task I was given has finished.' As he spoke he held a finger to his lips. 'Why don't we go out for dinner for a change? Who knows when we'll get the chance again.'

Taking the hint, Bea made inconsequential conversation as she changed out of her work clothes into a pair of jeans and sweater. They then both walked out into the cool evening air.

Gunter looked around casually. 'Sorry darling but the level of paranoia at work is at fever pitch these days and although I'm second in command of the department for internal security I wouldn't put it past someone to have bugged everyone's home accommodation. I may have just caught the paranoia bug myself but there's no point in taking risks.'

'Hopefully, it will all be over soon, one way or another.'

'You're right of course. Now what did the British say?'

'Firstly, they agree with your assessment of the eighteenth. They think it will be some sort of coup, especially with Gorbachev being away. Also, it's a Sunday and there will be less people around. They have no idea what form it will take though. Any ideas on that?'

'Not really. Our Head has been in meetings almost constantly but we never hear what they're about. Many of the meetings are over in the central government departments and the White House anyway. So, what have you arranged with the British?'

'It's a simple dead drop like we used to use in the old days. You know the children's playground just past the house?'

'Yes, let me guess, the old tree?'

'Clever boy, you. There's a split in the trunk and when you're standing there it's almost impossible for anyone in the surrounding apartments to see you. When we have a message for them I put a vase in our front window with flowers in it, otherwise we keep it empty. And before you ask I bought some plastic ones today, so we'll always have some available. They say they will check three times a day. If they have a message for us they have an old red Lada which they will park opposite until we've done the pick up.'

'Sounds pretty simple but it should work.'

'Gunter, what's going to happen? Have you any idea at all?'

'Sorry darling, you know as much as me. Frankly, it could go either way. In a few days we could be back to the old Soviet Union or maybe we could all have just taken a great leap into the unknown.'

Chapter 36

18 August 1991

'Bloody hell Rupert, have we got it all wrong?' Jon was looking worried. It was past midday on the eighteenth and absolutely nothing had happened. The previous two days had been a total anti-climax. The window in Bea's apartment had remained steadfastly empty of flowers. Intercepts of communications from the government were purely routine. It was as if the whole of Russia was holding its breath. The weather had been glorious. Jon and Rupert had spent hours sitting in bars enjoying the sun and trying to assess the mood of the population. Everyone seemed happy but there was definitely an air of anticipation.

They were now back in the Embassy sitting in Rupert's office. 'No Jon, something is going to happen soon. I'm quite sure.'

Just then one of Rupert's staff appeared. 'Flowers Rupert, the message will be here in a few minutes.'

'See, I told you so. Now, why do I get the feeling that this is it?'

Within ten minutes, Rupert held an envelope which he quickly opened and scanned the contents before handing it to Jon. While Jon was reading it he gave instructions to get in contact with London.

'What does this mean Rupert? What the hell is this State Emergency Committee?' Jon looked puzzled.

'I'm pretty sure it's the leaders of the coup. And look, they've sent envoys to the Black Sea. There's only be one person they can be visiting. They must want to have discussions with Gorbachev.'

Before Rupert could say more, another member of staff came in. 'London report that they have intercepted mobilisation orders for tank and infantry regiments in the Moscow district. They're passing it on to the Dacha as we speak.'

'Well, if there was any doubt before, there's none now,' Rupert said. 'We need to get a high level briefing together and make sure the Ambassador is fully in the picture and then we will just have to wait and see what the next step is going to be.'

Vladmir put the old war time phone down. 'Boris will be back later this afternoon but I've passed on the information. It seems the plotters are trying to cover both options. Presumably, by going to talk to Gorbachev, they are trying to get him to come in with them but it would appear they're also about to send a team out here to try and convince Boris to do the same thing.'

'Thank goodness Bukov managed to keep Boris out of the loop until now. I wonder what they would have done had they been able to talk to him before.' Sergei observed.

'You know Sergei, this all seems incredibly amateurish. They seem to want to stop the Union Treaty but don't seem to know who they want to side with them. One thing is for sure they can't have both Gorbachev and Yeltsin. That would never work.'

'Maybe they don't mind as long as they get one of them. If Boris goes over, then the treaty is definitely dead. If Gorbachev does, presumably it will be a condition imposed on him.'

'But if he refuses to accept that and if Boris does likewise where does that leave them?'

'With nowhere to go except to take power directly themselves. Can you see the Russian people accepting that after all these years of openness?' Sergei looked worried.

'One thing we don't know is who is actually in charge of this so called Safety Committee. However, my bet is that it's either Kryuchkov of the KGB or Yanayev the deputy Soviet President. Well, I know both of them and I have to say it doesn't fill me with much confidence. Neither are potential leaders of our country or the union. What is Boris going to do when the delegation arrive? Did they say?'

'He's not going to speak to them. He will be in no fit state to talk until tomorrow. At least that is what they'll be told. With his previous track record, they will probably believe that. That leaves him in a position to act tomorrow depending on what this so called Safety Committee decides to do.'

Gunter was sitting at his desk. He had little to do but his boss had told him to stay until dismissed. Something was going on but no one was saying what. His secretary buzzed through on his intercom. 'Sir, you've been asked to go to Comrade Kryuchkov's office straight away.'

'Tell him I'll be there in a minute,' Gunter replied as he stood up, thankful that at least something seemed to be happening. When he arrived at the head of the KGB's palatial office he realised he was the only one present.

'Gunter, come in. Thank you for attending so promptly.'

Gunter looked at Kryuchkov. He looked tired. There were bags under his eyes and he seemed anxious about something.

'I am about to let you in on a secret which won't be a secret much longer but I have an important task for you. Please take a seat.'

Gunter did as he was told and waited for Kryuchkov to speak.

'I expect that everyone is aware that the government is very unhappy with this forthcoming treaty which will effectively turn the Soviet Union into a Republic?'

Gunter merely nodded.

'Myself and the Soviet Deputy President, amongst others, have decided to take action. This afternoon we sent a delegation to Foros where President Gorbachev is on holiday. We asked him to sign a state of emergency until the matter is resolved. I suspect you won't be surprised to hear that he refused. He even rang me for clarification but despite my urging still would not budge. Consequently, we have placed him under house arrest for the moment.'

Cold water ran down Gunter's spine. It was really happening. He forced himself to remain calm.

'The only other politician we might be able to rely upon is the Russian President, Comrade Yeltsin. He returned from Kazakhstan this evening and went to his Dacha. Unfortunately, it appears that he has once again fallen foul of the vodka bottle and could not be roused. We need to speak to him urgently and before he can return to the capital. If he refuses to cooperate then he will have to be arrested as well. We have prepared somewhere to hold him if necessary. Tomorrow, we will announce a state of emergency until this is all resolved. We may have to deploy troops and impose a curfew.'

'Very well comrade but what do you want me to do?' Gunter didn't like the way the conversation was going at all.

'We intend to intercept President Yeltsin tomorrow morning if he attempts to leave his Dacha. If he stays there we can deal with him later but we cannot take the risk of him turning against us and coming to Moscow. I want you to go to the road block we are establishing on the only road out of his house and if he attempts to pass it you are to arrest him. We need a high ranking and trustworthy officer to ensure that this is accomplished.'

Gunter forced himself to keep a straight face but inwardly he was starting to wonder at the competence of his leader and his plotters. They had issued an ultimatum to Gorbachev without apparently any fall back plan. The only other legitimate politician who might support them had not even been spoken to and their only option was to arrest him if he refused to cooperate. Of course, Gunter knew why Yeltsin had not been contacted. It was his actions that had ensured that it hadn't happened. But surely they should have ascertained his position before going to Foros? This was madness and of course what they didn't know was they were using exactly the wrong man for this task.

'You can trust me Comrade Kryuchkov,' he responded sincerely.

Chapter 37

19 August 1991, morning

Rupert put his head around Jon's door. 'Jon wake up, listen to the radio.'

Blearily Jon looked at this watch. It was just after half past six. He had stayed up late the previous night just like everyone else but eventually succumbed to fatigue. He quickly rolled over and turned on his bedside radio alarm clock. It was already tuned to the TASS station.

A stern voice was saying something. 'I repeat, this is an announcement from the State Emergency Committee headed by Deputy President Yanayev. President Gorbachev has been taken ill and is no longer able to fulfil his duties as President of the Soviet Union. Consequently, Deputy President Yanayev is taking over the duties of President for the meantime. Because of the nature of this emergency, all citizens are urged to remain at home. For the foreseeable future, all demonstration have been declared illegal and a curfew will come into force from eight o'clock tonight until eight o'clock tomorrow morning. In Moscow and all major cities, troops will be deployed to ensure that peace is maintained. Further information will be provided in due course.' There was a moment's pause and the message started repeating itself.

'Oh bollocks, it's really happening isn't it?' Jon asked as he sat up in bed.

'Seems so. We've got word that tanks are starting to enter the city as well. They're heading for the White House and other government buildings.'

'But the White House is only just down the road from us. It's only a few hundred yards away.'

'Yup, looks like we're going to have a grandstand seat, which is probably why the Ambassador has ordered the Embassy closed. No one comes in unless they are nationals with an emergency and no staff are to leave. As I said before, interesting times.'

'But that means no one will be looking for any messages from the Bukovs.'

'I'm afraid that's right Jon but let's face it we've done all we can now. Events are just going to have to play themselves out and we can still pass intelligence on via the Dacha.'

'Right, just let me get dressed and I'll come down to the section.'

The morning dragged on. From the windows of the Embassy, they were able to see the line of tanks appear and surround the Russian Parliament building. What they also saw was that despite the announcement on the radio, people were converging on the area in their thousands. The television and radio were playing continual transmissions of Swan Lake. There were no further announcements of any sort. Most Embassy staff had gathered in the main reception area. Its large glass windows gave a good view of the outside and a large television was mounted on the far wall. After the second repetition of the ballet, someone had turned the sound down. Even Tchaikovsky could become wearing after a while.

Suddenly, the picture of prancing dancers was replaced by the Hammer and Sickle of the Soviet Union.

Someone called out, 'hey everyone, there might be something coming on the television at last.'

All heads turned towards the television screen as the volume was restored. A man's face appeared and announced, 'we now go to a press conference from the State Emergency Committee.'

A picture of a room crammed with people appeared. At one end, a table had been set up with eight men in identical sombre dark suits sitting before microphones. They all looked ill at ease.

'That's a bloody cheerful bunch,' Jon muttered to Rupert.

'They look more nervous than anything, I wonder if it's going wrong already,' Rupert responded. Then the man in front began to read from a clearly prepared speech. It was no more than a repeat of the early morning broadcast but then he opened the floor to the assembled journalists for questions.

'That's Yanayev talking. Look at his hands, they're shaking,' Rupert observed. 'They look like a bunch of old men completely out of their depth.'

The questions came thick and fast but the repeated response was that Mikael Gorbachev had been taken ill and was not in a fit state to manage the union. When one journalist asked if that meant he no longer had the black bag with the nuclear release codes in it, the reply took some time. Eventually, it was admitted that the codes were now back in Moscow.

Despite repeated and often hostile questioning, they all stuck to the line that Gorbachev was in no fit state to carry on as President but were very sketchy on providing any details. When challenged about the deployment of troops, again they insisted it was only a temporary measure, to ensure public safety.

When someone asked about the Russian President, Boris Yeltsin, the answer was that as far as they knew he was in residence in his Dacha but as this was the business of the Soviet Union not Russia it was outside his remit.

'In other words, they don't know what Yeltsin thinks,' Rupert said.

'Jesus, they can't be that incompetent, surely?' Jon replied.

As the session drew to an end, a pretty young girl in a green check dress managed to get noticed. 'Comrade Deputy President, are you aware of the fact that you have just committed a state coup?'

There was a moments silence before uproar erupted. No one had dared use the word coup until then and its effect on the men at the front was electric. At first, they all looked at each other in dismay. The Deputy President immediately denied anything of the sort but it was too late and minutes later the whole team withdrew without a further word.

The Ambassador who had been watching with everyone else called the room to order. 'Ladies and gentlemen, I think we can all agree that that was quite unusual. It would seem that this is indeed a coup. Notice that once asked, none of them were prepared to deny it. I'm afraid there's nothing we can do at this stage except sit tight and watch developments.'

Gunter's eyes felt gritty. He was tired but sleep was just a dream. He had arrived at the road block late last night. When he got there, there were already half a dozen KGB troops with their truck and a car containing a junior KGB agent from his own department. He immediately realised that if he briefed them on what he wanted, which was contrary to their original orders, there was a real risk that someone would report back to the main operations centre. His only hope was to wait until their target arrived and then order him to be allowed through. It was going to be difficult but he couldn't see another way. He was going to have to rely on the ingrained response of all Russians to obey someone of higher rank. A couple of hours sleep in his car had only served to give him back ache. Hopefully, it wouldn't be long before things were resolved. And of course being stuck out here meant he had no idea about what was going on in Moscow which only heightened his frustration and worry. His one consolation was that he had been able to stop by their flat and tell Bea what was going on. At least they had a contingency plan to fall back on.

The road block had been set up just as the pine forest thinned out on both sides of the single carriageway road. It consisted of a simple portable barrier painted red and white. Both sides of the road were bordered by a deep drainage ditch, so there was no way a vehicle could drive past. The heavily armed troops would put a stop to anyone trying anything stupid.

The KGB agent's name was Anton. He seemed quite young and quite nervous, probably because Gunter was so senior. Gunter had explained his presence simply by saying that the job was so important that he had been asked to ensure all went well, which was of course true, up to a point.

The morning dragged on with a few vehicles going through. The road really only served the private houses of the rich dotted along its length, so most traffic was domestic staff and some deliveries. Everyone seemed to have a frightened look on their faces and were reluctant to talk. Luckily, the troops had come prepared and the Sergeant in charge of the platoon had invited both KGB men to share a soldier's breakfast. That and the copious quantities of tea had helped ease the time by.

At first, Anton had wanted to talk but Gunter made it clear that he wasn't there for idle chat and the young man had soon subsided into silence. Suddenly, in the distance two black cars came into view around the far bend. Gunter asked the Sergeant if he could borrow his binoculars and he could immediately see that both limousines were flying the Russian flag from small flagstaffs on their front wings.

'This is our man everyone, standby please.' Gunter ordered, silently cursing the President. Those bloody flags were such an obvious sign of who was in the cars. Suddenly, it felt like the whole world had landed on his shoulders. History could very well pivot around this moment. He had to ensure that these cars were allowed past.

The first car drew up to the lowered pole and the driver's window wound down. Signalling to the Sergeant to stand back, Gunter went up to the window.

'Papers please,' he ordered while at the same time looking in the back. There were two men there but he didn't recognise either of them.

He examined the papers and handed them back. 'Wait here,' he ordered as he went down the line to the second car.

Again, he asked for the occupant's papers and looked in the back. Sure enough, seated on his own in the rear was the man he needed to let through. He looked angry and Gunter could see he was about to say something.

Leaning in through the driver's window he gave him a smile. 'No problem Sir, I'll clear you through.'

Pulling his head out he signalled for the barrier to be lifted and waved that the cars were clear to move on. For a second, the soldier on the barrier hesitated, looking confused. Anton had started to walk towards him.

'It's alright, I'm authorising the cars to proceed,' he called in a loud voice to the troops and the advancing agent. It was enough for the soldiers. They were there to obey orders and he was the senior man present. The barrier was lifted and both cars accelerated clear.

Anton reached Gunter. 'But Sir, wasn't that President Yeltsin? I thought we were ordered to arrest him? What's going on?'

'Young man, I make the decisions as you well know. Are you questioning my orders?'

Anton looked confused for a second. Then he clearly decided that it wasn't his problem, Gunter was far more senior than him.

'Sorry Sir, no I would never do that.'

'Good because we can all go home now. Our task is over.' Gunter strode over to the Sergeant and ordered him and his men back to barracks. He then told Anton to return to Moscow. A clearly confused young man got into his car and drove off. Once the soldiers had dismantled the road block, they also got into their lorry and headed back towards Moscow. Gunter got into his car. As he put his hands on the wheel he realised they were shaking. His problem now was that there was no way he could go anywhere near the Lubyanka or his apartment, anywhere in Moscow for that matter. However, that shouldn't be an issue for too long. He turned his car around and headed in the opposite direction to everyone else.

Chapter 38

19 August 1991, afternoon

Jon and Rupert were sitting watching the television although they might just as well have been looking out of the window at the drama unfolding only a few hundred yards away.

'So much for TASS trying to block out any news,' Rupert observed. 'No one seems to have told CNN and the BBC that they shouldn't be walking around with their cameras switched on.'

'It's not exactly the October revolution is it?' Jon remarked. 'All these troops and tanks around the White House yet there are thousands of people talking to them like they're out for a picnic and they've even managed to barricade them out of the building, it's amazing.'

'Hang on, isn't that Yeltsin?' Rupert asked as a man in a grey suit was spotted climbing on top of the turret of a tank. 'Turn the volume up Jon, he's saying something.'

They listened as Yeltsin's speech was captured by an unknown camera team.

'As the President of the Russian State, I declare that this coup is unconstitutional. I call for a general strike.' Yeltsin then turned to face some of the troops in front of him. 'You have taken an oath to your people and your weapons cannot be turned against the people.'

There was complete silence in the square. He then pulled out a piece of paper and continued as he read carefully from it.

'As President of Russia, I declare that in connection with the actions by a group of persons who call themselves the State Emergency Committee, I order that this committee must be considered anti-constitutional, and the actions by its organizers must be considered a revolution, which is a state crime. All resolutions, which are issued by the so called committee, must be considered illegal and they have no authority in the territory of the Russian Republic. Lawful power remains in the person of the President, the Supreme Soviet and the chairman of the Minister's Council. Actions by officials, who execute resolutions of the afore-mentioned committee, fall under the criminal code of the Russian Republic and they are to be prosecuted by the law. This decree is in force from the moment of signing.' He produced a pen with a flourish and carefully signed the paper before waving it to the crowd.

Cheering broke out. Russian flags were waved as Yeltsin climbed down off the tank and walked unmolested into the Parliament building.

'Bloody hell, that was well prepared and the troops just let him do it,' Jon said with amazement on his face.

'Well, he's been pretty well briefed. I wonder if he would have been quite so brave if he hadn't been party to all the intelligence we've been passing him. He must have worked on that declaration all night.' Rupert observed. 'What interests me is that the troops seem paralysed. Not one of them made any move to stop him.'

'Well, he is their President after all. Of course, it begs the question of which authority they are actually answerable to. Is it the Soviet Union or is it Russia?'

'When you've managed to have a country with two Presidents that is always going to be a problem.'

Jon snorted in amusement. 'They've really got things in a mess. I just worry about what happens now. With Yeltsin inside Parliament we've lost touch with him.'

'Not necessarily, we can always use the telephone. It's a bit late to worry about calls being intercepted now.'

'And Gorbachev? Do we know what's happening in Foros?'

'Not really. There's a complete communication blackout which is hardly surprising. Whatever happens over the next few days I guess he's out of it.' Rupert responded. 'But we just have to pray that things don't explode. Who knows what the coup leaders will do now?'

Vladimir Kryuchkov was about to explode with rage. He had just turned off the television where Yeltsin's speech had been shown across the world. Standing silently on the other side of his desk was the agent who was meant to have stopped the bloody man getting into Moscow.

Kryuchkov turned to the young man who was visibly shaking with fear. 'Tell me again what that traitor Bukov did?'

'Sir, he simply ordered us to let the cars through. What was I supposed to do?'

'And where did he go after the cars were allowed to pass?'

'I don't know Sir. He ordered us all back to Moscow but I didn't see him follow. He must have gone the other way.'

'Tell the duty officer to get up here and bring a map of the area,'
The man fled.

A few minutes later Kryuchkov was studying the map. The road led up towards a wooded area where he knew many of the rich of Moscow kept their country houses. It petered out after a few miles, so Bukov must have gone to ground somewhere in the region.

He turned to the duty officer. 'Get me a list of everyone who owns a Dacha in this area and when you have it, bring it to me. Oh and also get Bukov's secretary to come along as well.'

He didn't have long to wait. He was well aware that the whole building would know of the disaster by now and also how he was reacting to it. Good, let them all feel a little fear. When this situation was sorted out there would be some reckoning within the KGB. Bukov's name would be at the top of the list.

There was a knock on the door and a remarkably pretty young girl came in with a sheet of paper in her hand. She was followed by the duty officer.

'Have you looked at the list young lady?' he asked sternly.

'Yes Sir,' she answered, clearly terrified to be in his presence.

'Well?'

'Sorry Sir, what do you want to know?'

He sighed in exasperation. 'Come on girl. Do any of the names on that list strike a chord? Was your boss interested in any of them?'

She looked at the list again and hesitantly pointed to one name. 'Comrade Bukov did do some research on this man Sir, although most of it was from the files and in Berlin.'

Kryuchkov looked at where she was pointing. 'Vorodov. Where have I heard that name before? Can you get me all the files he was looking at?'

'Yes Sir, right away,' the girl also fled.

He turned to the duty officer. 'Get hold of Alpha Group. I want a senior officer and the Sergeant who was manning the road block in here straight away.'

The duty officer didn't wait to be told twice.

An hour later Kryuchkov had read the files and had a pretty good idea of who Vorodov was and what agenda he was working to. There was a knock on the door and two soldiers came in. The KGB Alpha Group was a very elite force of soldiers and as of this moment only answered to him. The Sergeant looked worried. The Captain who accompanied him just looked obedient.

'Sergeant, I don't hold you responsible for what happened this morning, is that clear? You did what you should have done and obeyed orders.'

A grateful look of relief crossed the Sergeant's face. 'Yes Sir, thank you Sir.'

'And Captain you are?'

'Sir, Captain Gregori Vitsin.'

'Very well, I have a task for both of you and whatever number of troops you deem necessary. But first, have you seen what is going on in Moscow at the moment?'

Both men looked to be struggling to know how to answer.

'Don't worry, everyone in the city has. I just have one question. Are you still loyal to me and will you follow legitimate orders?' Kryuchkov knew he was taking a risk even asking the question but he had to know. After the Lithuania debacle, even Alpha Group might be starting to side with Yeltsin.

'Sir,' the Captain responded. 'You are our Commanding Officer. We do not get involved in politics.'

Kryuchkov considered the slightly evasive answer. It would have to suffice. 'Very well look at this map. This is what I want you to do.'

Gunter was sitting with Vladmir in a small room at the rear of the Dacha. He had briefed them of the morning's work. They had then watched the events unfold outside the White House.

'Well, it seems your intervention may have turned the tide of history Gunter,' Vladmir said with admiration. 'One little action with such a large result.'

'I just wonder what the idiots in Moscow will do now Vladmir. The whole thing has been incredibly badly managed so far. It's almost as if they don't want their little coup to succeed.'

'Not the least because of your actions in wrong footing them my friend.'

'Maybe but I'm worried about what Kryuchkov will do. He's a vindictive bastard and I think we should put our contingency plan into operation. I've already called my wife and told her to get out and go to our pre-planned rendezvous.'

Just then Sergei appeared. To their surprise, he had the satellite radio case in his hand.

'Message from London. It appears some of Alpha Group may be mobilising and they've suggested that we move location as a precaution. I've packed up the radio and told them we will get back in contact when we are at the alternative location.'

Gunter looked at Vladmir. 'It seems the decision has been taken for us.'

Chapter 39

19 August 1991, early evening.

The convoy of Alpha Group troops consisted of two trucks led by a UAZ Kozlik four wheel drive utility vehicle. In the front of the Kozlik were the Sergeant who was driving and Captain Vitsin. The forty troops in the trucks behind had been carefully briefed and were armed with light assault rifles only. They all had strict instructions only to use them as a last resort. The Captain had briefly considered an airborne assault but as the target was surrounded by a tall pine forest he had ruled it out. He also wanted their approach to be as quiet as possible. Which was why, when they were several miles away, he ordered the Sergeant to pull into a side road and halted the convoy.

The troops all disembarked and he gave his final orders. Two men jumped into the Kozlik and drove off. The rest of the men spread out and headed into the trees. They were carefully separated enough so that each man could still see the next one either side of him. It took over an hour to cover the direct route to the Dacha and once they could make it out through the trees the Captain signalled his men into position surrounding the old hunting lodge to ensure there were no avenues of escape.

Once he received a nod that all his men were in position, he beckoned to the Sergeant and they carefully made their way over to the road leading into the grounds. They carefully studied the building. There was no sign of life but that meant very little. If their intelligence was correct, there would only be three people inside; the owner, his companion and the quarry they were hunting. It was still daylight and would be for several hours yet so there were no lights to be seen and no obvious signs of activity.

Staying in the woods, they walked back until they were out of sight of anyone looking. The Kozlik was parked up waiting for them and they both jumped into the back seat.

The small vehicle drove sedately up to the front door. There was no sign that they had been noticed. The Captain considered knocking but knew it would be a waste of time. He beckoned to one of the soldiers who came up to the door with a large metal door ram and nodded to him. The soldier slammed the ram into the door which barely moved it was so massive. Luckily, the lock was a modern one and not so strong and with a crash the door flew open after the second blow. The four men charged in with weapons raised.

'This is the KGB,' the Captain shouted into the large empty hall. 'Everyone here is to remain where they are.'

Silence was the only response. With methodical care, they started to clear the building but the Captain had already come to the conclusion that their quarry was gone. It didn't take long to prove him right. It also looked like great care had been taken to remove anything incriminating. There was food in the kitchen and clothes in the cupboards, even books in the large library at the rear. However, everything was neat and tidy and there was precious little to tell him of the character of the owner or his guests.

One of the troops came in and reported that they had found a field telephone wire in one of the flower beds. The Captain ordered the man to follow it but he soon came back and reported that it had been cut and there was no direct sign of where it had led. A quick look at the map gave him a pretty good idea as there was only one other Dacha in the direction. But it didn't help apart from confirming what he already probably knew.

Just then, one of the soldiers came up to him. It was the man who had driven the Kozlik around by the road.

'Sir, I think you should know that while I was driving here, a car came past me the other way. I couldn't see how many were in it but I thought you should know.'

'What sort of car?' the Captain asked, seething that the man hadn't come forward earlier but understanding why all the same.

'An old black Volga Sir. Sorry I didn't say earlier Sir, should I have done?'

Biting back a sharp retort, the Captain reined in his feelings. He had been very careful to tell his men to respect his orders, which is really just what the man had done.

He went outside and looked at the gravel drive. Sure enough, tyre marks led around one side of the house to a garage which was empty. He ran back into the house where there was a telephone in the hallway. Lifting the receiver, he was relieved to get a dial tone. Quickly dialling the number, he realised it still might be possible to catch his quarry.

In Vladmir's old Volga there was a sigh of relief from all the occupants as the small military vehicle drove past without any sign of recognition.

'What do you think? Are they going to the Dacha?' Vladmir asked.

Gunter answered first. 'Quite possibly but they would have sent more than one small car with two soldiers. We need to keep our eyes out. If they've put up a road block, we're in serious trouble.'

No one answered but the level of tension in the car rose noticeably. A few minutes later they spotted two military lorries parked down a side road but they were clearly empty.

'Looks like we would be having visitors about now,' Sergei observed wryly.

They drove on for several more miles but when the main highway into Moscow came into view with no further sign of the military, there was a collective sigh of relief.

Pulling on to the main road Vladmir increased speed. 'How far to the airfield Gunter?'

'Only about thirty kilometres Vladmir, stay on this road until I tell you to turn off.'

Vladmir followed Gunter's directions until the small airfield came into view. It had originally been a satellite airfield for fighters protecting the city in the Second World War. In recent years it had been allocated to Kamov for their Moscow facility. There was a grass airstrip which was fine for helicopters, two hangars and a modern office block. Next to the new building was the old original military block which had been converted to provide temporary accommodation for people on site. It was rarely used but provided for visitors and staff who had to work late. Bea often used it for just that reason.

The car drew up to the main gate where an old man seemed to be the only person present. He came to the passenger's side of the car as soon as he recognised Gunter who wound down his window.

'Hello Boris, it all seems rather quiet today?'

'Yes Mister Bukov, most of the staff have gone home now, those that turned up at all today with all that's going in the city. I have a television in the guard room so I've seen what's going on. The facility will be closed now until further notice. Your wife is already here though and she told me to tell you to go straight through.' He peered through the window at Vladmir and Sergei. 'And these are your guests? You're vouching for them I take it?'

'Yes, they are here to visit the facility. However, with what's happened today we will just have to see what happens. Either way, we will be staying the night and see what tomorrow brings.'

The old man waved them through the gate and Gunter directed Vladmir where to drive. They parked up behind the accommodation building with the car well screened from the road.

Bea was waiting for them and came out to greet Gunter and shake the hands of the other two men. Once they had their cases from the boot, including the satellite radio, she ushered them in, out of view. Gunter briefed her on what had happened on the road and afterwards.

'Thank goodness you managed to get away in time Gunter. What do you think they would have done if they had caught you?' Bea asked with a worried look on her face.

'Probably just locked us up for the moment. I think Comrade Kryuchkov has far more important things to worry about at the moment, don't you?'

Vladmir who had been listening, joined in. 'That's right Madame Bukov but that would not be a good place to be if this coup succeeds. And we need to re-establish communications with the British as soon as we can. Can you help Sergei find a location for the radio please?'

Bea nodded. 'In a moment but you probably don't know the latest news.'

'What's happened now?' Vladmir asked.

'That's the strange thing. In some ways, nothing at all. The gang of eight, which is what everyone is calling them now, seem to have disappeared. Nothing's been heard from them since that dreadful press conference. Some more tanks have appeared but gone to various other parts of the city. However, there are now estimated to be over one hundred and fifty thousand people protesting in Moscow with similar numbers in Saint Petersburg and other cities. Nothing has been heard from the White House either although people have been going to these new American restaurants, Pizza Hut and McDonalds and taking food into the Parliament building. The soldiers are doing nothing to stop them. The curfew should have come into force and again the troops are not enforcing it. It's crazy.'

'Stalemate,' Gunter said. 'Yeltsin has made his position clear. The plotters have said their piece. Now we wait to see who will blink first.'

'Or fire the first shot,' Vladmir said with worry on his face.

Chapter 40

20 August 1991, morning

Jon hadn't slept well but neither had anybody else in the Embassy. Apart from the gravity of the situation stressing everyone out, their proximity to the centre of the action had meant continual noise all night. Car horns were regularly sounded and someone had managed to set up a sound system so that it sounded like an all night disco was going on just outside. He was gloomily looking at his plate of eggs and bacon when Rupert plonked himself down next to him.

'Morning Jon. Looks like another interesting day to come,' Rupert announced cheerfully.

'There are just too many bloody interesting days at the moment Rupert,' Jon replied. 'It seems like most Muscovites are treating the whole thing as an excuse for a party. They didn't shut that bloody music down until after five this morning.'

'Well, at least you've managed to get some sleep. I've been up just about all night. And as for the music, anything that keeps this situation even close to normal has to be a good thing.'

'You're probably right. So what's the latest thinking amongst the intelligencia?'

'If by that you mean my lot, then we're all still bloody worried. We're back in contact with Vladmir and his people, including Bea's husband but they're now ensconced in their secondary hiding hole. Not sure there's much more they can contribute but it's always useful to have help on the ground if needed. I need to talk to you about that in a minute. However, the real issue is this stalemate. We've heard nothing from the so called Safety Committee and there has been virtually no communication traffic to their military overnight. And as far as Yeltsin is concerned, he seems to be simply waiting to see what's going to happen next and why not? The ball is firmly in his opposition's court.'

'So, what might happen today Rupert?'

'I'll turn that round Jon. What would you do if you were in the coup leaders place?'

Jon snorted in amusement. 'Not get in such a sodding mess in the first place. But on the basis that that is where they are they've either got to capitulate or break the deadlock in their favour. Presumably, they've got Gorbachev safely under wraps. So their main problem is the man in the White House. If he hadn't managed to get there things would be quite different. It seems the soldiers are reluctant to do anything other than sit in place. It would seem extremely unlikely to me that they would now obey any orders to open fire on their own people. So, if the conspirators are really serious, they're going to have to provoke something. If I was a ruthless hardliner, I think I'd try to engineer some form of confrontation that would give me the moral high ground and make the troops angry and on my side.'

'Go on Jon.'

'Well if I could get a sniper well positioned or even several for that matter, they could fire on the crowd or even better, on the troops at the same time and all hell would probably break loose. It would then give me the excuse I needed to storm the White House and also properly establish martial law.'

'You know what you've just described, don't you Jon?' Rupert asked with half a smile on his face.

'Eh? What do you mean?'

'That's just about exactly how the nineteen seventeen revolution started. I'm pretty sure these coup leaders know that and also just how many citizens lost their lives in the process. I just pray they have the sense not to try it.'

Jon looked surprised. 'So I'm guessing most of those people on the streets know as well. They're even braver than I thought.'

'I suppose its safety in numbers coupled with a real desire for change. One thing's for sure, nothing will ever be the same here. Now, I've got a little favour to ask if you don't mind?'

'Here we go,' Jon smiled at his friend. 'Doing you favours always ends up with me in trouble.'

'No, it's quite simple. My lords and masters have decided we need to retrieve our radio. Vorodov's not in any real position to influence things anymore and it would be in neither party's interests if it was discovered. We could ask them to destroy it but the bean counters would never allow that, they cost a fortune.'

'What do you want me to do?'

'Simple really, you know the way to the Kamov facility and it would save time and me getting hopelessly lost if you navigated for me. And come on Jon, if you're like me you're going stir crazy stuck in here. I've cleared it with the Ambassador. So, fancy a look see for real?'

'I can't think of anything I'd rather do Rupert. When do we leave?'

Captain Vitsin was very tired but it only seemed to serve to increase his drive. He hated it when someone got the better of him. Before leaving the Dacha, he checked in with the Lubyanka. He had then ordered most of his people back to barracks keeping just two troopers and his Sergeant. He had also requested any detail on the black Volga. The car was a rarity dating back to the fifties and so shouldn't have been hard to spot. The trouble was that nearly all of the civilian police had been recalled to attempt to control the situation in the centre of the capital. No one had reported seeing the car and so they were reduced to literally driving around looking for it. After an evening of fruitless searching, he had been ready to give up but when he checked in with the Lubyanka he had been ordered to stand down for the night and start again the next morning.

He had returned to Moscow surprised that the crowds he had been hearing about were nowhere to be seen. In fact, the city was eerily quiet. The White House was over a kilometre away from Lubyanka Square and seemed to be the magnet that was attracting all the people. He had spent much of the rest of the evening studying the city map as if staring at it would reveal the whereabouts of the old black car. In the end, he decided to turn in. Just before he fell asleep an idea came to him. It was too late now but he would check first thing in the morning.

It was easy enough to check the files and when he saw the wife's employment record he had an idea of where his quarry could be hiding. It was a long shot but the best he could think of. A quick stop by the Bukov's apartment confirmed that the woman hadn't been seen for at least twenty four hours and her car wasn't parked where it normally was. One nosy neighbour had even said that she had seen the wife leaving with bags early the previous day. So maybe his hunch was right.

Wasting no time, he directed the Sergeant to drive to the north west of the city. It hadn't been as easy as the previous night and the traffic was bad. It took almost two hours to get clear and onto the road leading to the Kamov Bureau's facility. The first thing they did was simply drive past and look carefully at the layout. The whole airfield was surrounded by a high wire fence. There appeared to be only one way in, with a small building and barrier across the road. A large modern office block was adjacent to two old hangars, clearly relics from the last war. There was also a much older two story brick building to one side. There was no sign of a large black Volga.

They pulled up well clear of the main entrance. The Sergeant spoke first. 'No sign of anyone there Sir. It looks like the whole place has shut down.'

'I suspect they've suspended work while this crisis is on.' The Captain replied. 'And that should make things easier for us.' He came to a decision. 'We seem to have two options. Firstly, we could cut the wire and try a covert approach but we're not even sure that they are there. They could be anywhere in those buildings or even the hangars. So what we're going to do is drive up to the gate. There was someone in the guard hut as we drove past. We'll simply ask and then take it from there.'

Two minutes later the Kozlik pulled up at the main entrance and an old man came out to meet them with a puzzled frown on his face. 'Can I help you officer?' he called as he walked over. 'The facility is closed until further notice.'

The Captain held out his identification badge. He spoke in a friendly tone. 'I understand that a woman called Beatrix Bukov works here. She wouldn't be on site today would she?'

The old man didn't answer. Four armed soldiers asking for anyone was a clear indication of trouble. The Captain's identification showed that he worked for internal security. What could he do? 'Yes Sir, she brought in some visitors last night. They were meant to be touring the facility today. I don't know what they will do now but I haven't seen them this morning yet.'

'That's fine and where will they be?' the Captain maintained his friendly tone.

'Over there Sir. The old brick building is used for temporary accommodation. They stayed there last night.'

'Very good. Now, this is official business so please don't ring and tell her we're coming.. That wouldn't be a good idea. Do you understand?' The Captain's voice had gone cold.

The old man suddenly looked frightened and he simply nodded in acknowledgement. Then the Captain had an idea. He quickly went into the guard's office and pulled the telephone wire from the wall and smashed the receiver with his rifle butt. He would rather have left one of his men there to ensure no warning was given but he only had three men with him and he couldn't spare any of them. This would be just as effective.

He got back in the car and turned to his men. 'There's no time for a subtle approach as you might just have noticed. I want one man to go to the rear of the building as soon as we arrive. Sergeant, you and the other come with me. We go in armed but absolutely no shooting unless we are fired on first, is that clear? We want Bukov and anyone with him arrested, nothing more.'

The car roared away from the entrance and was in front of the accommodation block within seconds. They all jumped out and one of the soldiers ran around to the rear while the three others, with the Captain leading, went to the front door. It was unlocked and they went straight in. There was a simple entrance hallway with doors on either side and a stairway ahead of them leading upstairs. Before they could react, an old man came out of a door to one side.

'Yes Captain, can I help?'

'Who are you?' the Captain asked curtly.

'I might ask you the same question,' the old man answered, clearly unfazed by the rifles held casually by the three soldiers.

'Answer me please and where is Comrade Bukov?' The Captain asked, clearly trying to keep the anger out of his voice.

'Listen son, I was facing the Nazis before you were even a glint in your parent's eyes. You don't intimidate me and you don't speak to me like that.'

The Captain suddenly realised that whoever this man was he wasn't the one he was after and he was trying to buy time. He pushed past him in to the room he had emerged from. It was some sort of common room with a number of chairs and a coffee machine in the far corner. It was also empty. There was a door at the far side. He ran towards it. It wasn't locked. There was a short corridor with a door on either side with the standard picture of a man on one and woman on the other. He heard the sound of a toilet flushing. The door with the man's picture on it opened and a very tall man with an angry frown in his face appeared.

'Comrade Bukov, you are under arrest,' the Captain announced.

Chapter 41

20 August 1991, midday

Jon had found it far more difficult to navigate to the Kamov airfield than he expected. He hadn't really been paying that much attention when Bea had driven him. Or rather he had but it was primarily focused on which potential accident site Bea was looking for next. On top of that, the city was in semi-chaos and they had been forced off the correct route several times. They were driving one of the Embassy's old Ladas rather than one with diplomatic plates and were dressed in the current Moscow fashion of T shirt and jeans. Rupert wanted to keep the whole visit simple and low key.

'Not far now Rupert,' Jon called as he studied the map. 'This is the outer ring road now and the entrance we're looking for is about half a mile up here on the right.'

'About time Jon, driving in this country is bloody terrifying.'

'You try it with one of the locals behind the wheel mate. Then you'll understand the real meaning of terror. Hang on here we are.'

They pulled up at the gate and an old man came out. Jon immediately recognised his face. 'Hello there, we're here to see Bea Bukov. You might remember me I came to visit a while ago.'

The old man peered in. 'Hello Sir, yes I recognise you but I wouldn't recommend you come in today. The facility is shut down until this crisis is resolved.'

Jon got the impression that the man was worried about something. 'No, it's alright she's expecting me. Just give her a ring. I'm sure she'll confirm it.'

'I'm sorry Sir but you can't come in today. I can't let you in. You'll have to come back when we are back to normal.' The man turned and went into his guard room.

Baffled, Jon turned to Rupert. 'Something's seriously wrong here Rupert.'

'I agree. We need to get in. Let's see if we can persuade the old bugger.'

The two of them got out of the car and went into the guardroom. The first thing Jon noticed was the damaged telephone on the man's desk.

'Now look, I said the facility is closed,' the man's voice was angry.

'Boris isn't it? Bea told me a little about you. You were a pilot in the war?' Jon asked.

He looked a little mollified by Jon's remark but stuck to his guns. 'Sorry Sirs, I just can't let you in.'

'Why not? We know that Bea is here and she's expecting us. What's happened to your telephone? There's something very wrong here and you're not telling us are you?' Jon was starting to get angry now.

The old man seemed to deflate. 'Some KGB soldiers came here a few minutes ago. They said they were looking for her and smashed the phone to stop me ringing ahead and warning her. You really can't stay. They were all armed. You really don't want to go in. I know what those bastards can do.'

Jon turned to Rupert. 'Fuck, just a routine visit to collect something? Now what the hell do we do?'

'Even if they arrest them they'll probably do nothing more than hold them until this is all over and then they should be fine.' Rupert responded but then a thought struck him. 'Shit we can't let them find the radio though.' He was interrupted by the sound of a distant shout. Rushing to the rear window they could see two figures, one holding some sort of case, disappear into the small side door of the nearest hangar. Suddenly, what could only be one of the KGB soldiers appeared waving his rifle and continuing to shout. He suddenly stopped and ran back to the brick building behind him.

'Shit, I'm pretty sure that was Bea and Vladmir,' Jon said. 'They're hiding out in that hangar. I know the layout. I was there the other day. There's another small door on the far side but unless they get out pretty quickly they're going to be trapped.'

'Right come on Jon,' Rupert called urgently. 'If we drive around the main office block we should be able to approach the hanger from the far side and we won't be seen.'

The two men ran to the Lada and Rupert gunned the engine. The red and white wooden pole offered no resistance and splintered as they hit it.

'I've always wanted to do that,' Rupert grinned at Jon. 'Just like in the movies.'

Jon didn't answer. He had caught a glimpse of several men running out of the brick building. They didn't seem to be looking their way as they were heading towards the hangar. He prayed they wouldn't be heard.

Rupert drove the car the opposite way down the tarmac road and around the front of the main building keeping as close to it as he could. The next building was the hangar. The Lada shot across a small gap and Rupert slammed on the brakes as they came up to the side door.

Hopefully, the soldiers approaching from the other side hadn't seen them.

Jon ran to the door and pushed the latch. It wasn't locked. He poked his head inside. Taking up most of the room inside was a Shark but around the walls were various items of ground equipment and tools. There was no sign of Bea or Vladmir.

'Bea its Jon,' he called loudly. 'We saw you run in here, where are you?'

There was a sudden noise from the rear of the hangar and the two fugitives appeared. Jon and Rupert ran to them.

'What on earth are you doing here Jon?' Bea asked.

'Trying to help you, no time for questions, is that the radio?' he queried looking at the suitcase she was holding.

'Yes it is,' Rupert answered for her. 'We need to hide it if nothing else. Those soldiers will be here any moment.'

'We've barred the door we came in and the main doors only open from the outside with a special winding handle.' Bea replied. 'We were going to try to get away through the door you came in through.'

Suddenly there was a loud bang on the door on the far side of the hangar and a voice called out in Russian although it was impossible to make out the words.'

'Bugger we're trapped now.' Jon said, 'Even if we get out to the Lada they've got rifles. They're bound to have sent someone around that side. We'd be sitting ducks.'

'At least let me jam that door,' Vladmir said. 'I know how to.' He ran back behind the helicopter and came back with large metal rod. 'There are several of these. I can jam the fire door handle with it.'

At the same time, Bea went over to the Shark and opened a fuselage panel at the rear. She pushed the radio suitcase inside and closed the panel.

'No one will think of looking there but what the hell do we do now Jon?' she asked anxiously just as a loud banging noise was heard from the door Jon had just come in from.

Jon looked around, there was nowhere to go and nowhere to hide. 'Good question Bea, any ideas Rupert?'

'There are four of us and we're unarmed. Bea any idea how many soldiers there are?' Rupert asked.

'There were at least four and they all carried rifles. They've got Gunter and Sergei back at the accommodation block.'

'So there could be four but more likely at least one has had to stay to guard them but let's face it we're going to have to give ourselves up.' Rupert looked despondent. 'When they find out we're British nationals the shit will really hit the fan even if we do have diplomatic immunity.'

'Yes and with the current situation who knows how well disposed they will be towards any of us, immunity or not,' Vladmir said. 'Things are getting desperate. We've no idea exactly what orders those soldiers have been given.'

'So, you're saying we should resist them somehow?' Jon looked really worried. 'They hold all the cards.'

The banging on the nearest door started again and then a voice could clearly be heard. 'This is Captain Gregori Vitsin of the internal security forces. This building is surrounded and everyone inside is guilty of resisting arrest. You are required to open this door and surrender to me. If you do not, we will shoot the door open and I cannot guarantee your safety. You have five minutes to respond.'

'Well that answers one question,' Jon said. 'We either give up or fight. If I said I've an idea how we might just turn the tables on these guys will you all agree to give it a go?'

'That rather depends on what the idea is Jon,' Rupert responded. Bea and Vladmir nodded agreement.

'Alright, I'll tell you but first I'll need Bea's approval to damage some of her company's property.'

Chapter 42

20 August 1991, early afternoon.

Captain Vitsin was worried. The situation was getting out of hand. He knew that two companions to the man he was seeking had run into the hangar and seemed to have barricaded themselves in. However, his specific orders were to detain Bukov and he already had the man in custody and under the guard of his Sergeant. Should he even continue trying to arrest these others? But it was the way they had tried so hard to escape that made him suspect there was more to the situation. He hadn't had time to question his two captives and strongly suspected that the two escapees where the owner of the Dacha they had raided and the other was Bukov's wife. Both must be tainted with the crimes of Bukov himself. He made his decision. Looking at his watch he realised that over five minutes had already expired since he had made his ultimatum. He looked at one of the soldiers and nodded.

The soldier waved the others clear and pointed the muzzle of his AK47 close to the door where there was a lock mechanism clearly visible. He fired a short burst of automatic fire. The sudden noise was deafening and shards of metal flew everywhere. He put his shoulder to the door but it wouldn't budge. He looked in query at the Captain who simply nodded again. This time he pointed the weapon on the other edge of the door and fired twice at the exposed hinges at the top and bottom of the door. This time it worked and he was able to pull the door open towards him. The Captain and other trooper went to help and within seconds had ripped the door clear. There was a metal bar jammed in the opening mechanism clearly visible as the door fell to the ground. They waited for a moment and then carefully looked through the open doorway. The lights were on and there was some sort of helicopter parked in the hangar but no sign of movement.

'This is your last warning,' the Captain called into the echoing space. 'Give yourselves up or face the consequences.' Silence greeted his demands. He nodded to his two men and with their rifles held ready, the three of them entered the hangar.

Jon had been watching carefully for the right moment. He and his companions were hiding behind a large ground power unit mounted on a trailer twenty feet back from the door. The others were all lying down with their hands over their ears and with their eyes shut. Jon was gripping a piece of rope that went up to one of the beams supporting the hangar roof. It then carried on across the hangar and dropped down to the cockpit of the Shark.

As soon as all three men were well inside the hangar and just starting to fan out, he pulled the rope as hard as he could. He knew he should take cover but he couldn't tear himself away from watching what would happen next. It wasn't every day a helicopter pilot got to do what he was doing. The rope did its job and pulled out the ejection seat handle of the Shark.

The initial explosion was rather disappointing. There was a large detonation as six explosive bolts fired simultaneously. It was immediately followed by the sound of six rotor blades falling off and hitting the hangar floor. In flight, centripetal force would have flung them violently clear. Here in the hangar, they just dropped to the floor with a tremendous racket. The reaction of three soldiers as a large helicopter seemed to tear itself to bits in front of their eyes almost made Jon laugh. They all stopped and froze at the spectacle in front of them with almost identical expressions of astonishment.

It didn't last for long. If Bea was to be believed the delay was just under a second. There was an enormous bang and crash and the cockpit canopy of the Shark exploded. A bright gout of flame shot upwards as the ejection rocket cleared the machine and embedded itself in the hangar roof. The noise was overwhelming. Unable to fly to its full distance which would allow it pull out the seat from the helicopter, the rocket motor continued to burn in the roof. Immediately the hangar filled with choking fumes and deafening noise. It didn't last long. It was only designed to fire for a few seconds but the effect on the unprepared soldiers was exactly what Jon had hoped for. What he hadn't expected was the amount of smoke. It was acrid and already making his eyes water. Remembering his fire-fighting training, he threw himself to the floor. The air was much cleaner down near the ground.

'Now,' he yelled to his friends and they all crouched up and sprinted as best they could towards the door and the coughing, choking soldiers. Jon thanked God he had vetoed turning off the lights. If it had been dark as well, they wouldn't have even been able to get themselves to the exit, let alone take out three armed men. Jon saw one of the soldiers ahead of him and although never a fan of the sport, he managed to carry out a pretty effective rugby tackle. They both fell to the floor and Jon managed to snatch the rifle. He belatedly realised the soldier was barely struggling. Looking around, he could just make out the shapes of other figures through the thickening smoke. He could also see the halo of light from the open door. Suddenly their innovative method of attack had turned into a rescue mission as he dragged the almost unconscious soldier outside. Once in the clear, he took great whoops of clean pure air before leaving the soldier on the ground and plunging back into the chaos. Vladmir and Bea pushed past him with another slumped body but he could see that the man Rupert was grappling with was putting up a more effective fight. Jon ran over and jammed the muzzle of the AK47 into the man's back.

'That's enough,' he shouted into his ear. 'Drop your weapon. We need to get out of here.' As he said it he looked up at the roof really worried that they might have set the whole place on fire but there were no signs of flames for which he was really grateful. Rupert had managed to disarm the man and they half marched, half dragged him out into the clear daylight. All three of them were coughing hard as they reached safety.

'Is the hangar on fire?' Bea asked between gasps.

'I don't think so,' Jon replied. 'I had a look and couldn't see any sign of it but with that much smoke it's hard to tell.'

'It's only steel sheeting on the roof so there's not really anything to burn,' Bea replied. 'We should be safe here for the moment.'

'Should we try to open the main doors to let the smoke out?' Rupert asked.

'No,' both Bea and Jon replied simultaneously. They looked at each other and laughed, Jon then starting coughing again, so Bea explained. 'That would just let more oxygen in and if there is a fire it would make it far worse.'

'Oh, good point,' Rupert replied. 'I'm Rupert Thomas by the way.'

'Hello Rupert, Jon has mentioned you. What are we going to do with these three?'

They all turned to look at the three soldiers. The one who had been struggling with Jon and Rupert spoke. 'I am Captain Vitsin of KGB internal security and I strongly suggest you return our weapons to us and surrender. What are you going to do, shoot us?'

Vladmir answered. 'Of course not but we have no intention of being incarcerated by you either.'

'So what are you going to do? You have already betrayed your country,' the Captain sneered.

Vladmir looked offended at the man's words but before he could say anything more a loud voice came from behind them.

'Do as the Captain orders please, drop the weapons.'

They all spun around. Standing twenty yards away by the corner of the hangar was another soldier. He had Gunter and Sergei in front of him with their hands handcuffed behind their backs. His rifle was pointing at Gunter's back.

'Well done Sergeant,' Captain Vitsin said. He started to get to his feet but Rupert gestured with his captured rifle for him to stay still.

Jon looked at Rupert. 'Shit, this wasn't part of the plan.'

Bea spoke up, looking at the Sergeant. 'Or what? Are you going to shoot my husband in the back in cold blood?'

The Sergeant looked taken aback. He wasn't used to people questioning him, especially when he was holding the rifle. The woman was almost as big as her husband and looked very, very angry.

'What do I do Sir?' he asked looking pleadingly at his Captain.

Before anyone else could speak, Vladmir held up his hand. 'Stop everyone, just stop, this is getting crazy.' He could see several other people about to interrupt. 'No, just listen to me for a moment all of you. In case none of you here know who I am, my name is Vladmir Vorodov. I was a tank commander in the last war and I'm a Hero of the Soviet Union. But that all means nothing because first and foremost I am a Russian. I fought the war for Russia and all the days since I have worked for Russia. Captain let me ask you a question. Who is your ultimate commander?'

The Captain looked at the old man standing ramrod straight in front of him. 'I am a member of the KGB Alpha troop and I work for Comrade Kryuchkov who is head of the KGB and has given me a direct order to arrest Comrade Bukov.'

Vladmir looked him in the eye. 'You're wrong Captain and that is because Comrade Kryuchkov has to work for someone himself and that man is your ultimate commander is he not?'

The Captain thought for a second and reluctantly nodded his head.

'So who is that?' Vladmir continued relentlessly.

'The President of the Soviet Union, Michael Gorbachev.'

Vladmir laughed. 'Come on Captain, please don't tell me you didn't see the press conference on television yesterday morning. They may be claiming that Gorbachev is ill but what did your head of the KGB say when that young girl accused him of leading a coup against comrade Gorbachev? Did he deny it? No he didn't. In fact all eight of them got up and left at that point. So I ask again, who is your ultimate commander?

Is it the leader of an illegal coup that has incarcerated the man you say you follow or is it by any moral standards someone else now?'

The Captain didn't answer he was looking perplexed.

Vladmir continued inexorably. 'Several months ago there was the most democratic election held in Russia for many years and the man elected to be President of this country, not some disintegrating empire was Comrade Yeltsin. So the real question for you Captain is, are you a Russian? Because if you are, the only legal commander you now answer to is currently occupying the Russian Parliament building. There is no other legal authority.'

'And you work for President Yeltsin? You and all the others here, whoever you are. That is why Bukov allowed him to pass through the road block that Comrade Kryuchkov ordered for the very opposite reason?' The Captain sounded angry and confused.

'Captain, we are all on the same side here, can't you see that?' This time it was Bea talking. 'My husband and I are patriotic Russians like you. In nineteen seventeen there was a despot oppressing this country and we rose against him and replaced him. Can you not see the parallels? But the big difference this time is that there is an elected head of state already in place.'

The Captain looked one by one at the faces of all the people staring back at him. His mind was whirling. The problem was that he agreed with just about everything that had been said. He had been trained for years to obey his superiors but at the same time he still had a mind of his own. It had been easy, maybe too easy, to hide behind his duty and ignore his doubts. He looked at the old warrior in front of him. He knew what the man would say if he used the excuse that he was only following orders. The man would say that that was the excuse nearly every Nazi in the last war had used. The thought made him smile inwardly. He was a better man than that.

He looked over at this Sergeant. 'And you Sergeant? How do you see this?'

The Sergeant looked surprised to be asked and then a faint smile crossed his face. 'Thank you for asking Sir. I'm a Russian and always have been, just like all of us here. I saw that press conference as well and I wouldn't trust anyone of them as far as I could throw them. If President Gorbachev was here that would be a different matter but those people are trying to overthrow him. In fact, we don't even know what they've actually done with him. Sir ,we have no choice.'

The Captain made his decision, one he would remember for the rest of his life with pride. He turned to Vladmir. 'Very well, Sergeant, release those men.'

Chapter 43

20 August 1991, mid-afternoon.

Jon and Rupert were sitting clear of the others.

'What the hell do we do now Rupert? Do you think we can just disappear quietly while everyone else is busy?' Jon asked quietly so as not to be overheard.

'Let's just wait and see. We can't just leg it. I still haven't got the bloody radio.'

They were back in the common room of the accommodation block. One of the soldiers had been despatched to ensure that the old man on the gate hadn't rung any of the emergency services which thankfully without a functional telephone he hadn't been able to do. He had been told that all was now well and had no choice but to accept it. The smoke had cleared remarkably quickly from the hanger and there didn't seem to be any further danger of fire.

The Captain and Vladmir were still talking but it seemed that the argument had definitely been won. Even the two troopers seemed relieved at the change of heart of their officer.

Vladmir came over to Jon and Rupert. 'I've told Captain Vitsin the truth about you two. Sorry but he knew straight away from your accents that you're not Russian. There's been enough deception recently. He says he understands and he's promised me that he won't mention your part in all this, at least until you can get away and then you can of course deny it all happened in the first place,' he said smiling. 'So, I suggest you go back to the hangar, retrieve your radio and disappear and thank you for everything you've done. Maybe we can get together when this is all over and share a vodka together.'

Jon grimaced. 'Thank you Vladmir but I know you Russians and it won't be just one will it?'

'Probably not,' Vladmir replied with a grin. 'But just go. We're all going to stay here until the situation stabilises. We have a television and a large quantity of tea. The Captain says he's decided that he and his men are going to stay put with us.'

The two of them quietly walked to the door. As Jon went past Bea, he bent down and whispered quickly to her. 'I'll see you soon Bea. I hope you don't get in too much trouble with what I did to your nice shiny helicopter.'

'That's all right Jon. It was my decision come what may. I'll contact you when it's all settled down.'

With a final pat on her shoulder, the two of them made their escape and walked towards the still slightly smoking hangar to their car.

'Bloody well told you so Rupert,' Jon said when they were clear.

'Oh, what's that?' Rupert asked innocently knowing full well what Jon was about to say.

'Going on any of your so called 'simple little trips' always ends up in a bloody fiasco.'

'Hey, it wasn't me who thought it would be a good idea to make a helicopter blow itself up.'

'And if we hadn't, that bloody KGB Captain would probably have shot first and asked questions afterwards.' And then he added with a big grin, 'but it was rather fun wasn't it?'

'If you'd told me just how much smoke it was going to make maybe I wouldn't have been quite so keen but yes it will be something we won't be able to tell the grandkids about.'

For just a second a cloud went across Jon's face but then it cleared and Rupert didn't catch it. 'Right well here we are, let's get that box out of the Shark.'

The hangar was still smoky but nearly all of it had dispersed even if the smell would probably remain for ages. Jon looked up to the ceiling. The rocket was firmly stuck half through the roof. The last thing he wanted was the damned thing falling on their heads as they went to retrieve the radio. Stepping over a couple of the detached rotor blades, he went to the rear of the fuselage and opened the hatch, pulling out the suitcase. Turning, he handed it to Rupert.

'Right, let's get the clucking bell out of here old chap.'

'Would you mind Jon but with all that's happened I really think I ought to check in and I can use this to do so. It only takes a few seconds to set up.' Rupert asked.

'Fair enough, you can put it on the roof of the Lada. It's out of sight of just about everyone.'

True to his word Rupert had the antenna assembled and pointing at the right bit of sky within a few seconds. Not long after, he was talking into the small microphone attached to the earphones he had put on. While he spoke Jon looked around. Seeing even a small airfield like this totally deserted seemed odd and he wondered what had been going on in Moscow while they had been away. Hopefully, they would soon be back in the safety of the Embassy and they could put all this madness behind them.

Rupert interrupted his thoughts. 'You know that simple little trip we just finished?' He asked with an odd look on his face. 'It may not be over.'

'Oh for fuck's sake Rupert, what now?'

'Well, I got through quite easily and explained our situation. London tell me they've intercepted some signal traffic. They think the coup leaders tried to get the army units already in place to act. When that didn't work, they've tried to mobilise other units throughout the country but it seems no one will obey them.'

'That's good surely? Without the military in support, the whole thing just has to collapse.'

'Agreed but there's one military unit that answers directly to the KGB as we know all too well.'

'Are you saying they've ordered the whole of the Alpha Group out?'

'They think so but what they don't know is what the result of the order is. These are highly trained and very loyal troops. Look how much convincing Vitsin needed. If they get onto the streets of Moscow and are prepared to use force it could be a disaster.'

Jon looked worried. 'Rupert, this isn't our fight we've already gone too far. We can't get involved.'

'Normally I would agree with you but London have asked if we can talk to Vitsin and see if there is anything that can be done. He is a KGB soldier after all. They've given me authority to act if I see the need. Our priorities remain the same. British interests first but if we can do anything to hasten the end of the Soviet Union then we are free to act.' Rupert swiftly stowed the radio back in its suitcase.

They trudged back to the accommodation block with the radio. Inside the others had turned on the television and were watching the BBC World News. Cups of tea had appeared. They all looked round in surprise as Jon and Rupert opened the door.

'I thought you two were going to disappear?' Vladmir asked. 'Don't tell me something has happened?'

Rupert answered. 'Sorry all of you but you need to know this. I quickly checked in with London when I retrieved the radio. They have some intelligence that the coup leaders are getting desperate. Apparently, most of the conventional forces in Moscow have openly refused to act. However, there is an order to Captain Vitsin's group to mobilise and we think they might obey.'

For a moment there was a stunned silence. Then Gunter turned to the Captain. 'Will they do it do you think?'

'Possibly, it would depend on several things. I don't really know,' Captain Vitsin responded in a worried tone.

'And what would the objective be?' Vladmir asked. 'I can only assume that they would try to storm the White House and take out Yeltsin,' he continued, answering his own question.

'There would be a massacre,' Bea observed. 'All those crowds, they wouldn't stand for it.'

'Well then, it seems there are two issues. Will they obey the order and more importantly is there anything we can do about any of it?' Vladmir said. 'Where are the main barracks Captain?'

About thirty miles south of the capital, almost on the opposite side of Moscow to us. I know the Colonel who is in charge of the main troop. He's a good man but I can't answer for the General who commands the division.' Captain Vitsin turned to Rupert. 'Do we know anything more? For example the timing of the order and any detail about the task?'

'It was intercepted about an hour ago and heavily encrypted. We know what it was but it will take hours if not days to break the code sufficiently to read the order itself.' Rupert replied. 'If they obey, do you have any idea what they'll do?'

'Not really, it depends on the situation on the ground,' Captain Vitsin explained. 'I'm sure that by now they will have carried out reconnaissance in the city. My guess would be a quick airborne assault by helicopter and then extra ground troops to hold the perimeter. One thing I can be pretty sure about though is that they will not move far until dark and probably not attack until the middle of the night.'

'Look, this is all academic,' Vladmir said. 'We're over sixty miles away. What can we do stuck out here?'

'How about alerting the media somehow,' Bea suggested. 'Maybe they won't proceed if the story was made public.'

Gunter didn't like the suggestion. 'There are two problems with that idea my dear. Firstly would we be believed? And then even if we were, it could play into their hands. It would cause panic and that might make it actually easier to assault the Parliament building. It's not as if the people inside are even armed let alone in any way able to fight off a special forces assault.'

'What are the coup leaders saying in public?' Rupert asked nodding at the television.

Bea laughed, 'the current phrase everyone seems to be using is that they all have mysteriously caught flu. Apparently, they all went to their homes soon after the press conference and haven't been seen since.'

'You can bet they are still all talking behind the scenes though,' Vladmir observed. 'Otherwise these attempts at mobilising the military wouldn't be happening. This is the key moment. If they can't get anyone to obey orders then the whole house of cards will collapse. Their power base will be effectively destroyed. Then it will be up to Yeltsin and hopefully Gorbachev to sort out the mess but at least no one will be killed. If only we could get to the man in charge of these troops and talk to him. Captain Vitsin, you could make a good case as could I. But we can't get to them. You know I'm afraid that Bea might have had the only idea that we can use. Maybe we will have to take the risk and call the media.'

'So you think that if you could get to these troops and talk to their boss then that would be the best chance?' Bea asked.

'Yes my dear but we don't have wings and that would be the only way to get there in time.'

'Ah, but what would you say if I could provide those wings?'

Chapter 44

20 August 1991, early evening

'Can someone help me here?' Bea asked as she attempted to turn the windlass handle that opened the main doors of the second hangar. It was a much bigger building than the other one and the doors were massive.

'Here let me,' the Sergeant offered. He put his powerful shoulders to the windlass handle and the doors immediately started to grind open.

Jon turned to Rupert and spoke quietly. 'I think we should make our exit soon Rupert.'

'Yes but I really want to see what's in here Jon, don't you? It will only be a few minutes.'

The doors were half open now and Bea went in and turned on the lights. There were gasps from everyone. Inside were five helicopters. At the rear there were three of the archetypal Kamov twin rotor design of machine. Jon immediately recognised them as Hormone anti-submarine variants but all were surrounded by metal stages and clearly being worked on. On the right hand side was one of the ubiquitous Mil 8 transport helicopters, which slightly surprised Jon as it wasn't a Kamov aircraft. But what really took everyone's attention was the sleek, dark grey, machine on the left. For a second Jon thought it was another Shark but then immediately realised it looked subtly different. It had the same twin rotor system and large side mounted engines but the cockpit was very different. It was much wider, with space for two crew to sit side by side. Under its stub wings he could also see that there were missiles loaded and under the nose the muzzle of a large cannon pointed out. It looked menacing and very dangerous.

'So this is the one you didn't want to talk about Bea?' Jon asked.

'Yes, this is the Alligator and as you can see it's designed for a crew of two. It was brought here last week. There were going to be some demonstration flights to the military brass this week but I don't suppose that they will be happening soon. But it's not the Alligator that I want everyone to look at.' She pointed to the Mil 8. 'We use that as our company hack. Kamov don't really make a good utility machine. I am a qualified flight engineer on those and we have a very experienced pilot here don't we Jon?'

'What? Oh come on Bea you must be joking.' Jon protested.

'Oh, I thought you were talking about me,' Captain Vitsin interrupted. 'I'm qualified on that machine and so is my Sergeant. We can fly it even without a third crew member.'

Jon breathed a sigh of relief. That mad woman had been about to drag him into something really silly.

Vladmir looked at them all. 'You're saying we can use that machine to fly over Moscow and land at the Alpha Group Barracks. Won't that be dangerous?'

Captain Vitsin thought for a moment. 'There are specific routes to overfly the capital or we could go around. If we go very low we could avoid the civilian air traffic radar but the military ones would probably pick us up. Bea, do you know where I could file a flight plan?'

'Yes, we do it from the control tower over the telephone.'

'Fine, do you have an aviation map of the area?'

Bea went over to the Mil and jumped in. She came back a moment later with a folded map which the Captain studied.

'So, we file a flight plan to somewhere south of here and divert at the last moment. By the time anyone realises we are off course it should be too late. The only problem is that the area around the barracks is a no fly zone unless we are specifically cleared in and as we will ostensibly be a civilian flight they might take exception to us going doing that.'

'But I thought you said that no one would have time to react? Bea asked.

'Apart from a group of very nervous and heavily armed soldiers about to go into combat.'

'Oh shit, you mean they might not let us land?'

'No, I mean they might shoot first and talk later. Look, I don't know what the risks will be but you have to consider all the possibilities.'

'What about if we had an armed escort, do you think that would help?' Bea asked innocently.

Captain Vitsin gave her an odd look. 'You can't mean the attack helicopter. Is it actually armed? Those look like drill missiles to me and anyway who would fly it?'

'Yes, it is armed. The missiles are demonstrators as you have so cleverly seen although that wouldn't be so obvious from the ground. But I happen to know that the thirty millimetre nose gun is fully loaded. Air to ground firing was going to be part of the demonstrations this week. And as for operating it, I am qualified to fly as the gunner. I sort of talked the company into letting me qualify as part of the development team and we still have another pilot amongst us,' she said as she turned and looked pointedly at Jon.

'No Bea, that's a really, really silly idea,' Jon protested.

'Is it Jon? When we were passing the time after that crash in the mountains you told me there wasn't a helicopter in the world you couldn't fly. It was starting it up that was the problem. Well, I know how to do that.'

'Bea, come on, I was concussed and raving and anyway I'm a British national what the hell would happen if anyone found out I was flying a secret Russian attack helicopter against armed ground troops in the middle of a revolution? Rupert, help me out here for God's sake.'

Rupert was strangely silent while he looked around at all the faces staring at them. 'Jon could you actually fly that thing?'

'Oh for fuck's sake, not you as well. Yes, I probably could but come on mate, the risks.'

'It's simple Jon, I want to be in the other machine and I would feel a hell of a lot safer if you were riding shotgun.'

'What? Why on earth do you want to go in the Mil? This isn't our business.'

'Yes it is. Look, we've been fighting the Soviet Union for decades. Your whole military career has been based on that one fact. Suddenly, we have a chance to influence the one single moment that could change the world forever. This is without doubt the most pivotal moment of history in this half of the decade. I want to be a part of it. I want to try to help, don't you? And if getting that machine into the air with us makes it more likely that we'll succeed then I think you should do it.'

Jon looked at everyone. 'Look's like the decision has been made for me.'

An hour later Jon still couldn't shake off the feeling of unreality. Together they had managed to push both machines out onto the concrete hardstanding. Then Bea took him, Captain Vitsin and the Sergeant into a low building on one side of the hangar and they had all clambered into Russian flight gear. The soldiers were familiar with the equipment and between them they briefed Jon on its general use. Bea then explained the extra straps necessary to connect to the Alligator's ejection system which was the same as the Shark's. Jon really didn't want to contemplate using it, having had a first hand demonstration only a few hours ago but he also wanted to know enough to ensure he was safe.

Bea had pulled out some steps from the hangar and Jon had climbed into the right hand seat where the two of them managed to strap him in safely. Bea then went and walked around the machine doing the external pre-flight inspection while Jon tried to familiarise himself with the controls and gauges he would need to use in flight.

Bea then clambered in on the other side and one of the soldiers took the ladder away for her. She strapped in, plugged in her helmet and then flicked a switch on the dashboard. Suddenly Jon's helmet earphones woke into life. 'How does it look Jon?' She asked.

'I've got all the basic flying instruments sorted out and I presume this is a torquemeter?' he asked pointing to a large dial to the left of the attitude indicator.

'That's correct Jon,' Bea replied and quickly confirmed with him all the gauges he would need. 'Let's not worry about emergencies. I can handle most of them anyway.'

'What about if we lose an engine, is there anything specific I need to do?'

Bea laughed. 'No Jon, the aircraft is designed to be able to fly the whole of its flight envelope on one engine, so unless we have a fire which would mean we have to land then we can keep going. And anyway, these are proven engines that have thousands maybe millions of hours in other helicopters, they don't fail.'

'Hmm, unlike the bloody Gem engine in the Lynx then. You know Bea, part of me is terrified but then I keep thinking of all those aircraft that never had twin seats yet pilots managed to master them. In the Second World War a Hurricane pilot with a few hours on bi-plane trainers was given the pilot's notes and then told to get airborne, even the Lightning jet started out life without a training variant.'

Bea realised Jon was talking to calm his nerves and kept silent.

'Right, I'll stop burbling then. Start her up Bea and let's see if I can really make this thing fly.'

Bea carefully went through the start up routine. The aircraft, like most Russian designs, had a small gas turbine auxiliary power unit so no external power was required. Once all systems were up and running she looked over at Jon. 'Ready to start engines and rotors Jon?'

'Oh, you start up the engines with the rotor brake off don't you?'

'Yes of course, is it different in western machines then?'

'Yes, I'll tell you about it sometime. So you want me to let the rotor brake off then?'

'It's the big red handle to the left of your seat. Pull it up to release it and then let it drop all the way down.'

Jon did as instructed and was treated to the slightly surreal effect of the two rotors starting to turn in opposite directions above his head as Bea started the first engine. All too soon, she had gone through the pre-take off checks with him and it was time to get airborne. Jon settled himself into his seat and made himself relax. It was only a bloody helicopter after all and he had thousands of hours of experience.

He looked over at Bea. 'Ready?'

She nodded.

'Check left please.' He made sure there was no one near on his side. All the others were standing well clear next to the Mil 8 which had yet to start up. They were giving Jon a head start to get familiar with the Alligator.

He was about to push in some rudder pedal to compensate for the torque reaction as he pulled up on the collective and then berated himself. With no tail rotor, that wouldn't be necessary. Spinning around the first time he lifted into the hover would have been really embarrassing.

With a steady pull on the collective, the Alligator lifted smoothly into the hover. Jon immediately noticed two things. It was incredibly stable and the vibration levels were very low. Carefully, he experimented with the controls. Spot turns were easy, as was sideways low speed flying. He suddenly realised he was enjoying himself. This seemed to be an easy aircraft to fly.

'Ready for a quick circuit of the airfield Bea?' he asked.

'Whenever you are Jon, you seem to be doing well so far.'

Jon lowered the nose of the helicopter, pulled in some power and transitioned into forward flight. Fifteen minutes later they returned to hover next to the Mil which now had its rotors turning.

Bea called on the radio using their agreed callsigns. 'Kamov One this is Kamov Two, we are good to go, endurance is two hours over.'

'Two this is One, my endurance three hours, flight plan has been filed, stay as close to me as you can so we are one radar echo. I will make all radio calls on normal frequencies keep this one open for private communication.'

The Mil lifted into the hover and Jon flew the Alligator to within two rotor spans and the two machines transitioned away towards Moscow.

Chapter 45

20 August 1991, evening

Jon still felt he was in a dream. He was flying a Russian aircraft so secret that NATO knew nothing about it, in formation with another Russian helicopter as they flew over Moscow which was in the throes of a revolution. For a second he wondered just what the Group Captain somewhere down there on the ground would make of it. He chuckled wryly to himself because he knew he would never be able to tell the story.

Although he was having to concentrate to keep close to the Mil, he'd never liked formation flying in helicopters at the best of times, he still had time to relax slightly and think of what was to come. 'So Bea, how does this cannon work? It's not in a turret like the one on the Apache.'

'No, it's a semi-fixed design as we feel that the turret would make it less accurate especially at long range. Turret mountings will always have some flexibility. Generally, we leave it fixed fore and aft and the pilot aims the aircraft to aim the gun. Isn't that how the cannon worked that you had fitted to your Lynx during the Falklands?'

'Exactly and this is the sight I take it?' Jon asked pointing to a glass panel mounted on the top of the cockpit coaming.

'That's it, if I power up the weapon a little cross will appear which is your aiming mark. I can also control it through my optical system in front of me but let's just keep things simple.'

'Let's just hope we don't have to use it.'

Although the Alligator was capable of very high speed, the Mil could only trundle along at about one hundred knots, so it took them over forty five minutes to be routed around the city by Moscow air traffic. It seemed that their deception of keeping the two aircraft close together was working because no one queried their activities. Kamov One was well known to the local controllers. Once clear of the city to the south, the Mil slowly altered course more to the east as if to just clear the exclusion zone around the military complex they were actually aiming for.

Bea was following their course on the helicopter's tactical display. 'We'll be going low level and turning any moment now Jon.'

Almost as the words left her mouth, the radio came to life on their private frequency. 'Two this is One, go.'

The Mil turned hard to the left and dropped out of the sky. They had been flying at five hundred metres. Jon followed them down until the altimeter was showing fifty. Bea changed frequency on the main UHF radio in time to hear the Mil calling the small aviation control centre at the army base. At first there was no answer. It took several minutes before a voice responded to their calls.

'Alpha base, this is Kamov One, I am a Mil 8 helicopter with passengers who urgently need to talk to General Karpukhin, over.'

'Kamov One standby, you are not to close this area unless cleared, is that understood?'

'Kamov One affirmative.' The radio went silent and the Mil started to orbit round in a circle waiting for a reply.

It didn't take long. A different voice came on the radio. 'Kamov One, the General is not available. This is Colonel Yenin, to who am I speaking?'

Jon now recognised the Captain's voice on the radio. 'Sir, this is Captain Gregori Vitsin of Alpha Group, I am flying the aircraft. I have several people on board who need to talk to you urgently about your current operation.'

'How do you know about that Vitsin? Aren't you meant to be based in Moscow? What on earth are you doing in a helicopter infringing my airspace?'

'Sir, we really need to talk in person, request permission to land at the main barracks.'

'Sorry Kamov One, we are under strict orders and you should not be here. You are ordered to clear the area and return to wherever you came from. Any attempt to come any closer will be met with lethal force, do you understand? Over.'

'This is Kamov One understood Sir, out.'

The Captain's voice came over the radio on their private frequency. Two this is One, we have a few minutes while the Colonel waits in the control tower to see what we do. Plan B, over.'

Jon felt a wave of fear and excitement wash over him. They had discussed this as a contingency but he had been praying he wouldn't have to do it.

Bea looked over at Jon who nodded. 'One this is Two, understood, follow as fast as you can, out.'

He dropped the nose of the Alligator and allowed the speed to build up. Soon they were at the aircraft's maximum speed of one hundred and seventy knots and flying only a few feet above the ground. Suddenly,

Jon remembered the time he had done something similar in the Falklands. This time he prayed there wasn't another aircraft around that was trying to shoot him down, although there might well be a lot of angry troops on the ground trying to do just that very soon. He had a rough idea of the layout of the area from Captain Vitsin and knew he was heading to a small helicopter landing area on the northern edge of the main barracks. He was following the road but flying off to one side. Suddenly there was a column of tanks, they were all stationary. None of the turrets moved but Jon caught glimpses of the heads of soldiers in the turret hatches turning to watch them as they thundered past. Then in the distance, he could see buildings appear. Aiming to keep them just to the right of the nose, he started looking for anything that might be a control tower.

'Can you see anything that looks like a landing site Bea? Because I bloody well can't,' he asked anxiously, still scanning ahead.

'There Jon, just to the left of that building with the water tower by it.'

'Got it, didn't realise it would be so small. Call Kamov One.'

'One this is Two,' Bea said over the radio. 'One minute over.'

'Holding at three kilometres out until called, over,' came the immediate answer.

'Understood, be aware of tanks on the approach road.'

'Bea, arm the cannon and give me fire control please,' Jon asked.

She didn't answer but made the main armament safety switch and turned on the gun arming system. Suddenly a small white cross appeared in Jon's targeting display.

The small landing area was approaching fast now and Jon had to decide when to slow down. It could be difficult to wash off speed and still stay low. He decided that prudence was in order. In a Lynx or a Sea King, he would know exactly how much room he would need but he had no experience in this machine. On top of that, he was going a great deal faster than in any other helicopter he had flown. He lowered the lever and pulled the nose up to compensate, while still keeping the nose pointing towards the little building with the glass cupola. He immediately realised he had left it too late and they were going to overshoot. Desperately trying to stay low he pulled the nose up really hard and all but lowered the collective to the floor but even so he found that he was having to put more and more rudder pedal in to keep pointing at the control building. He then discovered something else about the flying characteristics of the Alligator. With only a short tail and no tail rotor to run out of authority, it flew sideways almost as well as it flew forwards. Instead of overshooting his target he managed to bring the machine skidding sideways into the hover almost facing back the way they had come. It probably looked very impressive from the ground, only he knew how close he had come to completely bolloxing it up.

'Your radio Bea,' he said.

'Alpha Base this is Kamov Two over, I would like to speak to the Colonel please.'

They could see several people in the control tower looking out at them. The voice that answered sounded shaken. 'This is Colonel Yenin, who the hell are you and what is going on? Over.'

'Colonel, my name is Bukov, my husband is a senior member of the KGB in Moscow and I work for the bureau that built this helicopter. We have accompanied Kamov One here because we urgently need to talk to you and we thought you might be reluctant. I request that Kamov One be allowed to come in and land.'

'Or what Comrade Bukov? You may have sneaked in here in that machine but trust me you won't get out unless I say so.'

Bea looked at Jon. 'How about those cars parked next to the building?'

'You sure? One probably belongs to the good Colonel.'

'All the better as a demonstration then.'

'Fair enough,' Jon ruddered the nose of the helicopter around until the cross hair was on the right hand car of a line of six and pressed the firing button on his cyclic control. The aircraft shuddered as the cannon shells poured into the car. He then brought the nose slowly to the left and the row of cars simply disintegrated one by one. In a few seconds, they were all reduced to smoking scrap. He brought the nose of the helicopter back to point at the control tower.

'That's what Colonel.'

There was silence for a heartbeat and then the Colonel came back on the radio. 'Kamov One you are cleared to land.'

Chapter 46

20 August 1991, late evening

You could cut the atmosphere in the room with a knife. Colonel Yenin and three of his senior staff had taken the crew of both helicopters into the large room below the control tower. Armed guards had met the crews and passengers as they had disembarked from the two machines and escorted them there without a word being spoken. The guards left the room and the door closed with an ominous bang.

The Colonel was a tough looking, grey haired man with piercing blue eyes that were creased with anger. He took a seat on the edge of the only furniture in the room, an old trestle table and turned to Captain Vitsin. 'Give me one good reason for not immediately placing you under arrest Captain.'

'Sir, that is your prerogative. I only ask that you listen to what these people have to say first.'

'And who exactly are these people?' He held up his hand. 'No one else speak. Captain, you tell me.'

'Very well Sir. This man is Comrade Gunter Bukov. He is Deputy Head of the Department of Internal Security at the KGB.'

At those words the frown on the Colonel's face turned to puzzlement.

'Doesn't know much about what's going on in Moscow then,' Jon muttered to Rupert through the side of his mouth.

Captain Vitsin continued. 'The lady is Beatrix Bukov, his wife. She works for the Kamov helicopter bureau and she was responsible for providing the aircraft that we arrived in.'

'And for destroying my car,' the Colonel hissed.

'Er, yes Sir. The three soldiers are under my command and might I request that they leave us? Anything they've done has been under my orders.'

The Colonel nodded and the soldiers left the room with relieved expressions.

'This is Comrade Vladmir Vorodov. He is a retired war time Tank Commander and a Hero of the Soviet Union as well as being a very influential industrialist. The man next to him is his assistant Sergei. Sorry I don't know his given name.'

Rupert looked at Jon as the Captain continued and they exchanged worried looks but the Captain ploughed on.

'Sir, the other two men are British, from the Embassy in Moscow. The pilot is the Deputy Defence Attaché, Commander Jonathon Hunt and the other man is Mister Rupert Thomas from their intelligence section.'

The last announcement left the room in silence.

The Colonel looked stunned. 'Very well, you've certainly got my interest. Who is going to tell me what this is all about?'

Gunter stepped forward. 'Colonel, as you now know, I am the deputy of the department that has responsibility for your command and control. I have been away from Moscow for a couple of days on departmental business but I take it that you have been ordered to mobilise and get ready to go into the city?'

The Colonel looked worried. His face showed the internal conflict going on. Eventually, he spoke. 'Yes Comrade but my orders come from the head of the KGB himself.'

'I understand that Colonel and what is your assessment of the likely outcome of such an action?'

'There will be casualties of course but I have to do what I am ordered to do. You of all people should understand that.'

'Of course, rather like when you were ordered into Lithuania in January, thirteen people died and then the politicians denied they had given you the orders.'

The Colonel looked like he was sucking a lemon. 'A fair point but I still have to obey orders and my General has also confirmed the instruction.'

Vladmir looked at Gunter with a raised eyebrow. Gunter waved to him to talk. 'Colonel, I am Vladmir Vorodov. At the start of the Second World War the Nazis murdered my family after raping my mother and sisters. In fact, they murdered my whole village. I was lucky to escape. I walked over a thousand miles until I was able to join the Red Army where I became a tank commander. Even now I can't forgive those savage bastards for their actions even though one could argue that our retribution was just as savage.'

'While I sympathise and understand, even admire your story Comrade Vorodov, what does this have to do with the current situation?' The Colonel asked.

'During those terrible years, I fought for one thing only. I fought for mother Russia. I had no thought of creating an empire out of the ashes and wouldn't have cared less if someone had told me that that was what it was all about. That said, while it worked I supported the union. When the war was over I found wealth and was able to build a business that has been successful. I watched all the ludicrous actions of that monster Stalin and the psychopathic pervert Beria. When they were swept away there was some sense applied by our new rulers but never enough. I was able to see what the West was achieving because I was in a privileged position through my businesses. When Gorbachev came to power, he inherited a corrupt and hopelessly inefficient system. At first, like many, I supported him but it soon became clear that he still thought that all the Soviet countries would stay socialist if they were given more freedom. He was soon disabused of that idea but having rescinded the Brezhnev doctrine there was nothing he could do. It was at that stage that I called together a small group of people who would be influential if matters got out of hand. As you can see, that's exactly what has now happened. Why do you think all the conventional armed forces have refused to act? In all my actions I have wanted to protect my country only. Although I may not have agreed with Gorbachev's methods, I fully support his aims, as do most of the population. If this coup succeeds, do you really want the old hardliners back in power? Because that is what will happen and it can only be achieved through bloodshed. You know how many people are surrounding that building. Do you want hundreds or thousands of innocent lives on your hands? And then we will probably have to go into the Baltic States and Georgia and Chechnya and the Ukraine and God knows where else to re-establish our authority. Do you want open warfare on multiple fronts?'

The Colonel looked worried. 'And what are these two British men doing here?'

'Simple Colonel, they've provided the intelligence we needed to ensure that the President of Russia was able to fulfil his duties without interference from the gang of eight.'

'And one of them shot up my bloody car.'

'Colonel, I will personally buy you a new Mercedes when this is over,' Vladmir replied with a grin.

'I'll hold you to that Vorodov.'

'Sir, may I also make a point?' Captain Vitsin asked. 'As I hope you can understand, I was in the same position as you only a few hours ago.'

'Go on young man.'

'Sir, somehow we have ended up with two Presidents. Both democratically elected but one has been deposed. The orders you have received have come from the illegally constituted committee that has deposed the President of the Union of Soviet Socialist Republics. Their orders are to detain or even kill the only man who has any right to rule in this country.'

'But they say that President Gorbachev is ill and they are only ruling in his absence.'

Muted guffaws of laughter greeted his remark.

'Alright, I saw the press conference as well. So what are you saying I should do?'

Vladmir stood forward, this was the absolute key moment. 'Stand down your troops Colonel and then tell the gang of eight that you only obey orders from legally elected politicians.'

Two hours later, their transport pulled up in front of the British Embassy. Rupert and Jon jumped out. Jon was still in his Russian flying gear and had even managed to keep hold of his flying helmet. It would make a great souvenir if he was allowed to keep it.

As the car drove away, Rupert turned to Jon. 'Not a word about this except to the Ambassador, he can then decide what to do next.'

'Understood Rupert, although I suspect there will be some guys at Boscombe Down who will want a word at some time. But boy am I relieved that the Colonel was convinced. I would hate to think what would have happened if they had come into the city. I wonder what will happen now?'

'Anything is better than a bloodbath Jon.'

They turned and walked up the steps into the Embassy. They confirmed that the Ambassador was in and made their way to his office. As they were walking along the corridor, Group Captain Pearson appeared.

He took one look at Jon and frowned. 'Hunt, what on earth are you doing dressed like that?'

'Oh, hello Group Captain. I would love to tell you, really I would.'

'But then I would have to shoot you,' Rupert finished off for him.

Epilogue

Vladmir's Dacha, ten days later.

Vladmir raised a glass of vodka in a toast. 'To the new Russia gentlemen.'

Glasses were raised and the toast repeated. The original group were meeting for the last time. Vladmir had decided they were no longer needed and no one disagreed.

'The only thing I really don't understand,' said Sergei. 'Is what Gorbachev thought he was doing when he got back to Moscow? He missed the biggest propaganda coup of his career. If he had just gone straight to the White House and stood on a tank like Yeltsin did, he would have been the hero of the day and re-established his authority. Instead, what does he do? He goes home for goodness sake and then the next day just goes to work as though nothing had happened.'

'Maybe he really was just exhausted,' Gunter said. 'His wife had suffered a stroke or heart attack on the flight back and maybe he was more worried about her.'

'Of course, the current conspiracy theory doing the rounds is that he engineered the coup in the first place,' Vladmir remarked. 'If they lost, he would come back in triumph. If they won he would come back as their leader and be able to reverse some of his more radical reforms. In other words he couldn't lose.'

'But why then not capitalise on his return?' Sergei countered.

'Who knows?' Vladmir replied. 'I'm sure we'll all find out in the end and now President Yeltsin has the power and Russia might just be able to take a more meaningful role in the world.' He raised his glass again, 'to interesting times my friends.'

Author's Notes

Once again let me separate fact from fiction.

The rescue at the start of the book is based on elements of several I was involved in and others from around the early eighties. One night, when I was duty SAR crew at Culdrose we were scrambled to go to an ore carrier in the Channel that had taken on a list in a Force Ten storm. When we launched, she was listing at ten degrees by the time we arrived she had capsized. Only one survivor was recovered. The weather pattern I describe is just as it was that night.

Salt build up in the engine intakes and on the rotor blades of a Sea King was a real problem even up to as high as fifteen hundred feet. The end result could be engines surging due to the choked airflow.

Sorry about Helen! But when I wrote the prologue to my first book in the series, Jon admits to a journalist that he never managed to hang on to a good woman for any length of time, so she had to go. But doing it this way allowed me to get Jon to thump the stupid journalist, something I guarantee I will do for real if one ever asks me that banal question.

All the helicopters that I mention are real, the KA 52 Alligator and Mil 8 are still in service in Russia today. The single seat, KA50 Shark wasn't so successful although it was offered as a candidate to the UK Attack Helicopter programme in the mid-nineties. The distinctive Kamov twin rotor design is yet another way of getting over the issue of needing to counteract the torque a helicopter's main rotor. It docs lead to a very complicated rotor system which is probably why no one else has gone down exactly that same route. The ejection system is exactly as I describe.

I moved the Italian European Rotorcraft Forum back in time a couple of years. But the story of the Russians misbehaving at the final dinner is absolutely true. I was sitting at the next table.

In 1995 I wasn't able to attend the ERF which was a shame as it was in Moscow. However, a colleague did and as part of the visit he was invited to fly to a closed city where they produced gas turbines. Jon's similar visit is based on my recollections of the feedback I was given. This included the flight in an old aircraft with rusty wings (I saw the photos). On the way back they had to land early as they had run out of fuel. The flight crew then asked the passengers to help out with their credit cards to buy enough gas to get back to Moscow!

'Protection, Location, water, food' was the mantra of military survival in my day. However, although we were taught how to snare food, how to resist capture and how to survive, we were never taught how to cope with wild animals. And no, I've no idea what wolf tastes like.

In 1977 I took up my first appointment as an Air Engineer in the navy on 772 Squadron at RNAS Portland. We flew Wessex Five aircraft and one of our duties was Search and Rescue. On the second Friday afternoon after I had joined, there was a deafening bang from the hangar as someone accidentally fired the emergency cable cutter of one the aircraft's rescue winches. The first thing it taught me was that these things always happen on a Friday afternoon just as you are trying to sneak away on weekend leave. However, who would have guessed that thirty seven years later it would give me the idea for a plot line in a book I was writing?

Could Jon have flown the Alligator? It really annoys me when I read novels and the hero jumps into a helicopter and flies it away. Not because of the flying bit, most machines are similar enough in that respect but you would need hours studying the aircraft's manuals to know which switches to make just to get the engines going. So, by having Bea to do the hard bit, I believe I could have flown it, so therefore Jon could have as well.

My slightly cheap shot at the RAF not shooting down anything since WW2 is not really true although it is a myth put about by the Fleet Air Arm. However, the tally is only about four Egyptian aircraft in 1948 and possibly some during Suez but those are unconfirmed. They have also shot down two of their own in air to air mistakes. It may be an unfair criticism of the RAF but the Fleet Air Arm has been far more successful in the same time frame in Korea and the Falklands, which make the politicians decision to scrap our Harrier Fleet all the more stupid.

My descriptions of the end of the Stasi in East Germany are factually accurate. There really was a Division of Garbage analysis, which just shows how out of hand that country had become before the Wall came down.

Trying to discern the true facts of the attempted coup in 1991 is like trying to knit fog, herd cats and nail jelly to the wall at the same time. Conspiracy theories abound and even after many of the main players have published memoirs or given interviews there is still doubt about what really happened. I have established several things though:

Boris Yeltsin was not approached by the plotters in advance even though they did sound out nearly all the other Soviet country's leaders. No one can explain why.

When he came back from Kazakhstan that evening he couldn't be spoken to for whatever reason…….

A KGB road block was set up the next day to stop him. There was even accommodation set aside to hold him incommunicado afterwards. The road block let him through.

All the conventional armed forces refused to respond to orders to attack the White House.

The final straw for the coup was when the KGB Alpha forces also refused.

There is a strong feeling that one of the reasons that Yeltsin was so confident was that he was getting real time intelligence from overseas.

The sequence of the events leading up to the coup and the political situation that was in place at the time are accurate, as is the description of the events of the three days of the coup. Sending in food to the White House from Pizza Hut and McDonalds did happen for example. The girl in the green check dress really did ask if the Safety Committee were conducting a coup and caused uproar in the process.

Gorbachev's unexplainable actions on his return are also described as they happened. It gave Boris Yeltsin the leverage he needed. On Christmas day that year, Gorbachev resigned as the one and only President of the Union of Soviet Socialist Republics and on Boxing Day the Union was dissolved. The Cold War was over.

Jon (and Brian) will sail again

The players:

The Mil 8 (NATO Name Hip) one of the most prolific helicopters in the world

The single seat Kamov KA 50 Shark (NATO Name Hokum Λ)

The twin seat Kamov KA 52 Alligator (NATO Name Hokum B)

Retribution

Now out – the next book in the series and some questions get answered:

1995, the vicious war in the fragmented former Republic of Yugoslavia is moving to an end game. The United Nations have troops and observers in the country but are finding it impossible to act. Thrust into the maelstrom of rape, murder and ethnic cleansing, the newly promoted Captain Jonathon Hunt joins the UN Protection Force UNPROFOR and finds himself being drawn into the struggle. The only way the war is going to end is if the might of NATO becomes fully committed to stop the fighting. Jon plays a major part in the momentous events that finally convince the world that the war has to end. At the same time, investigations by MI6 allow him to finally discover the truth about why his wife died so tragically three years earlier. In both cases, retribution is called for.

Printed in Great Britain
by Amazon

62551957R10129